A Girl Named Charlie Lester

also by Carissa Halston

Cleavage

A Girl Named Charlie Lester

a novel

Carissa Halston

Hi Stephanie,

Enjoy!

Aforementioned Productions

Boston - New York

Published by Aforementioned Productions
www.aforementionedproductions.com

Book design by Randolph Pfaff

"Ballad of Reading Gaol" © 1898 by Oscar Wilde.

"Bad Driver" © 2004 by Carissa Halston. First published in *Fables*.

Alis's poem (page 48) written by Paul Marques.

ISBN 978-0-6151-6546-2

Printed in the United States of America

September 2007
First Edition

This book is for all the boys I ever kissed and all the girls I wanted to, but didn't.

Prologue

Charlie Lester's parents are dead.

Sometimes, she doesn't remember that.

Sometimes, she remembers what her brother used to tell her when she was nine years old.

"Mom and Dad aren't really dead, ya know," he'd say. "They sent us to live with Aunt Jean because they don't really love us. They never really loved us."

At seventeen, she figured out that the latter part of his story was kind of true.

Her best friend, Abby Quinn, lived downtown.

Abby was a video game addict. She also liked tattoos. "Not because I want to rebel or anything," she'd say. "I just think they're cool." If she had ever done anything to rebel, it was dropping out of high school to become a professional masseuse.

By the February prior to Charlie's graduation, Abby had three tattoos: a pisky hanging from her nipple, a leprechaun peeking around her hip, and a gnome nestling between her cheeks. She was one of those girls.

She cajoled Charlie into tagging along for her fourth. Charlie was quick to jump at the chance to escape Jean's white-picketed prison. Whenever she wanted to leave the house without Jean knowing, she would dangle from the second story of her aunt's imitation Tudor, close her eyes and release. She learned to tuck her legs on impact. Afraid that Jean had heard the thud, Charlie would run like hell was at her heels until her breathing felt acidic. Only then would she slow her pace to a frenetic walk.

When they were about a block from Inky Doodles—Abby's tattoo parlor of choice—Charlie said, "Maybe I'll get a tattoo."

"I'd pay to see that," teased Abby.

"What? I could get one."

"Yeah, I bet," Abby laughed. She rejoiced in mocking her friend. "'Umm, sir, do you really have to use the needle? I've seen them in those little machines for fifty cents and you can put those on with water!'"

"I'm not really sure why you hate me," said Charlie, holding open the door to the parlor. "After you." Abby walked in; Charlie followed. They approached the counter.

"Appointment for Quinn, four o'clock," Abby said to the guy behind the desk. He had his black hair pulled back in a long ponytail. His pork chop sideburns were turquoise. His goatee was black. Silver rings were on every finger. He had five facial piercings. His T-shirt read: If you like your jaw the way it is, you'll stop fucking staring at me. Charlie was swooning. She quietly, yet excitedly, poked Abby's back.

"You're the…sprite?" the tattooist asked. "Five inches high, three inches wide, right shoulder blade?" Abby nodded. "You're getting a soda label tattooed on your back?" he asked, arching his left eyebrow, causing the barbell which jutted through to catch the light off the neon OPEN sign.

"Yeah, I'm getting a soda label tattoo," Abby said, low-lidded. "I brought a picture." She retrieved a photo from her back pocket and unfolded it. It was a fairy introspectively gazing into her reflection in a puddle.

Knowing that Abby designed all her own tattoos, Charlie leaned close to her ear and whispered, "Very nice."

Abby's eyes narrowed. In an instant, her expression changed to sticky sweet and, grinning widely, she said, "Oh, and my friend was wondering if you had time to squeeze her in." Charlie's eyes widened so you could see the entire iris.

Stephen—the guy with the sideburns—leaned over and smiled, "If you can wait, I'll do yours."

Charlie nervously smiled. "Um…okay…"

Fifteen minutes later, Charlie was in the chair.

"So," said Stephen, "where would you like it?"

"Umm…" Charlie tried to think of a place where it would be painless. Other than her hair, nothing came to mind. "How about between my shoulder blades?"

"Okay, take off your shirt," said Stephen.

Charlie swallowed hard and audibly. She took off her shirt.

"Do you have a picture?" he asked.

"Uhh, no," replied Charlie. She explained that she wasn't quite sure what she wanted, but she wanted something personal.

"Okay, so tell me about yourself," said Stephen.

Charlie made a long story short.

"I know something perfect," he said. And after that, there was only the sound of the needle, and the pain.

Twenty-five minutes and fifty dollars later, Charlie had a tiny black sheep on her back under a swatch of paper towel and some tape. She bought a tube of A+D ointment and sat down to wait for Abby. She took great care not to sit back.

Abby walked out, sans shirt, fifteen minutes later. The red soaking through the paper towel on her back almost matched her bra, red with tiny black flowers. She saw Charlie sit up and wince when she came out. "You're kidding. You actually got something? Let me see!"

"Abby, it's just a piece of Brawny with some tape over it," Charlie groused. "You can't see anything."

"Well, what's it look like?" asked Abby, excitedly.

"It looks like someone injected ink under my skin with a big fucking needle. C'mon, let's go," said Charlie.

"Wait a minute, where's your dream date?" Abby asked, meaning Stephen.

"*That* replaced him and he left as soon as he could," muttered Charlie, motioning to the girl standing behind the counter. She wore her hair in two candy cane braids and her arms covered in tiger lilies and skulls. Charlie stalked out the door and down to the street. Abby tossed her money on the counter and followed without a word.

They reached Abby's house and Charlie asked, "Has it been an hour yet?"

Abby leaned over and hit the comb on a plastic rooster holding a guitar. The rooster's eyes opened and its beak moved unsynchronized with the pseudo-eighties hair band song that blared out. It crowed. "Woo! It's six! Oh! Clock! Woo!" said the little clock.

"Must you do that every time?" asked Charlie, gazing balefully at the plastic rooster. "Can't you get a normal fucking clock?"

"Dude, kiss my ass. My cock rocks," said Abby.

"I'm sure it does," replied Charlie.

"To answer your question, Captain Moody, yes, it has been an hour. Into the potty you go." Charlie and Abby marched into the bathroom. They hadn't talked about the tattoo since they got there. Abby played video games and Charlie sat, uncomfortably brooding, in a dusty black bean bag chair.

"Okay, take off your shirt," said Abby. Charlie did as she was told. She clutched her midriff self-consciously. "Turn around." Abby eased off the tape but the paper towel stayed stuck to the fresh wound. "All right, lean over the tub." Charlie fiddled with the hot and cold water knobs until the water was warm enough to tolerate. She contorted herself below the faucet until the water ran over her back. She gritted her teeth at the water's first contact with the tattoo. After a minute or so, she saw the paper towel hit the tub's floor with a satisfying plop. Abby squeaked out a chuckle. "My God, that is *so* you."

"Whatever, just help me clean it up," said Charlie.

Abby put the specified mild soap on Charlie's back and Charlie let out a little yelp. "Sorry, it's cold."

When they were done, Charlie sat up and walked to the mirror. "Jesus, it looks like my hair is bleeding black leaves." Her hair was a light brown and cut very close to the scalp except two black tufts in the front, which hung down in her face. Abby threw her a towel.

"So, cut it."

"I can't; I'll look like a guy. No human male looks at me now, I'm *not* cutting my hair," said Charlie.

"First of all, you would not look like a guy. Your tits stick out like fire cones. Secondly, I'm pretty sure that—Stephen, was it?—was staring at you hard."

"Stephen, and yes it was, did that so I'd help him make his quota for the day."

"I really don't think fifty bucks was all that important. Maybe you just scared him off with that I'm-an-independent-woman-and-I-don't-need-you-so-don't-even-try-to-be-slick thing you do," said Abby.

Charlie looked at Abby with a clenched jaw and said, "Yeah, you've got me all figured out. And I think it was because I talked too much, not too little. I told him about all the shit with my aunt."

"Speaking of your aunt, don't you think she's going to freak out?" asked Abby.

"Look at my complete lack of surprise. I could drop dead by bleeding from the face and she'd bitch at me for staining the carpet," Charlie replied.

"Remember, the offer still stands to move in here," said Abby.

Charlie took a deep breath, "Nah. I think I want to get my own place. Besides, I'd eventually strap dynamite to that clock of doom," Charlie smirked. Abby smiled and whipped her with a towel. "Hey, I'm injured here."

"Yeah…I'm such a bitch."

"You said it. Well, I guess I'm delaying the inevitable," said Charlie. "I ought to take off. Thanks for a memorable afternoon. I won't hug you for fear of induced bleeding."

"Give me a call tomorrow," said Abby.

"Later."

Jean didn't see Charlie's tattoo. Charlie was able to smuggle in the ointment and antimicrobial soap without her aunt's noticing.

She did not, however, reach her bedroom without incident.

"Excuse me, young lady," Jean called in her crisp tone which she reserved for instances in which she wanted to remind Charlie of her inferior age.

Charlie froze. *Why fight it?* she thought. She dragged her feet into the kitchen.

"I know you don't care, but—"

Here comes the guilt…

"—how do you think it looks to the neighbors when they see you drop from your bedroom window and then run like you just made off with a family heirloom?" Charlie sighed as if she were incredibly weary. She was. "How do you think that reflects upon me?"

"I'm sure it looks really awful," Charlie said in a low tone. She didn't mumble or whisper. She merely sounded defeatist.

"You'd be correct in your assessment. How am I to explain why you would behave in such a manner?"

"You could tell them the truth," Charlie suggested.

"Which is?"

"That you're not my mother and I can't stand living with you and ever since Lee left, you've gone out of your way to be even more menopausal than usual."

I can play the age card too, you cunt.

Jean raised her hand just once. More than once was rarely necessary.

"You'd be wise to remember who you're speaking to, young lady."

"That's not true, actually," Charlie said, rubbing her jaw. "If I were at all wise, I'd have told the cops years ago about your special brand of child rearing."

"And who do you think they'd believe?" Jean raised her chin and spoke like an athlete with home field advantage.

"It doesn't really matter. The question would always be in their minds. One child who ran away and the other who suffers the abuse at her guardian's hand."

Jean laughed. "You have a smart answer for everything. Well, I have a news flash for you, little lady. You better get used to these four walls, because you won't be seeing anything else until after graduation," said Jean.

"That's not for another four months!" Charlie exclaimed. Jean raised her nose in the air. She was in control, her favorite position.

"I'm glad they're still teaching arithmetic in that school," said Jean, and strolled out of the room on her high horse.

Charlie did her best not to cry. She didn't want Jean to know she'd gotten to her. Slowly, calmly, she walked to her room and gently shut the door.

She took her comedy and tragedy masks down off the wall and stood in front of the mirror. "Okay, baby, show me happy." She held up the comedy mask. "Beautiful. Show me sad." She held up the tragedy mask. "Yes! Show me manic depressive." Both masks were held up. "Oh, yeah, color me deranged. I could put on my very own one-woman kabuki show. If only I had a machete," Charlie mused.

She returned the masks to the wall. Her cheek was pink and slightly puffy from her aunt's slap. It was nine thirty. Charlie changed into her polyester blend, imitation silk pajamas and got into bed. She rolled onto her side and hoped she wouldn't end up on her back before morning. Her breathing became rhythmic but she wasn't asleep, nowhere near it. She was pacing herself, she didn't want to be overtaken. Little by little, bit by bit, the tears came. And for what felt like the millionth time in her life, Charlie cried herself to sleep.

Chapter One - Eight years later

Charlie glanced both ways before crossing the street. Her black canvas bag slipped off her shoulder to the crook in her arm. She grunted and tossed it back to her shoulder. As she approached the slope of the next hill, a breeze kicked up and mussed the part in her hair she had struggled so hard to achieve less than an hour prior.

"Jesus H. Christ," she muttered. Down slipped the bag to her elbow. "Fucking books…" she said in reference to the bag, containing two books, one fiction, one non-fiction, and two notebooks, one for fiction, one for non-fiction. She reached the top of the hill and glanced down at the view which lay before her. It was less than scenic.

The streetlights had been installed the year before to give the streets a more historic look. Charlie didn't remember any historic references to the Gap and the Dollar Store. She took a deep breath, exhaled and whispered, "Ahh, consumerism."

Charlie plunged her hand into the pocket of her bulky green corduroy coat and clutched her keys. So began her ritual descent, down past Kinko's, past McDonald's and Starbucks, past Charlie's favorite building—it had been remodeled to house offices, but sold pianos in the early twenties—to stand in front of The Book End, Charlie's home away from home.

She unlocked the door, flipped the light switch and plugged in the phone. She banished her bag to the drawer below the one where the scissors were supposed to be. They'd been missing for the past two weeks.

Two hours earlier, Charlie had sat in her apartment. Her living room was full of tangible memories. A typewriter for which she'd been meaning to buy a new ink ribbon, if only she knew how to change it; a guitar case which was chronically ajar from being stuffed to the gills with books and DVDs, the guitar, like the scissors, gone, but she knew where that was; an open box of cigars on her mother's old desk; pictures and postcards of places she'd never been. Vacations taken vicariously through Dick and Jane.

A thesaurus with sticky notes lining the pages sat atop a cardboard box filled with photos. Stacks of CDs waist-high leaned against two stately bookcases. Among the throng was a futon in the bed position, also covered in books; a folding chair with DRY CLEAN ONLY clothes draped over it and a bean bag chair, black, lost and abandoned in the corner.

Charlie had sat in the middle of the room on the floor, legs spread to a V. She had scribbled a few paragraphs in her notebook—the fiction one—before she started doodling in the margins.

A cigarette had loitered idly in her mouth, unlit.

She had glanced around the room, from the guitar case to the desk to the futon to the bean bag chair. Charlie had sat there for a moment, taking it all in. She had then stood up, grabbing her bag, dropped her cigarette and left.

She liked to think she wasn't materialistic. *It's just stuff,* she'd tell herself. *I only keep the things that have sentimental value.* Sentimental meaning that which made her doubt the direction her life had taken and wonder if her fuck-ups were irreparable. She only went through this every other day, torturing herself the entire way to work while she was supposed to be relaxing and readying herself for another day of customer interface.

A bell clinked behind her. Spot strolled in. He presented Charlie with that male speechless greeting that looks like a backward nod. "What up, G?" he said.

"Not much, home slice," Charlie replied without looking up. "Have you seen the scissors?"

"Nope. Sorry," replied Spot.

"I'm beginning to think one of the customers lifted them," Charlie said, while rechecking all the drawers.

"Maybe Potty Man took them," said Spot. "Maybe he was making little paper dolls out of all those dirty books he buys."

"One day he's gonna hear you call him that, then he's going to follow you home, and the next day, we'll find your tongue in the mail."

"Yeah. And you know how he'll do it? With your fucking scissors," he quipped and leaned back against a bookshelf.

Charlie looked around the shop. "I'm more than certain that there are books to be shelved," she dismissed him with a wave of her hand. "And no skimming in front of the customers."

"How many times must I tell you, boss lady? It's not skimming. It's research. I need to be able to recommend fine literature to the unknowing slobs that frequent this establishment," said Spot.

Charlie counted out money for the register and said, "Oh, as opposed to the slobs that work here. 'Work' being the operative term."

Ring, ring…

"Book End, this is Charlie."

"Hello," said a gruff voice. "Do you sell newspapers?"

"No, sir, we do not," said Charlie.

"I'm a woman with five children."

Of fucking course.

"Sorry about that, ma'am. But, we don't carry newspapers," replied Charlie.

"Well, what kind of bookstore doesn't sell newspapers?" demanded the woman.

"We deal mainly in books, ma'am. A newspaper is a periodical," said Charlie.

"Don't you talk to me like I'm stupid! I know what a damn newspaper is!" she yelled, irately.

"Ma'am, it was not my intention--" Charlie started.

"I'll just go to Borders or Barnes & Noble!" the customer threatened and slammed the phone in Charlie's ear.

Charlie stared blankly at the receiver. "I'll draw you a fucking map."

"What was that?" asked Spot.

"Apparently the mental ward is letting the patients play with the phone again," said Charlie.

Spot shrugged and set off to work.

Gwen read *Rare & Out of Print Books: Where to Find Them and What They're Really Worth* as she walked into The Book End.

"Hi Gwen," Charlie said.

Gwen continued to read her book, but held up one index finger, silently asking Charlie to wait. After a few moments, she closed the book. "Goddammit, I should be British."

"I'm fine, Non Sequitur Lass, and how are you?" said Charlie.

"No, I'm serious. What I just read clinched it," said Gwen. "Who is my favorite author?"

"Jonathan Carroll," replied Charlie.

"Exactly. I just read that Jonathan gets the attention he deserves across the pond. Do you have any idea how hard it is to find someone who even knows who he is?"

"One doesn't become English, my dear."

"T.S. Eliot did. He was born here and then moved to England later. You can find his works in several British literature anthologies," protested Gwen.

"That just goes to show you how little work one truly does to collect work for an anthology," Charlie retorted. "Besides, Eliot didn't become British, he merely moved to England and lived as close to a British life as an American can."

"I guess. Have you ever heard him read his stuff though? He even *sounded* English."

"Affected accent."

"Well, what about Edward Gorey and Paul Theroux?"

"What about them?"

"They're both Americans who people think are British."

"But they don't pretend to be British," Charlie explained. "Most people also thought Edward Gorey was dead long before he actually passed away. People are stupid."

"And lucky for us," Gwen said, "Some of them even read."

Charlie regretfully nodded.

"Hey, where's Spot?" Gwen asked. "That bitch owes me money." Charlie couldn't help but smirking anytime Gwen swore. She was five-four and her voice hadn't deepened since the release of Hangin' Tough. Luckily, Gwen's mother sent her to diction classes so rather than sounding like Mickey Mouse, she sounded more like Marilyn Monroe but even the idea of Marilyn Monroe using words like "cunt rag" and "douche bag" made Charlie giggle like a tipsy debutante. The fact that Gwen lightened her already blonde hair to a platinum white didn't help.

"He's shelving, I believe," answered Charlie. "I wonder when 'bitch' became a derogatory term for both males and females," she added as an afterthought.

"I think it was around the time homosexuality and bisexuality were trendy. 'Oh, I think I'll be gay this week.' No offense," said Gwen.

"None taken, but I'm not seeing your point," returned Charlie.

"It has been my experience that gay men refer to each other as bitches. It adds to the catty aura. And when it was incredibly fashionable to come out of the closet, the phrase became more widespread and so was used by gay men and fag hags alike. The latter are usually known to have at least one hetero male companion, and we all know how infuriating men can be--"

"People in general can be infuriating, not just men," interrupted Charlie.

"Point taken, but when said fag hag gets pissed at her hetero counterpart, I'm sure the term 'bitch' is used on more than one occasion."

Charlie blinked at Gwen. "That was astounding, informative and disturbing all at once."

"I'm going to take that as a compliment."

"Do as you will," said Charlie.

Gwen glanced down the aisles for Spot and yelled, "Hey, bitch! Where's my twenty bucks?"

Charlie was printing out the inventory sheet when a sandy haired, disheveled man skittered into the store.

"May I help you, sir?" asked Charlie.

"Uh, uh…yeah." He gave a sideways glance to his right and then his left before continuing. "Do you, uh, have *The Anarchist's Cookbook*?"

"We usually carry it, but let me check." Charlie punched the title into the computer and pressed enter. "No, sir, we're out of it. We can certainly get it for you though," Charlie offered.

"That would be awesome," said the customer, sounding greatly relieved.

"Okay, I'll just need your name and phone number please."

His eyes bulged. "Do you really need that?" he asked.

"Yes, sir, so we may contact you when your book arrives," said Charlie, nodding and smiling.

"Oh…um, okay, then, never mind," he said. The unkempt man lingered in front of Charlie's counter, shifting from one foot to the other. Charlie realized he was still standing there.

"Is there anything else I can help you with, sir?" she asked.

"Uh, yeah. Do you have any…uh, weed books?" he asked.

"Weed, as in gardening, like dandelions, weed books? Or weed, as in, 'No, officer, I swear it's oregano,' weed books?" asked Charlie.

"I…think I'll just browse," he said and inched away.

"You do that."

Gretchen, Moira, and Ruth were punctual, as always, for their Tuesday outing to the bookshop. On that particular Tuesday, their outfits smacked of an LL Bean catalog. Gretchen wore a pink polo shirt with matching pink slacks. Moira followed suit in sky blue, as did Ruth in celery green. Ruth approached the counter slowly, decrepit old bat she was, while Gretchen and Moira went to peruse the women's studies section.

"Hi, may I help you?" asked Charlie. She hated dealing with these women, but they bought a lot of books.

"Yes," said Ruth, in her calm, business-like tone. She took a few eons to retrieve a magazine clipping from her purse. Charlie almost offered to do it for her. "Do you have this book?"

It was the latest biography on Princess Diana. Charlie was pretty sure, by her count, it was number 36,027. Give or take a few.

"Yes, Ruth, I'll run and get it for you," said Charlie, hoping Ruth wouldn't follow her. Ruth barely had the strength to hold her own weight, much less walk, but when Charlie turned to look, she saw Ruth making her decelerated way to follow. Charlie reached for the book and awaited Ruth's arrival. Her breathing was labored.

"My goodness. Such long legs, you must have a mighty stride, young lady," said Ruth.

"Yup. Here's your book. If you need anything else, please let me know," said Charlie, making a beeline for the front of the store. She was stopped by Gretchen.

"Excuse me," said Gretchen. "I'd like to order some books."

"Okay," said Charlie. She grabbed some order slips and a pen and said, "Do you have titles for me?"

"Of course," replied Gretchen, seeming put out by the very question. She handed Charlie a list of titles and quantities. "As you know, I am the librarian for our church and receive--" Charlie interrupted her.

"A fifteen percent discount, I'm well aware, Gretchen. I'll make a copy of the list and give you a call when your books arrive," said Charlie.

"Thank you." Gretchen left the counter to continue browsing. As Charlie was copying the list, the phone rang.

"Book End, this is Charlie."

"Hi, I'm looking for a book," said the voice on the phone.

"Okay…" replied Charlie.

Silence.

"Do you have the title?" Charlie asked.

"Oh…uh, no," answered the voice.

Moira approached the counter. Charlie clenched her jaw.

"It's Dr. Shapiro's new diet book," continued the voice on the phone. Charlie put down Gretchen's list and cupped her hand over the receiver. "I'll be right with you, Moira." Moira nodded.

"Do you think you might have that?" the woman on the phone asked.

"Uhh, let me check," said Charlie. She rapidly tapped on the keyboard and a search for *Shapiro* brought forty-eight results. "Ma'am, do you know when it was published?"

"No, I'm sorry. I know it's Dr Shapiro's new diet book," she answered. Moira drummed her fingers on the counter loudly. Charlie cupped the receiver again.

"Spot? Little help?" she yelled.

"Okay…" he replied and sauntered to the front of the store.

There were three diet books published that month by Shapiros. "Ma'am, do you know the author's first name?" asked Charlie.

"Um…" she hesitated. "I think it's Doctor."

Charlie closed her eyes tightly. "No, ma'am, I'm sorry, we don't carry that."

"Oh, okay. I'll check back soon!" said the voice cheerily.

"Okay, thanks," said Charlie and hung up.

Spot was trying to decipher Moira's hieroglyphic chicken scratch. Charlie went back to copying Gretchen's list.

Ruth was moving at her snail's pace to the register when she stopped, doubled back and then moved forward again. She made it a few feet before sighing heavily and then moving, resigned, back again. Charlie couldn't help herself.

"Ruth. Did you need something?"

"Well," she looked at Charlie as though she'd misplaced something. Charlie imagined, if anything, it was her wits. "I was wondering if Dan Brown's book is out in soft cover yet."

"No, ma'am. That recently came out in hardcover. It takes nine months to a year for a book to come out in paperback."

"How much is the hardcover?"

"With tax? Twenty-eight forty-five."

"That's almost thirty dollars!" Ruth explained. Charlie smiled joylessly.

"I'll wait for it to come in at the library."

"Okay."

"Nine months to a year? Are you sure?" Ruth asked.

"Positive," Charlie said. "Isn't that right, Spot?"

"Not a word of truth in it," Spot said without looking up. He had finished helping Moira.

"He's brain damaged, Ruth, ignore him," Charlie warned.

"Really, young man?" Moira and Gretchen were now at Ruth's side.

"It's true. I am brain damaged," Spot said soberly.

"No, about the nine months."

"Oh, that," said Spot. "No, that's true."

Ruth nodded sadly. "Ladies? Are you ready then?" she asked the other two elderly women. They indicated that they were quite through. As they were shuffling toward the exit, Ruth stopped and looked Spot up and down. "I'm sorry about the damaging of your brain," she said solemnly.

Spot nodded and said, "So am I. Have a good day, ma'am. May Jesus be with you."

Ruth smiled and left.

Spot looked at Charlie and Charlie looked at Spot. They broke up with laughter.

"'May Jesus be with you.' You really do have brain damage," said Charlie, red-faced with mirth.

Summer of 1997

Charlie sat in her room, taking mental inventory of her belongings. Posters she could leave. She could give up much of her clothing. All her CDs would fit in her backpack. She could put some things into storage little by—

Her train of thought was broken by a knock at the door.

"What?" she said, knowing it was Jean.

"When the hell are you getting your ass out of bed?" replied the voice on the other side of the door. A hand tried the knob; it was locked.

I'm not in bed, you motherfucking succubus.

"Go away, I'm busy," said Charlie.

"Open this Goddamn door," her aunt demanded. "I want to talk to you."

"So, talk. I can hear you perfectly well now," replied Charlie.

"I can hear your smug little voice. If your parents were here..." Jean trailed off.

Charlie unlocked and opened the door. "If they were here, they'd be lamenting the loss of their son."

"So what? You're going to follow in his footsteps? Just leave with no word?" her aunt asked, not out of concern so much as an attempt to guilt Charlie into acting responsibly.

"Don't act like that would break your heart, Jean."

"And what do you propose to do after you leave here? I don't suppose college is in your agenda," Jean snapped.

"No, as a matter of fact, it's not," replied Charlie.

"Still have that ridiculous notion that you'll become an actress," Jean scoffed.

"Because that's completely unheard of, isn't it?" Charlie spat back at her. "I might as well peddle drugs. At least that's a lucrative business. I mean, hell, why do something I'm good at? No one does that any more."

"God, you don't have a fucking clue, do you?" Jean half-laughed. Charlie wore a bored expression. She was sick to death of having this conversation, but she wasn't going to let Jean win. "Who's going to feed you when you can't get a job? Listen to me, I'm far smarter than you are and I know what it's like out there."

"Once again, you automatically assume I'm going to fail," said Charlie. She was just going through the motions.

"Have you any idea how stiff the competition is for any job?" Jean asked.

"There will always be someone better."

"Your confidence in me is staggering," Charlie deadpanned.

"Use the brain God gave you and go to college," said Jean, disgustedly.

"Fuck you," Charlie replied and pushed past Jean to get down the stairs.

Jean held up an arm to block her. "We're not finished discussing this."

"I don't feel like listening to you bitch at me--" Jean held Charlie's lips together, forbidding her to speak.

"That is *enough*, young lady," Jean hissed at Charlie. Their faces were uncomfortably close.

Charlie pushed backward out of Jean's grasp and rubbed her now sore mouth. "What the hell is wrong with you? For fuck's sake, you act as though no one has ever disagreed with you."

"I'm doing this for you, you ungrateful—"

"I don't want it! Whatever you've chosen for me would make me miserable! It's not like I'm going to wake up one day and say, 'Wow, Jean was right! How foolish I've been!' You're not my mother. You will never, *ever* be my mother."

"Even if I were, it still wouldn't hold much weight. You are such a child. You will always be a child. But one day, little lady, you have to grow up."

"Spare me the existential bullshit, Jean. I'm sick of it." Charlie attempted to pass her once again. Jean tried to grab her arm, but Charlie put enough distance between them that she was just out of reach. "If you so much as touch me again," Charlie told her, "if you come near me in my sleep, I will go to the police. Now leave me the hell alone." Charlie stormed past her and out of the house.

Abby dragged hard on a menthol cigarette and blew the smoke in Charlie's quickly approaching direction. "What's up, ho bag?" she said, smiling sweetly.

"I," said Charlie, standing at the bottom of the stairs connected to Abby's porch, "am not in the mood."

"What crawled up your ass and laid eggs?" asked Abby.

"Nothing. Just that evil harpy I live with is pushing me over the edge. I hate not being eighteen. I wonder if I can move out anyway," Charlie mused.

"Doubtful. You have to get all this signature shit from your guardian if you want your own place before you turn eighteen," Abby replied.

"She's such a bitch. She gives me crap for everything. I don't want to do what she wants me to do with my life, so she jumps down my throat and says I'll do what she wants or she'll turn into Hitler and put me in an oven or something."

Abby turned a skeptical eye toward Charlie. "Did she really say that?"

"Well, no. But she might as well have," said Charlie.

"Listen, I'll make a deal with you," said Abby. "We can go get your shit now, put some in storage, put some over here and you can stay here until you turn eighteen."

"Abby…that's in, like, five weeks," reasoned Charlie.

"Yeah, but it'll be like a really long sleepover," said Abby.

"I don't know," said Charlie. "It would piss her off if I got all my stuff and just moved." She exchanged a mischievous look with Abby. "Fuck it, let's go."

Abby smiled, slapped Charlie on the back, and said, "That's what I like to hear. Let me get my keys."

When Charlie and Abby arrived at Jean's house, there wasn't one lit window. The porch light wasn't even on. The heaps of clothing and miscellaneous items littering the front lawn weren't even visible until the headlights hit them. There were CDs, photo albums, stuffed animals, and books, so many books. All her posters had been ripped off the wall; some had been torn in half. Even Charlie's desk had been pushed over on its face.

"That cunt. That evil, fucking, control freak!" said Charlie as she ran out of the car. "Look what she did! All my shit is ruined! There are grass stains all over my fucking books!" She flew to the front door, about to knock it down, when she saw a note taped to it. She flicked her lighter and held it close enough to read.

Charles,

> *You want out now? Fine. I couldn't care less. All of your belongings have been removed from the premises. Everything else is* <u>mine</u>*. If you have any qualms with my decision, you may take it up with the local law enforcement. Enjoy what you make with the rest of your life.*

Jean

Charlie tried the knob. It was locked. She fished her keys out of her pocket. It didn't work. Jean had changed the locks. Charlie pounded the door with the side of her fist. "Jean! Open the fucking door!" Charlie knew she was still in the house. Jean didn't have any friends, so she couldn't possibly have gone out. So many thoughts whipped through Charlie's mind. She wanted to wring Jean's wrinkled turkey neck. Charlie spouted syllables, the beginnings of expletives forcing their way out of her mouth. "Fu…ckyou…sonof…whore…" She continued banging the door in a cadence to match her swearing. When her forearm began to ache, she resorted to kicking. Non-stop. Marring the paint job which Jean had specially chosen out of an issue of *Martha Stewart Living.* Charlie screamed as she kicked. "Fuck! You! Fuck you! Fuck! Fuck! Fuck! Fuck you!"

Abby had started putting Charlie's belongings, or what was left of them, in the back of the car. She was almost done when Charlie had ceased her rampage.

Charlie was fuming. "Get me the fuck out of here before I set the place on fire," she said.

"Done and done," replied Abby, loading the remainder of stuff in the backseat of the car.

Abby lived alone. She wanted to be a masseuse. In an attempt to show her parents she was serious about her career, Abby dropped out of high school to work as a receptionist at a local spa. When her parents found out, they said, in no uncertain terms, that she was no longer welcome. Abby moved into a three-bedroom house with Amy and Reiss, a stripper and an incredibly queeny homosexual male, respectively.

Two years later, the house was empty, save Abby. Amy moved to New Mexico to be closer to her brother. Reiss capriciously moved to Florida to pick oranges. Abby moved all her things to the second floor of the house and set up shop on the first floor. She took out an ad in the yellow pages and hoped for the best. Business was slow at first, but she talked it up at the spa while her boss was out of earshot. After a few months, she had enough people on her client roster to stop answering phones and commit herself to massage. Charlie riled her mercilessly about it.

"You have to feel up old guys. You're like a socially acceptable prostitute," she said.

"No, I have to relax old guys and take their pain away. I'm more like a socially acceptable drug dealer," Abby corrected.

Abby propped the door open so they could unload the car easily. Charlie moved her things in without a word. Her face was cemented in a scowl. She practically threw everything on the floor. Abby grabbed her arm.

"Dude, what is your problem?" she asked.

"She fucking ruined all my shit," Charlie replied.

"Charlie, it's just stuff. She didn't hurt you, not physically anyway. Not today..." Abby wasn't making her point well. "Anyway, you don't have to deal with her anymore. And you chipped paint off her door, which was cathartic, right?"

"Yeah, I guess," said Charlie, not sounding at all convinced. She picked up one of her shirts. There was something inside it. She reached in and pulled out her comedy mask. It was cracked down the middle and the nose was chipped. "Motherfucker!" Charlie almost threw it against the wall, but restrained herself. She held it with both hands and pushed so hard, it broke. Charlie stared at the palm of her left hand. She flexed her fingers and blood streamed out of the heel. Abby ran for a paper towel and Charlie just started to giggle. She dropped the mask to the floor and collapsed in a heap, laughing maniacally. Abby returned and grabbed Charlie's hand.

"You lunatic. Hold still," she said. She applied pressure to Charlie's palm. Charlie was still on the floor cackling. "You want to let me in on the joke or is it a you had to be there thing?" Abby asked.

"I'm finally free of her. I'm free of that controlling, evil, malevolent twat and this is as close to suicide as I've ever gotten," said Charlie. She howled with laughter. "Just the irony. Sorry."

"You're messed up," said Abby. She looked around the room. "Listen, hold this still. You need to hold it until the blood starts to clot, okay? I'm gonna move your stuff upstairs."

Charlie regained her composure somewhat. "Okay." Abby grabbed an armful of stuff and made for the stairs. "Abby?" said Charlie. She turned. "Thanks. Really, I mean…thanks. Ya know?"

"Yeah. I know."

Abby came downstairs to check on Charlie once everything was moved. "Think you'll need stitches?" she asked.

"Nah," said Charlie.

"Don't shrug it off. That could get infected. Here, let me see," said Abby, reaching for Charlie's hand. She looked at the palm. It had stopped bleeding and there was barely any evidence of injury. "Luckily, it's not deep. But, I want you to put antibacterial ointment on that," Abby warned.

"Yes, mother dear," said Charlie and plodded off to the bathroom. Abby heard running water and Charlie yelled over it. "Hey! Can we do something to celebrate my freedom?" The water was turned off.

"Sure," Abby replied. "What do you wanna do?"

"I don't know," said Charlie, reemerging from the bathroom. "Can we get some drinks?"

"Uh, no. You're not even eighteen, much less twenty-one," Abby retorted.

"Neither are you. But that's never stopped you before. I'm not going to drink anything alcoholic and if I don't order any drinks, they've no reason to card me, right?" said Charlie, smiling widely.

"I don't know…" Abby hesitated.

"C'mon…please?"

Abby decided they'd go to a restaurant that had a bar, so if they ordered food first and alcohol later, maybe they'd only ask for Abby's ID. Abby's always reliable, albeit illegal fake ID. There was such an institution downtown called Caramel.

They waited for the host to seat them. The décor said, "We're laid back, but classy." The walls were covered in dark wood paneling. The restaurant was separated into two areas: the seating area, with booths and a few tables; and the bar. The former was well lit and white Christmas lights ran across the ceiling from corner to corner. Potted ivy plants were dotted throughout. In the bar, bottles lined the wall and there were lights angled from the ceiling to illuminate them. Other than that, the only light came from two arcade video games and a jukebox. The host approached Abby and Charlie.

"Good evening, ladies, two?" he asked.

"Yes," Abby replied and Charlie quickly echoed.

"Smoking or non?" the host inquired.

"Smoking," said Abby.

"Would you like to sit in the dining area or at the bar?" asked the host.

"The bar," Charlie answered before Abby could reply.

"Very good," he said, grabbing two menus, "please follow me."

Abby glared at Charlie.

"What? Look at it this way, there won't be any little kids at the bar," Charlie reasoned.

The host led them to a block of free stools. It was still early so only a few hardcore lushes were out. And they were too busy drowning their sorrows to notice the arrival of fresh blood. "Here we are, ladies. You can place your order with the bartender. Enjoy your meal." Abby pulled up a barstool. Charlie sat to her left.

Charlie looked at the wall of liquor. She glanced to the man sitting a few stools away. He looked seedy and degenerative and slimy. Charlie leaned over to Abby.

"This is so cool," she said.

"Just relax, okay? We're not supposed to be here and you are not getting a drink," said Abby.

"I know. But the host didn't question our sitting at the bar. So, don't worry. We're cool," said Charlie.

Abby shot her a skeptical look and lit a cigarette. The bartender made his way to them.

"What can I get for you?" he asked, starting with Abby.

"I'd like a gin and tonic and she'll have a ginger ale," said Abby, assuring herself that she would keep Charlie honest.

"Coming right up," the bartender replied.

Charlie opened her mouth to protest, but she couldn't find the words. She stared down at her bandaged hand.

The barkeep returned with their drinks, and Charlie reached for her wallet.

"I got it," said Abby, waving her money away.

"You sure?" Charlie asked.

"It's a celebration, isn't it?" she said, raising her glass. "To your freedom."

Charlie clinked her ginger ale to Abby's gin and tonic. "Indeed." And they drank.

As the evening wore on, people poured into Caramel. An hour and a half after Charlie and Abby arrived, there were no barstools vacant. People shouted drink orders over the din. Beverages were handed around and between and over and above Charlie and Abby.

"Two margaritas, rocks," a voice said. Two margaritas went past.

"A grasshopper and a mudslide," said another voice. And a grasshopper and mudslide passed.

"What do you have on tap?" asked a voice. Abby turned to look.

"Bud, Bud Light, Fosters, Corona, Guinness, Harpoon, Miller, Miller Light, Rolling Rock…" Abby nudged Charlie with her elbow.

"I'll have a Guinness." Charlie arched an eyebrow at Abby. Abby nodded her head toward guy ordering. Charlie turned to look.

It was Stephen, the tattooist from Inky Doodles.

Abby mouthed, "Say something!" to Charlie. Charlie shook her head.

The bartender went to get Stephen's beer.

"Uh, hi," said Abby to Stephen. He looked at her.

"Hello," he replied unknowingly.

"You work at Inky Doodles, right?" she said. The bartender handed Stephen his beer. He, in turn, handed the bartender money.

"Uh, yeah," he answered. He squeezed the lime over his beer and then dropped it in. He sipped at the head.

"A few months ago," Abby said, "we went to your shop."

"You royalty?" he said.

"I don't follow," said Abby.

"You said 'we,' I only see you, which would be 'I,'" Stephen reasoned.

"Oh, my friend, Charlie and I. You didn't do my tattoo, but you did hers," Abby replied, motioning to Charlie. Stephen smiled in recognition.

"Oh, yeah. Black sheep. How did it heal?" he asked.

"Good. Thanks," was all Charlie could say. She wanted to sit in his lap and wrap her legs around his waist. She refrained.

"Okay…well, I'll see you around," said Stephen, walking past them to leave.

"Uh, can we buy you a drink?" asked Charlie. He looked at his mug of beer, still mostly full. She felt two inches tall.

He grinned and said, "Sure. I'll be right back." He headed in the direction of the dining area and returned with a chair.

Chapter Two – Talking Shop

Charlie's fingers danced across the number pad, entering strings of ten digit serial numbers. Spot would unpack the boxes, double-checking the inventory and read the ISBNs to her. They rarely spoke during this, unless it was to confirm a number or read back the digit in full. Charlie broke the silence. "I wonder what people did before the number pad."

Spot held a stack of books in one hand as if weighing them. "Hunted and pecked, I suppose."

"Mm," Charlie replied. She stopped then and looked at him. "Spot, if you could do anything, what would you do?"

"Fly," he responded immediately.

"No, not like that. I meant for work."

"Oh." He sat on the remaining boxes from the day's shipment and peered off at nothing. "I'd go on tour," he said, so pleased with his answer that he couldn't help but smile.

Charlie grinned in kind.

"What would you do?" he asked her.

Charlie's smile fell away. She lolled her head from left to right. "I guess I'd do this," she said. "Work for myself. Work with my friends. Be surrounded by books. Daydream if I wanted to." She exhaled a half-laugh.

"What?" Spot asked.

"I'm not quite sure when that happened."

Moving House

Charlie was a virgin. This was not a matter of choice. She'd gone to the same school district all her life, so she'd known everyone. It's hard to find someone attractive when you've seen him eat paste. The last time any of her classmates had been remotely attractive, it had been during dodge ball in third grade. A nasty girl had taken a dislike to Charlie and so singled her out by whipping the ball toward Charlie's head. Nick Emberson caught it before it reached her. He smiled at Charlie and said, "That probably would've hurt." She returned his smile, awkwardly and just nodded her head. She had held a torch for him through tenth grade, but at that point, he had become a cheerleader-banging jock. Charlie's interest in high school guys ended with Nick. She met much more entertaining males through Abby. However, the interest was rarely mutual. Before Stephen, no one had really made her a serious offer for sex.

Charlie had heard all the stories though. It really hurts. You'll bleed. It's terrible. It's an experience you should only have with someone you truly love. It's unlike anything you've ever felt. That much buildup for anything isn't good, but enough cannot be said about the magical act which is sex. The closest Charlie had ever been to intercourse was cyber sex. She had stumbled on to the internet when she was fifteen and filled out an online profile. She started up a correspondence with some guy a few states away who had a lot of time on his hands and an inordinate amount of it was spent online. He asked what she was into, her reply being music, art, and theatre. He said he wanted to fuck her in half.

Um, okay.

The only thing she learned was that talking dirty didn't do it for her. When she fantasized about sex, it was mostly quick snippets of kissing and heavy breathing. She didn't really know how to proceed from there. She'd seen endless reels of porn. She had an older brother and his collection of pornography rivaled most fetishists on the East Coast. He was not a fetishist himself, he was, instead merely a sexoholic. He liked talking about it, watching it, doing it, everything. And he felt the need to share it all with Charlie.

She knew all about oral sex. She knew most girls didn't like it. She knew most guys didn't do it. She knew sixty-nining was doing it simultaneously. She'd never experienced any of this, but she knew about it. She knew if there were someone she wanted to have sex with, if she were pressed for a candidate, it would be Stephen. He was very unlike the males Charlie was used to. He didn't stare at her in that "you're a freak" way, he didn't call her a dyke, and he didn't ask about Abby after five seconds. Charlie had feared that last part the most. Abby was sexy. Not just attractive, but sexy. She was confident and able and smart and when she knew what she wanted, she went for it. She could break most guys with a smile, but didn't. Many an object of Charlie's affection had fallen to Abby's charm. And she really couldn't blame them. Thankfully, Stephen had no interest in Abby.

"She's too skinny," he'd say. "You can see her ribcage through her shirt. That's not right." That, among other things, told Charlie that she need not worry about a possible attraction between Stephen and Abby.

That first night in Caramel, Charlie listened while Abby and Stephen argued about everything from politics to whether or not folk singers should be shot. When Abby's bladder filled and she left for the ladies' room, Stephen had reached the happily inebriated level. He looked at Charlie and said, "So, you haven't said much this evening…"

"I know very little about the subject at hand."

"Ahh, that's all right. I'm not a fan of overly opinionated people, anyway," replied Stephen.

"But you seem to be rather opinionated yourself," Charlie reasoned.

"That's true. Tact is a quality I admire in others. It's something I don't have the ability to master. So, I usually throw caution to the wind and find my foot in my mouth later." To this, Charlie nodded. She sipped her ginger ale. Looking at the blissful expression on Stephen's face and judging how much time she had left before Abby returned, she chose her words carefully in her head before speaking.

"Forgive me if I'm about to be too forward," Charlie began, "but, I've wanted to kiss you since I first saw you and I was wondering if it would be all right if I did that now."

Stephen stared at her blankly before a smile slowly crept to his face.

"Right now?" he asked.

"Yes," she replied evenly.

He leaned forward and she leaned to meet him. Their lips touched and stopped for a moment, unmoving. Charlie then felt Stephen's arm around her waist and she fell into him. She slipped her tongue into his mouth. He tasted of beer on its way to being stale. That didn't stop her. Their kiss lasted for ten more seconds and when Charlie took her first breath of fresh air, it was thick with smoke. That was mainly because Abby was blowing it in her face. She'd returned to the table during the floor show.

"Oh, hi," was all Charlie could manage.

"*Hello*," Abby purred. "Did I miss anything?"

Stephen had kept his arm around Charlie. He pulled her closer and said, "Nope. Just getting acquainted."

From that point on, Charlie knew there was no love loss between Stephen and Abby.

"So, you're goth, right?" Stephen asked Charlie. They sat in his room, not facing each other. He was at his desk, doodling. She sat on his bed, cross-legged, scribbling in her journal with a black crayon.

"Um…well, not exactly," she replied, looking up from her book.

"Okay…"

"Well, it's hard to categorize oneself into just one group. Like, if I had to describe you, I'd say you were a punky, body mod guy," said Charlie.

"Okay…" he repeated.

"See my point?" Charlie asked.

"Well, yeah, but only because we're talking about me. I don't fit into one category. You do," Stephen insisted.

"No, I don't," Charlie protested.

Stephen made no attempt to disguise his eyeroll. "Your hair is naturally brown; you dye it blue black. You wear a shitload of eyeliner and black nail polish. If I had to guess, I'd say you have a frequent shopper card at Hot Topic and you laugh in the face of mortality with that bauble resting against your rather impressive rack." The last part referred to Charlie's large silver ankh.

"So, if you have me all figured out, Mr. Socially Conscious, why bother asking in the first place?" Charlie demanded.

"Well, you don't act goth," Stephen replied simply. "You don't listen to Sisters of Mercy. You hate Vermouth. Not once have I ever heard you remark about 'the scene'…and yet, you're remarkably brooding."

Charlie was going to throw a barb in return. She tried to think of a witty remark to sling at him, but all she could think of was, "Fuck you," followed by a harumph and a baleful glare.

Stephen leaned over and mussed Charlie's hair. He shook it with both hands until it stood in a satisfactory state of dishevelment. He smiled and said, "Perfect."

Charlie hid her face for embarrassment. In doing so, she masked the tear of joy that found its way down her left cheek.

Charlie and Stephen were walking to his apartment when he asked, "So, what does it take to get you off?" It wasn't as up front as all that. There was segue, but there the question stood.

Charlie laughed and replied, "Physical contact," and kept walking. Stephen grabbed her from behind.

"You all wet now?" he asked.

"Yeah, let's do it here," she smirked. His face shifted from flirtatious to let's-get-it-on in no time. Charlie was seconds away from saying, "Please don't. Not here," when Stephen raised his eyebrows and she remembered his question. "I don't really know, I guess. I've never had sex before, so I'm not sure." They continued walking.

"Okay," said Stephen. He changed gears. "What do you do when you masturbate?"

"Um…" Charlie hesitated. "Nothing really. I, uh, don't do that either."

"Get the fuck out of here," Stephen said. He stopped walking and squinted at her. "Really?" She nodded. "Huh. I mean, you're not the first girl I've ever known who doesn't, but they're few and far between. Most girls I know can't orgasm during sex, which is unfortunate, but they can come because of masturbation."

"It's not that I'm repressed or anything," Charlie felt the need to explain herself. "When I was younger, I didn't even think about it. No urges, ya know? Then when I got to my teens, I thought it was gross. Stupid girl posturing. Then I met a couple people who seemed pretty cool and they talked about it openly," meaning Abby and her housemates, "so I figure, there's nothing wrong with it. I've just never done it, myself."

"I guess we'll see if you're an exception to the girls can't come rule," said Stephen.

"All right," said Charlie. They reached Stephen's building and went inside. His apartment was on the fifth floor; they walked up in silence. Before they went in, Charlie turned to Stephen. "Um, when we actually, do have sex," she said, "if I yell or anything, tell you to stop or whatever, just ignore me, okay? I want to get it over with, not that it won't mean anything to me, but I just want to get it out of the way and I don't want you to feel weird about it."

"Okay. That's fine," he said. He smiled at her and ushered her into the apartment. This reassured Charlie more than she could have said.

Once inside, Charlie finally met Stephen's infamous roommate. Up until then, he'd never been home. He had a full time job which demanded most of his free time. He got up when he saw them come in.

"Hey, what's up?" he said to Stephen.

"Not much. This is Charlie. Charlie, this is Derek," replied Stephen.

"Hi," said Charlie, extending her hand. "It's nice to meet you."

"Nice to meet you," said Derek. He glanced back to the television. An infomercial was starting. "Look at this. See that chick in the nice suit?" There were two women onscreen. One was wearing a suit and maddeningly pink lipstick. The other was wearing a shirt that didn't quite fit and grimy leggings. They were standing in front of a trailer.

"Yeah?" said Stephen.

"She look familiar?" asked Derek.

Stephen looked closer. "No. Should she?"

"She used to do porn," he replied.

"No shit? Anything I'd have seen?" Stephen asked.

"She was the chick who did that food series. Every one of her early stints had some food escapade in it. My favorite is the one when she shoved a stick of butter up that dude's ass. After that, she moved on to 'arty' porn. She'd paint herself all over and then roll around on this huge canvas, fucking some guy's brains out. Now she hocks makeup on the home shopping networks. It's ridiculous."

"And what charming makeup she's wearing now," said Charlie.

"Yeah, really," said Stephen. "So, what's with the Grape Nuts, Derek?" Stephen pointed to the box of cereal Derek held. "I thought you hated that."

"No, I figured it out," he said. He looked to Charlie. "See, when I first started eating this, it really pissed me off. It's called Grape Nuts, but it tastes neither like grapes nor nuts. It tastes like gravel. And it's cereal, so you're supposed to add milk. But the texture is such that it sucks up all the milk, so you use up half a gallon on one fucking bowl. So, I didn't eat it for a long time. But, I figured out a new use for it. Watch."

The three of them sat on the sofa and watched the screen. Derek turned up the volume. "Here you can see," said the porn star-cum-Avon lady, "when using the pore minimizer in conjunction with the foundation and blush, it results in less clogged pores." Derek threw a large handful of cereal at the screen.

"It's fewer, not less, you fucking cooze!" he yelled. As far as first impressions go, Charlie was fairly amused at this point. "See, I can take my frustrations out on the cereal and the slutty cosmetics monger. Can you imagine the interview she had to go through to get that job? 'Yeah, what is your previous experience with makeup?' 'Uh, I wore a ton of it on the set of Meals in Heels 5.'"

Charlie didn't know what she'd expected in Derek. After all the stories she'd heard about him: "Derek gets ass *all* the time. Just about every day…" "Derek has this crazy immunity to every drug imaginable. He can be tripping on anything, and you can't even tell. No hallucinations, nothing." Or, Charlie's personal favorite, "There was this one time Derek was at this bar, completely piss drunk and this chick started hitting on him. *Hard.* She might as well have put her panties on his head and done a lap dance on his face. So, the guy she's there with starts flipping out, saying she'd been flirting with everyone, from the bartender, who was female, to the bouncer, who was not. What does this bitch do? Fucking blames it on Derek. Says he was drunk and pawing her. He was drunk, yes, but interested, no. Well, the meathead boyfriend has heard enough at this point. He starts pushing Derek off his barstool and Derek, who has said nothing up 'til now, looks at him and says, 'Hey. Cuntrag. Don't start with me. Your lady came up to me, not vice versa, and practically wiped her cunt on my dick. And,' said Derek, staggering because he's still very drunk, 'I could get more pussy than you and your rug-munching girlfriend combined.' That was all this guy needed to hear. He grabbed Derek's mug of beer and smacked him across the face with it. That's how Derek got that scar above his left eye."

All Charlie could say was, "Your reputation precedes you."

"Uh-oh…what does that mean?" he asked warily.

"I just heard a couple stories," she said. "Like the one about your bar fight."

"Oh, this?" he asked, touching his scar. "Two stitches. The other guy got five. *And* I fucked his girlfriend. Chicks dig scars."

Charlie knew what it was. She'd expected Derek to be taller. Someone with such a voracious appetite for everything from women to drugs, one would expect him to be larger. Somehow the physical appearance would explain the need. But he was just a guy in a T-shirt and a pair of jeans. Average height, a little on the skinny side. Kind of scruffy looking with a beard in chronic need of a razor. From the stories, Charlie felt he looked too…normal.

She looked around the room. It was definitely male domain. No wall hangings. The furniture was minimal. The most characteristic thing in the room was a cardboard cutout of R2D2 which had been propped up in the corner. The living room spilled out into the dining room in the shape of a chunky L. The kitchen was an offshoot of the dining room, and beyond that one could see the beginnings of a hallway, but not what lay afterward.

"Didn't you say you wanted to show me something in your room?" she asked Stephen.

"Fuck me if that doesn't sound like bad porn dialogue," said Derek. Stephen kicked the side of his leg.

"Shut up," he said to Derek. Then, to Charlie, "Go ahead back." She led the way toward the hallway. The bathroom was the first door on the left. The second was a linen closet. The only door to the right opened onto Derek's room, and at the end of the hall, there was a door covered in pencil sketches. The largest was of a girl lying on her back, arms behind her head, naked. Her eyes were closed and her back was arched. There were a few of dragons, some Celtic knot works, a couple skulls, and the hearts and flowers gallery was inserted, smallish, at the bottom.

"Are these them?" Charlie asked after taking it all in.

"No, those are just prospective tattoos…some of them I've been commissioned to design, some of them are just for display in the parlor," Stephen replied. With his hand, he nudged the door open. A sickly blue light trickled out of the room, but other than that, it looked like a black hole. Charlie felt it reminiscent of science fiction novels and was trepidatious to go any further. Somewhere in the back of her mind, she knew dark, evil monsters lived in black holes. She hadn't noticed that Stephen had walked in already and was surprised when he flicked the light switch to ON. It was then that Charlie saw the origin of the blue light. Stephen's aquarium was on a table next to his bed and from it oozed a neon blue haze.

"Oh, you have fish!" she said and realized how naive she sounded.

Yeah, space cadet, that's what aquariums are for. Idiot.

"Three…just got them today. Thing One, Thing Two, and Red," replied Stephen.

There were two long fish with stubby fins that had zebra markings. Charlie didn't see the third fish. She looked against the faux sea setting background, but still saw nothing.

"Um…I don't see the third. I see the two zebra fish, but I don't see another one," Charlie said to Stephen.

"Yeah…Red's over here," he answered and pointed to his dresser. In its own fishbowl swam a small red fish with a flowing tail and willowy dorsal fin. Stephen sprinkled some food into the bowl. "Did you have a good day, Miss Red? Yes, you did." Charlie chuckled at hearing Stephen talk in a baby voice to his pet. He was so big and he would put on his "Do I scare you? Good," face. Seeing him act like a girl was almost shocking.

"Why isn't she in the aquarium?" Charlie asked.

"Because she'd kill Thing One and Thing Two. Hers is a very vicious breed," Stephen replied.

Stephen's room had a minimalistic decor. His desk was in the corner farthest from the door. An open case full of paint tubes stood below and papers were scattered on the desktop among inkwells and brushes. Against the opposite wall was Stephen's bed, full sized and without a frame. There was no blanket, only two fitted sheets, one for the mattress and one for the box spring. Both were white. Next to the desk was the aquarium. A closet and Stephen's dresser occupied the two remaining walls. The walls, like in the living room, were bare save a few drawings tacked above Stephen's desk. Charlie walked over to examine them more closely.

"Oh, don't look at those," said Stephen, waving her away. "They're just sketches. Reference pieces. Shit to work from."

"Ahh," Charlie said as though that whisked away her curiosity. She flopped down on his bed and looked up at Stephen's silhouette against aquarium light. "So…what do you want to do?"

"So? How was it?" Abby asked over breakfast the next day.

"It was, um…painful…and dry…and, uh, awkward," said Charlie. "Who knew sex was so much like a root canal?"

"Sex is nothing like a root canal," said Abby. "Getting a root canal is like giving a blow job with an unlubricated condom while wearing an O ring." Abby's eyes glazed over with nostalgia.

"Right," said Charlie. "so, what I was just talking about was sex with Stephen."

Her attention snapped back to Charlie. "Yes. And you said it was what?"

"Awkward," Charlie replied adamantly.

"Awkward? In what way?"

"Awkward in that I never had anything anywhere near my vagina, much less in it and now I've had a huge fucking cock thrust in and out of it."

"It was huge? Really? How huge?" Abby asked excitedly.

"Oh shut up. That's not the point. I don't need this kind of stress."

"Listen to you…'this kind of stress.' You're so young, it's almost cute," Abby teased.

"What is that supposed to mean?" Charlie said indignantly.

"The next time Stephen wants to have sex, you'll suck it up like every other woman has since the dawn of time. If you would've just given it up to Jeff Lindy back in tenth grade, you wouldn't have had this problem."

"But his ex said he was a minute man," said Charlie.

"Exactly," Abby responded while dragging on her menthol lite.

Charlie crossed her arms and pouted, "You're no help."

"Your problem is you need everything to be perfect and it never will be," said Abby, smiling contentedly while studying the end of her cigarette. Her eyes met

Charlie's. "Even when things feel as right as possible, there's always going to be one little snag, and if I know you—which I do—it's going to drive you insane."

"This isn't a little snag, Abigail," Charlie insisted.

"Yes it is, Charles," said Abby. "The major problem is the dryness. If you were wet, it wouldn't be as painful. And if it were less painful, it would be less awkward, so I think you know what you need to do."

"No, not really," Charlie snapped.

"You need to take your finger and shove it in your hole until you figure out what you like, retard."

Charlie looked at Abby, head down, eyes up, and said, "You cannot be serious."

"Fucking hell, you're so uptight."

"It's not a matter of being uptight. I don't give a shit who touches themselves or when or where or whatever. I just have no intention of doing it myself," Charlie insisted.

"You're telling me you've never been horny?" Abby asked.

"Sure I have."

"When?" Abby demanded.

"In the back of Jeff Lindy's car," Charlie said immediately.

"You're a liar, and even if you weren't, that situation was a matter of pheromones and stimuli. I'm talking about when you're just sitting there, minding your own business, whether it be watching TV, reading a book, painting your nails, or polishing your dildo, and you feel a little…ya know. Tingle in your nether regions…"

"I cannot believe we're having this conversation," said Charlie.

"Don't change the subject. Have you no urges, woman?" Abby asked.

"Maybe, once or twice. I don't really remember. It's not like I mark my calendar over these things," Charlie scoffed.

"Maybe you should."

"Right…next time, I feel a cuntache coming on, I'll be sure to grab my engagement book."

"Oh no…when it happens, you need to get in an empty room and go to town," said Abby, smirking.

"That's it. This discussion is over. No more," said Charlie. She grabbed her mug of coffee and sped out of the room. She could still hear Abby snickering as she left.

A week later, Charlie called Stephen's apartment.

"H'lo?" answered a distant voice. Something in its tone said, "I don't want to be bothered."

"Um, hi, it's Charlie, is Stephen there?" Charlie managed to squeak.

"Yeah, just a second." Charlie assumed it was Derek. A hand brushed the receiver to muffle the yell. "Stephen! Phone!" Charlie heard Stephen's heavy footsteps across the hardwood floor. "It's Charlie," said Derek. Stephen took the phone.

"Hey, what's up?" he said.

"Nothing really, I was just wondering what you were up to," Charlie said, attempting to sound nonchalant. She had been thinking about him all week.

"Not a lot. Just sitting here watching Derek throw breakfast foods at the 19-inch," Stephen replied. Charlie envisioned Grape Nut anthills surrounding their television.

"Sounds riveting," she said.

"It's quite educational. I'm learning new words," said Stephen.

"Yeah…so, have you eaten yet?" Charlie ventured.

"About twenty minutes ago," Stephen replied. He chuckled. She imagined that was at Derek's antics though she couldn't be sure.

"Did you want to go see a movie or something?" she asked.

"Nah, everything that's out right now sucks," he sighed.

"Okay…would it be all right if I came over?" Charlie asked.

"Sure," said Stephen.

"Great. Be there in a few," said Charlie and she hung up. She walked into the living room where Abby was apparently blowing up little worms with other little worms. "Hey, I'm going out."

"Uh-huh," said Abby, not taking her eyes from the screen. Charlie walked in front of the TV to get to the door. "Have some nice sex," Abby said right before the door closed.

"Hey, if you have time while I'm gone, don't forget to fuck yourself," Charlie replied and shut the door behind her.

Meanwhile…

"What was that about?" Derek asked.

"Eh, Charlie's coming over," Stephen replied and made his way to the kitchen. There was a portion of the wall cut out so he could still be seen from the living room. He grabbed a beer from the refrigerator.

"Dude, what is your problem?" said Derek, turning the TV off.

"What are you talking about?" Stephen asked after a swig and a wipe.

"I'm talking about your lack of affection for the girl whose ass you slap this week," Derek answered.

"You're one to talk," Stephen said accusatorily.

"Not the same. I've never met a girl who was interested in me for more than my funny drunk stories and fourteen inch cock," said Derek.

"Starting where? At the spleen?" Stephen scoffed.

"My point is that you need to show, for lack of a better phrase, a little love and tenderness."

"Derek, you are the last person who should be giving advice on being cold. You were with the same girl for three years and the closest she got to seeing the inner you was the time you jizzed in her eye. I don't see you going out to pursue the love of your life."

"Okay, first of all, I'm not pursuing shit, but neither are you. This girl is chasing you and you're not even showing her a good time," said Derek.

"She has a good time," Stephen interjected.

"Let me finish." Stephen waved him on. "She wants to spend time with you.

If I had a nice, young girl who called me and wanted to do shit for me, I'd snap that up in less time than you can say I haven't been laid in over a year."

"So that's what this is about?" Stephen asked Derek.

"No, but eventually, you're going to get to the point when there's no one who will give you a second look and you'll be regretting that sweet girl you snubbed or pushed away."

"Why don't you marry her then?" Stephen snapped.

"If she weren't so fucking enamored with you, I might consider it. And I'm not saying you need to get married. All I'm saying is you're taking her for granted."

Stephen opened his mouth to reply and then figured he wouldn't bother.

"And, by the way," said Derek, "I jizzed in Sara's eye because she liked it like that."

"Yeah, whatever," said Stephen.

There was a knock at the door. Derek got off the couch to answer it.

"Hey Charlie, come on in."

"Hi Derek, thanks." Charlie immediately walked over to Stephen and gave him a hug.

"I missed you," she whispered, hoping he wouldn't hear. She felt self-conscious saying it in front of Derek and Stephen always made her feel slightly stupid for saying it at all.

"Yeah…" Stephen trailed off. He had heard her. "So," he said, pushing her away to face him, "what's up?"

"I was just wondering if I could talk to you about something," said Charlie.

"Sure," he said. Stephen pulled up a chair in the dining room.

"Umm…out of earshot?" she asked, motioning to Derek.

Derek shot Stephen a look and mouthed the words, "Be nice."

Stephen said, "Okay, we can talk in my room."

"Thanks." Charlie walked down the hallway to Stephen's room and turned to see him enter and close the door.

"Are you okay?" Stephen asked noncommittally.

"Yeah," Charlie responded. "It's kind of, umm… I was talking to Abby the other day and she sort of suggested… I was trying to figure out what would make our sex easier."

"Our sex is uneasy?

"Not that it's not good. It's just…umm, painful? And since I'm kind of new to this, I was wondering if you'd be willing to try some stuff with me…to make it, ya know…less. Painful."

"What kind of stuff?" Stephen asked, sounding moderately interested.

"Would it be all right if I just went ahead and did it?" Charlie asked hesitantly.

Shady images flashed through Stephen's mind. Charlie whipping him while he was tied to a chair, her pissing in his mouth, him, face down, ass up, while Charlie fisted him. "Sure," he replied.

She turned the lights off. The room filled with weak, blue aquarium light. Charlie pulled Stephen to her and pressed her mouth against his. Her right hand traced his spine to his head and grabbed a handful of hair. She didn't let go. He palmed her ass and lay her down on the bed. He began to disrobe.

"Wait," she said. She took a quick breath in to speak, but then let it out loudly. "Christ, I don't know how to ask this."

"What?" he asked.

"I don't want you to think that I'm not enjoying this…because it's nice. Really nice. But, Abby said that I needed to…" Charlie stared at the ceiling. She didn't want to say *masturbate* aloud. "Sorry," she said. "This is just kind of embarrassing."

"We can do whatever you want to do, Charlie," Stephen said.

"All right." She took a deep breath. "I'm going to…masturbate. You can, uh, watch, I guess. Or help. Or masturbate too. Or…whatever…" She closed her eyes. Slowly, she took her clothes off. She heard the weight of Stephen's pants hit the floor. She opened her eyes, just once, to see him looking at her. He reached out and ran his hand up her leg. She touched the general area around her crotch, unsure of what she wanted. Once her hand was there, Stephen worked on himself. The harder she rubbed, the wetter it got. She didn't put her hand anywhere near her slit. Not even a finger ventured past her labia. She tried it with two hands. Stephen leaned against her and put his dick against her inner thigh. His breath was hot on her neck.

"I want to fuck you," he whispered.

"No, wait," said Charlie. She had to detain him somehow. She needed more time. She pushed Stephen on his back and kissed from his hip to his cock. She continued touching herself while she blew him. She was crouched between his legs and almost flat against her stomach. Her hands could barely reach past her pubic hair and she was beginning to lose feeling in her fingers. Her forearms started to ache and, defeatedly, she stopped. She retreated to the end of the bed and curled up in the fetal position.

"What's wrong?" Stephen asked.

Charlie didn't reply. He touched her back and felt her breath stagger. "I'm fine," she whispered. It was barely a sob.

"Are…can I…?" Stephen didn't know what to say.

Charlie sat up and hastily wiped her face. She hugged her sides and tried to regulate her breathing. "I'm sorry."

"No," he said. "Don't, I just…I don't know what to do to help…" Charlie felt around on the ground for her clothes. She pulled them on and stood to face Stephen.

"Listen, I'm sorry. I'm retarded or something. I'm gonna get going," she said.

"Uh, okay," he replied.

A twinge of pain shot through her. She was hoping he'd tell her to stay. She simply nodded.

"I'll call soon," she said and went out the door.

By the time she reached home, Charlie's face was still red and swollen from crying. She went straight to the bathroom to splash some water on her face.

"That was a quickie for the books."

Charlie gasped and turned around.

Abby was standing in the doorway.

"Jesus, what happened?" Abby said when she saw Charlie's face.

"I really don't want to talk about it right now."

"Did he hit you?" Abby demanded.

"No! Oh my God…no," Charlie shook her head. "I just really can't talk about it right now.

"What the fuck happened? You come home looking absolutely awful and you just say you don't want to talk about it? At least tell me if you're all right," said Abby.

"I'll be fine," said Charlie, returning to the sink. More splashing and then she turned the faucet off. She toweled off her face and looked at her reflection. "I suppose I do look rather heinous, don't I?"

"You've looked better, I must say that," Abby replied.

Charlie sighed and sat on the bathroom counter. "Shit." She looked at her friend. "Remember what we talked about the other day?"

"About your inability to touch your own hoo-hoo?" Abby smirked.

"Fuck you," said Charlie, her comment lacking malice. "Upon your insistence, I tried to…ya know…"

"Touch your own hoo-hoo?"

"Would you knock it off?" said Charlie. "I went over to Stephen's and I figured I could masturbate and then we could…whatever. But, I didn't know what the hell I was doing, and I just fucked it all up and got upset and I left."

"So why don't you go do it now?" Abby asked.

"Do what now?"

"Don't make me say it again," Abby replied.

"What the fuck is the point of that? I thought I needed to be wet for the sex? Why would I do it when he's not here?" Charlie asked.

Abby looked at her for a few seconds and then raised an eyebrow. "Are you serious? Honey, when I said you needed to figure out what you liked, I meant for you to do it on your own and then tell Stephen and have him do it for you. It's called foreplay." Charlie squinted one eye and tilted her head.

"Oh," she said. "But I'd feel kind of weird about telling him what to do."

"Fine. Have it your way and have your shitty sex."

"You are such a pain in my ass," said Charlie. "I don't know why I tell you anything."

"Neither do I. If you need any more advice, I can draw you a picture of hand positions."

"Be still, my heart," Charlie scoffed.

"I knew you'd feel grateful."

Charlie stood in Stephen's apartment, staring at his wall. In between a potential tattoo sketch and a poster for Meat Beat Manifesto was Stephen's degree, framed. "You graduated from Yale?" said Charlie, with an air of disbelief.

Stephen's eyes were closed. He sucked in part of his cigarette and an equal part ashed away. He held it in, letting the smoke saturate the roof of his mouth.

Charlie waited patiently for his face to turn red. Stephen blew the smoke out through his nostrils, opened his eyes and said, "Yup."

"*You* did," she repeated.

He smiled and said, "Yeah."

Her mouth hung open; he leaned over and tapped the bottom of her chin, shutting it. "What was your major?" she asked.

"Tattoo artistry, obviously," he answered, in another puff of smoke.

Charlie hesitated.

"Really?" she said finally.

"No." Stephen laughed with his cigarette clenched between his teeth. "Dude, you're such a tool. I have a degree in Russian."

"You have a degree…in Russian. Stephen, you live in Connecticut," said Charlie.

"Yeah. I was supposed to be an exchange student, but, to piss off my parents, I decided not to go."

"Did it work?" she asked.

"Oh yeah. But not as much as my being a tattoo artist," answered Stephen. He mimicked the voice of his father, "'You're doing *what?*'" He coughed heavily. "'What kind of fucking job is that? What are you, a fag?' Yes, father, I draw pictures on people's skin and therefore engage in sodomy with other men. You have me all figured out, you fucking Mongoloid Neanderthal."

"I thought you got along with your parents," said Charlie.

"My dear," Stephen replied, "no one gets along with their parents. It's just the way things are. It's like having some fine young girl ask her stereotypically sleazy frat brother boyfriend if he ever looks at other girls. Of course not, he lies. In fact, it doesn't even have to be that specific. Any guy who says he doesn't gaze at the scenery is a fucking liar."

Charlie's brow lowered. "What about you?" she asked.

"What about me?" he repeated, still nursing his cigarette.

"Do you look at other girls?"

"Yes." His eyes were closed again. The apathy in his answer bothered Charlie. She knew he was aware of her hurt.

"Well," said Charlie, standing up, "I'm gonna get going."

With one eye open, Stephen grabbed her waist and pulled her to his lap. "Just because I look at other girls doesn't mean I don't care about you. You see some girl, you wonder what it would be like to screw her. We are only mammals, after all." Charlie pursed her lips to stop from saying whatever. For as often as she said it, she vehemently loathed the word. "C'mon," he said, "haven't you ever seen some girl you wanted to fuck?" He moved his eyebrows up and down. She couldn't help laughing.

"Shut up. You're such a jerk."

Abby and Charlie sat in the bagel shop across the street from home/work.

"Charlie, I bet if you showed Danny your tits, we could get free bagels," said Abby. Danny owned the shop. He was visibly in his late forties at the youngest. He had teeth the color of the sun and 214 short hairs on his head. Every time

Abby and Charlie were in, he called Charlie "his sweetheart".

"Why not show him *your* tits?" Charlie grinned.

"Wouldn't be good enough," Abby teased. "He wants to see yours." The two girls were walking away from the counter to a table. "I bet he's watching us walk away."

"He is not," Charlie protested.

"If he is, you're paying for my next carton of cigarettes," said Abby.

They both turned.

Danny's eyes shot down and he scrubbed the counter furiously. Abby could be heard laughing from outside.

"So, how's that sexy piece of ass of yours?" Abby scoffed.

"Stephen's fine, thank you. How's your nonexistent piece of ass?" Charlie asked.

"Thanks. I appreciate that."

"You started it."

Charlie was carrying a stack of towels from the laundry room to the linen closet when the phone rang. Her eyes widened as though a safe had been dropped on her foot.

"I'll get it!" she yelled, tossing the towels on the nearest available surface. She leapt over the sofa and just barely caught the phone. "Hello?" she said excitedly. "No, it's okay, bye."

Abby was playing video games not two feet away. "Who was it?" she asked.

"Wrong number," Charlie sighed.

"Oh. Still folding towels?"

"Refolding," Charlie said and collected the towels from where they'd landed. Abby smiled. It was nice to have help. The phone rang again. Abby heard the rhythmic pounding of Charlie's running.

"Got it!" she exclaimed while sailing over the sofa. "Hello? Oh, yeah, just a sec." She passed the phone to Abby. "For you," she said, more than a little disappointed. She returned to her work.

Charlie was washing dishes about an hour later when, over the water, she thought she heard ringing. Without turning off the faucet, she ran, plate in hand, to the living room.

Abby waited until Charlie was practically upon her to answer it.

"Hello?" said Abby.

"Hey, is Charlie around?" Stephen asked.

Abby looked up at her friend/co-worker/roommate and smiled. "No, sorry," she said.

"Okay. It's Stephen. Could you tell her I called?"

"Will do."

"Okay, bye."

"Bye," and she hung up.

Charlie's face fell a mile. She looked at the clock. Six forty-five. She'd been hoping he'd call. Slowly and sadly, she started back to the kitchen.

"By the way," Abby began.

"Yeah?" said Charlie.

"You're doing a great job."

"Thanks," she replied quietly.

"Oh, and Stephen called."

Charlie bolted upright. "What? When? Just now? Why didn't you tell me?"

"You seemed busy."

Tossing the still wet plate at Abby, Charlie grabbed the phone. She held the phone in one hand and dialed with her thumb. Abby yanked it away by the antenna. "Hey!"

"Don't call him back yet," she said to Charlie.

"What? Why not?"

Abby shrugged and smiled. "Make him wait."

Charlie looked at her without moving. She didn't blink. She barely breathed. She spent thirty seconds staring at her before grabbing the phone back. "That's the dumbest thing I've ever heard."

"Know what I think is dumb? Being at his beck and call," Abby replied.

"That's not what this is. It's common courtesy. I'm returning a phone call."

"You're building your day around said phone call," said Abby. "If I wouldn't have picked it up when he called, you'd've leapt over the couch for the third time in two hours with a fucking plate in your hand."

"So?" Charlie snapped.

"It's just ridiculous."

"Don't act like you've never been this way over some guy you were fucking," Charlie responded.

"But, that's not all this is," said Abby.

"What does that mean?"

"You go through your day in a fog. You look at him like, 'Gee, you're dreamy,' and you do whatever he wants. What are you getting out of this relationship?"

"I have a good time with him. Is that a crime?"

"No, but you're being a lapdog," Abby said.

"I am not."

""You are. And if he were some great catch, I'd understand, but he's not, he's a—"

"Look. I know you don't get along with Stephen. That doesn't mean I can't like him."

"He treats you like shit."

"He doesn't."

Abby looked at her with sudden enlightenment. "Oh, Christ."

"What," Charlie snapped.

"You're in love with him, aren't you?"

Charlie attempted to reply but came up short.

"Does he know?" Abby asked.

Charlie avoided the question.

"Great," Abby groused. "That's just great."

Resigned, she handed Charlie the phone and headed for the door. Before reaching it, she said, "This is probably too late, but if there's any bit of sanity left in you, if there's some small part of you that's not his…try not to fall completely. This can't end well."

Charlie looked at the phone and then glanced after Abby.

Fuck.

She followed Abby halfway up the stairs. "Wait," Charlie said.

"What," said Abby.

"Why did you say that?" Charlie asked.

"Which part?"

"That it can't end well. Why not?" Charlie pressed.

"Charlie, really," said Abby.

"What?"

"Where do you think this is headed? Do you think you're going to get married, have kids, and a two-car garage?" Abby asked.

"I dunno," Charlie mumbled and sat on the stairs. Abby joined her. "We could get married," Charlie shrugged. "I mean, I don't know if that's what he wants, but ya know…I wouldn't mind." Abby snickered. "What?"

"My dearest friend, marriage is like college," Abby explained. "Everyone tells you what a wonderful experience it'll be…that you can't go through life without it. So, you're really excited when it starts, but after a few months, the novelty starts to wear off. It just becomes commonplace and you realize it's still life, just slightly awry. After a while, you begin to wonder whether or not all the effort you've put into it is worth what you're paying for it and, in the end, you realize it was a waste of time. Most marriages in this country end in divorce and most college graduates end up working retail."

"Abby, you've never been married nor have you gone to college," Charlie pointed out.

"But I know people who've done both. I knew a girl…when she was twenty-one years old, she decided she wanted to go to college. She hadn't spoken to her parents in three years. She applies for financial aid. They tell her she's not independent of her parents. Even though she's not spoken to either of them, she's still dependent on them somehow. And she won't be independent until she turns twenty-four, joins the military, has a kid, has a dependent who's not her kid, or… wait for it…gets married."

"What did she do?" Charlie asked.

"Well," Abby continued. "She married a guy who was completely in love with her. He knew it was only so she could attend college but he loved her, so they got married. He lavished her with attention to the point of suffocation, so they got divorced. She dropped out of college and is now waiting tables to pay off a student loan for a degree she doesn't have."

"So, what's you're point?"

"Marriage and college are for suckers. I'll leave you to think on that." Abby ascended the stairs as Charlie stared at the phone in her hand.

A long train of smoke slowly chugged its way out of Abby's mouth. She gulped a swig of coffee and let out a trademarked Diet Coke "Ahh!" She took a deep breath and said, "There's nothing like caffeine and menthol in the morning."

"I'll take your word for it," said Charlie, perusing a menu. They were getting pancakes at The Greasy Spoon.

Charlie let her fingertip roam around the rim of her coffee mug. She took hers decaffeinated and black. She couldn't stand sweeteners and she didn't deal well with caffeine. Most of the wait staff would roll their eyes and be put out that they had to get two different kinds of coffee. One girl actually said, "Why get decaf? There's no flavor and it puts you to sleep."

Charlie just smiled and said, "Thanks, I'll keep that in mind." The waitress got a three-cent tip.

Charlie felt if you really want to tell a waitress that she needs to work harder, you don't leave without tipping. Always tip. Not because you have to, but because if you don't, she'll think you forgot and just shrug it off. If you really want to point out how shittily she's done her job, leave anywhere from two to five cents on the table. Always in pennies, then you can stack them to make them more noticeable. Show that you made an effort because she didn't.

"What're you getting?" Abby asked Charlie.

"Short stack. You?"

"Three buttermilk," Abby replied with a tone of satisfaction in her voice.

"So," Charlie spoke while looking down and alphabetizing, counterclockwise in the holder, the different flavored syrups, "what's your big news?" Apricot, blueberry, maple, raspberry, and strawberry. Satisfied with her organization, she looked up.

"What?" said Abby, feigning surprise.

"Your news. The reason why we're here instead of Danny's. The reason you're going to choke down a heavy meal before," she checked the watch on her hip, "ten A.M."

Abby hated heavy food for breakfast. She could deal with cereal, a toaster pastry with a glass of milk, maybe. But the smell of runny eggs made her sick and the idea of having to eat an entire stack of pancakes appealed to her about as much as dissecting her own left breast. "So," said Charlie, "you going to tell me why we're here or will I be holding your hair back while you regurgitate those pancakes?"

Abby chuckled. The cigarette between her lips teetered up and down and she moved it to the ashtray just as the cherry fell. "How intuitive you are, my young lass. And I thought my, 'Mmm, yummy pancakes!' gig was actually working." She took another long drag and looked out the window to the parking lot. "Before I tell you, you have to promise to not interrupt because there's a lot I want to say and taken separately, it could be misconstrued. Okay?"

"Okay, I guess," Charlie replied.

"You have three months to find a new job." Charlie's face fell a mile. "Hold on, I'm not firing you per se, it's just that the lease is up on the house soon and I've found cheaper, more accommodating quarters elsewhere." Charlie started to speak, but Abby held up a hand. "It's not that you're not invited along, but the new place is a few states away and I figured since you and Tattoo Boy are so chummy, you'd be less than thrilled at the prospect of picking up and moving." Charlie turned down one corner of her mouth and sighed. "That's what I thought," said Abby.

Charlie and Abby stood on the sidewalk outside their old house, now mostly empty. A tightly packed moving truck was parked next to the curb.

"Well," said Abby.

"Yeah," Charlie reflected.

"My, what a Jerry Maguire moment this is."

"Yeah, except you're not as cute as Renee Zellweger and I'm not going to propose," replied Charlie.

"Oh, you're breaking my heart," said Abby. They both smiled. Charlie cracked on the inside; part of it streamed down her cheek. "Don't do that. If you start..."

Charlie wiped her eyes. "I'm just going to miss you, you big freak. I might even miss that stupid fucking clock of yours." That did it. They were both crying.

Abby looked toward the house. "Where are you going to stay?"

"Not sure yet," said Charlie, wiping her nose. "I'll stay at the house through the end of the month, I'll work my ass off, go apartment hunting and forward your mail."

Abby nodded. "Just don't fuck him in my old room."

Charlie laughed. "Deal." More smiling and sniffling. "Do I get a hug?"

They embraced for quite a while and Abby let out one quiet sob. With her head on Abby's shoulder, Charlie said, "You know, I lied."

"What?" said Abby.

"I won't miss that clock."

A smile crept to Abby's face. "No?"

"Not at all."

Chapter Three - Mark

Two thirty rolled around and Charlie shouted to the back of the store, "Spot! Gwen! I'm going to lunch. If anyone calls, I'll be back in an hour. Anyone is more than welcome to wait, but please don't page me unless it's an emergency, okay?"

Spot poked his head out from behind the self-help books. "What constitutes as an emergency?" he asked.

"Fires, death, plague. That sort of thing," replied Charlie.

"Is there anyone that falls under page worthy?" he asked.

"Uh, yeah," said Charlie after some thought. "God. If He comes in, page me and tell Him to wait."

"Will do. And while He's waiting, I'll tell Him all about your views on those commandment things," said Spot, grinning.

"You do that," said Charlie. She grabbed her bag from the drawer and went out the door.

At around three o'clock, a relatively good looking twenty-something male with brown hair and green, intelligent eyes came into the store clutching a battered paperback. Pinching the right arm of his glasses, he moved them higher up the bridge of his nose and tried to locate a sales clerk. Gwen walked past him, nose in a book, and froze. She walked backward, looked up and smiled sweetly.

"May I help you, sir?" she asked.

"As a matter of fact," he began, "you certainly may. I was looking for a map of this local area. I just moved in a few blocks away and I'm a bit out of sorts."

"Oh," said Gwen, walking around the counter, "well, we do have these complimentary maps of the downtown area. Most of it marks all the commercial spots. Eateries, knickknack shops, and your friendly neighborhood bookstore."

"Oh, I have no problem finding those. Thanks," he smiled one of those Hollywood smiles which made most girls check their make-up or change their underwear.

"Anything else I can help you with today?" Gwen asked dutifully.

"I think I'll just look around. Nearing the end of a novel," returned the heartthrob, waving his worn paperback in the air. "Can't be without reading material."

"Of course not. Feel free to ask if you need anything," said Gwen.

The customer was about to roam toward the back when he turned to her again and said, "On second thought, maybe there is something else you can do for me. I left my last residence in quite a rush and have found myself in this booming metropolis without employment. Are there any positions open here?" he asked.

"Well, my boss is out getting herself lunch right now, but I can page her. Wouldn't take more than a second," Gwen offered.

"Oh no, it's not that important. I can just wait until she comes back," he said.

"It wouldn't be a problem at all. Besides, she lives for these moments. It makes her feel like she's not wasting money on that little digital cube," said Gwen.

"I wouldn't want to interrupt her lunch," he said.

"Not to worry," Gwen assured him. "Lunch consists of a bag of gummy bears and a cup of a yogurt. She'll be here in a few moments."

"Well...okay. You talked me into it," he said.

Two minutes later, Charlie returned to the store, short of breath. She opened the door and inhaled deeply. Gwen ran up to greet her.

"I don't smell smoke," said Charlie between gasps. "I don't see corpses. This better be good."

Gwen, beaming, responded, "Oh, it's good." She pointed Charlie's face in the direction of the sociology section. The dark haired man was paging through a smallish black book of which Charlie couldn't make out the title. "And?"

"He's utterly lovely," said Gwen. "Can we keep him?"

"What are you talking about? He's just a customer," Charlie responded.

"He wants to know if we're hiring...if *you're* hiring," said Gwen, leering.

"Gwen, are you serious? We barely stay afloat with just you, Spot and I. God forbid Barnes & Noble should move in across the street," said Charlie.

"They won't. I'll protect you. Please? Just a few nights and weekends?" Gwen begged.

"We really can't afford it, Gwen. I'd love to say yes. I haven't seen you this excited since--"

"Don't say his name. I swear, if I hear it, I'll go vomit all over the Anne Rice books," said Gwen.

"Even the erotica section?" Charlie teased.

"Especially the erotica section. Listen though...seriously, you can dock my hours. Please. I need this. I haven't been laid in...Jesus, I don't want to think about it. If I keep this up, I'm going to have to go to the movies with my vibrator. At least I know it'll hold my hand in the dark," said Gwen, wistfully.

"All right. If it really means that much to you. How many hours do you want per week?" Charlie asked.

"I don't know...fifteen?" said Gwen.

"Fifteen? Jesus, how will you pay your rent?"

"I'll have to either sell more stuff or blow my landlord," Gwen retorted. Gwen was a freelance ceramist. She made everything from vases to mugs to sculptures and sold them to local shops on consignment. She did reasonably well with it. However, her main occupation at the moment was having a good time. It kept her mind off the recent string of "mistakes" made in the wake of Gregory. Gwen and Gregory had been together for four and a half years when one afternoon, Gwen came home to find their neighbor, Anton, banging him against the refrigerator. Gwen did her best to forget it and move on. A welcome distraction stood in the sociology section.

Charlie walked behind the counter and grabbed an application and a pen. "Here," she said to Gwen. "Give him this. Tell him to call back tomorrow to set up an interview."

"Boss...you're the best," Gwen squeaked. She ran over and gave him the application and he sat in one of the armchairs to hurriedly fill it out.

Charlie sighed disapprovingly and sat down to finish her lunch, the remainder of a yogurt cup. The applicant meandered over to the counter. She looked up as she saw him approaching.

"Hello. I'm Mark."

"Hi," said Charlie, extending her hand. "I'm Charlie. I own the shop."

"Ahh...small beauty," he said.

Confusion was writ on her face. "I'm sorry?" said Charlie.

"Charlie. Short for Charlotte, which means 'small beauty.' From the French," replied Mark.

"Actually, my name is short for Charles, which means 'man.' From my parents," she said, unimpressed.

"Oh," he faltered. "Well, here's my..." He handed her the application and the pen.

"Listen, don't worry about it. My parents were assholes. Come back tomorrow at...is two-ish okay?" Charlie asked.

"Yeah...uh, yeah." His lip curled to a smile. Charlie surprised herself by smiling back.

Masochism

Charlie put a quarter into the change slot of the payphone and dialed seven numbers. "Inky Doodles, this is Stephen," said a deep voice.

"Hi…it's Charlie."

"Hey, what's up," said Stephen.

"I was just wondering when you were gonna be around tonight. I wanted to make you dinner, if that was okay," she ventured.

"Can't. Hanging out with some friends from work," he replied.

"Oh…is it okay if I tag along?" asked Charlie.

"Can't. We're going out to a bar. Sorry."

"Okay, well--" said Charlie.

Stephen interrupted her; he was talking to someone else in the room. "What? No, I have an appointment at…wait, hold on a second." Then to Charlie, "Can I talk to you later?"

"Uh, yeah. Sure. Um, I guess I'll see you tomorrow," she said.

"Yup, bye." He hung up before she could say anything else.

"Bye." Charlie hung up the phone. She checked her watch. "What am I going to do with my evening now?" she asked of no one in particular.

In the four months prior, Charlie had scrambled to find a job, save some money and look for apartments. After a few weeks of earnest searching, Charlie knew that even if Linnmoore were half its size, she wouldn't be able to afford her own place. Not if she wanted to eat.

With no one to turn to and nowhere else to go, she asked Stephen who, in turn, asked Derek if she could stay with them for a bit.

"Do you really think that'll work?" Derek asked.

"I'd feel like an absolute dick if I said no," Stephen replied.

"No offense, dude, but you are what you are."

"Is that a yes or a no?" Stephen snapped.

"Why are you throwing this on me? You know I like her and wouldn't care if she moved in. It's not like she's my fucking girlfriend. Don't tell me you're afraid of hurting her, you've already done that. You afraid of her getting too close? Domesticizing you? She's not the type."

"Look, get off my ass. I don't want her to be homeless, okay? As long as she's happy, I'm still getting laid."

Derek ended the discussion with, "Your main priority."

Stephen told her it was fine. They split the rent three ways. The rest of her money went in the bank.

Charlie hadn't yet explored the surroundings of Stephen's neighborhood and she figured now was as good a time as any. Grabbing her journal, she headed out the door.

Usually, she took her walking time as time to think. But, since she didn't have a specific destination, she tried to pay attention to her environment. There was a small deli across from Stephen's apartment. A CD shop was in the adjoining building. She kept walking for a few blocks, passing streets with comforting names like Orchard Avenue and Hummingbird Lane. She went on until, on a dimly lit corner, she saw something promising. It was just approaching twilight, and in the dying light of dusk, she saw a café promoting their open mic night, scheduled for eight o'clock. That was in forty-five minutes.

Charlie sauntered in the front door and immediately loved the atmosphere. Tinted light bulbs hung on long chains from the ceiling. Triangular tables dotted the hardwood floor. There was a small stage with a microphone stand in the middle of it and, apparently, no spotlight. Next to the stage was a bar. There were bottles lining a mirrored wall which looked like they were filled with liquor, but upon closer inspection, one could see they were bottles of assorted syrups. One girl tended bar. She had shoulder length blonde hair and dark blue eyes. A few customers milled about, some reading, some talking, some obviously avoiding conversation. Charlie smiled and approached the bar.

"Hi, what can I get for you?" asked the friendly barkeep.

"I'd like a chocolate mint French soda, please," replied Charlie.

"Coming right up," said the girl. She quickly and expertly prepared the drink and set it before Charlie. "That'll be $2.50."

Charlie retrieved some money from her wallet, handed it to her, and went to find a seat. The clientele was obviously either still in or fresh out of college. There were always telltale signs. Some wore class rings. Some had college shirts. Some just had that look that said, "Mommy and Daddy paid for my $100,000 education. Aren't I a lucky little scamp?" Taking it all in, Charlie felt out of place. She had her knee high black boots on with an over sized black thermal shirt and a black skirt she found at a thrift store. Accessories included dark blue nail polish and a load of black eye liner. Charlie chose a vacant table segregated from the crowd and sat down to enjoy her drink.

'I can't believe this,' she wrote in her journal. 'I'm finally away from Jean, allowed to do whatever I want and I still can't do anything. What the fuck? I hate to pull that no one understands me melodramatic bullshit, but with Abby gone and no friends left to speak of, all I have is Stephen, who apparently isn't interested in doing anything other than drinking. I hate being underage. It's like this cosmic joke. Hey, you're finally 16…you get to drive. Yay. Hey, you're 18! You can move out! But you can't go anywhere. Jesus Christ, am I whiny tonight.'

A hand came into sight and knocked on Charlie's table. It was the blonde barista.

"Hey, open mic is about to start, and since I usually start it off, bar'll be closed for about fifteen minutes. Was there anything else you needed before I close up?" she asked.

"No. No, I'm set, thanks," replied Charlie.

"Okay, great," said the girl, smiling. There was something in her expression Charlie liked. She couldn't quite place it, but something in her face made Charlie want to know her.

The barista, dishrag in hand, swiped one last wipe of the counter and then moseyed up to the stage. She dragged a microphone with her and plugged it into a small amplifier. She cleared her throat which echoed throughout the room. All the junior league philosophers and the Abercrombie and Fitch shoppers and the anti-social malcontents and Charlie looked up. "Glad you could join us this evening. As usual, I'm Gwen. And this is our open mic night at Cool Beans, or as I like to call it, Better than Starbucks. To start things off, I'll be reading something I like to think of as Dark Dr. Seuss.

"'The vilest deeds like poison weeds,
Bloom well in prison air;
It is only what is good in Man
That wastes and withers there:
Pale Anguish keeps the heavy gate,
And the Warder is Despair.

For they starve the frightened little child
Till it weeps both night and day:
And they scourge the weak, and flog the fool,
And gibe the old and grey,
And some grow mad, and all grow bad,
And none a word may say.

Each narrow cell in which we dwell
Is a foul and dark latrine,
And the fetid breath of living Death
Chokes up each grated screen,
And all, but Lust, is turned to dust
In Humanity's machine.'"

A smattering of applause came from the audience. One of the hermits in the back and Charlie were the only sincere ones. Gwen took her bows and leaned in close to the microphone to whisper, "Who's next?"

No one stirred. Gwen stood on the dimly lit stage holding her grin and the dead air time. Someone coughed to the left of Charlie. And then the sound of a chair scraping the floor from behind her. A gangly figure came to the stage. Gwen abandoned it and pulled up a chair at a lone table in the front row.

A frail looking man stood before his peers, both 'man' and 'peers' being very loose terms. His hair, a light brown, was disheveled before that was stylish. He was skinny, almost painfully so. He wore a black, button down, cotton shirt and a pair of cheap, black jeans. He wasn't making a statement. He was merely not naked.

Charlie cringed watching him. She was an empathetic sponge. She was one of those people who couldn't watch an embarrassing scene in a movie without wanting to cry. Something in her related well to those in emotional turmoil. And this young man was a perfect example.

"Uhh..." he stammered. "My name is Alis."

Oh my God.

"It's short for Alister."

What is this? A bad 80s sitcom? Jesus...

"I, um...have this," Alis offered his voice shaky, waving a folded piece of paper weakly. He unfolded it. "I, ah, wrote it myself." And for the entire reading, Alis got to know that piece of paper. His eyes didn't move from the lines until he was done. What he said was this:

"A gaze that matters
For my heart does patter
Every time you pass by me
To the bar for a drink
I wonder to what you might think

About a time that me and you
For this time spent alone as two
I yearn for when we can be together
For a time that will last forever

Alas, the one you chose
In mine eyes should never go
Alone to my world
Looking upon that lovely strange girl

You would make me complete
Each day that you pass by me"

Charlie copied down every word. Her ear ached over the mismatched meter, and his poetic license made her want to cry. But it was honest and she wanted to believe that meant something. The girl probably had a bad dye job and acrylic nails.

At the close of Alis's recitation, a loud giggle exploded from the group of would be philosophers. Charlie leaned over to them and said, "Shut the fuck up, would you?" The catty flamer of the group flashed his brilliant, it-took-me-five-years-of-braces-and-two-years-with-a-retainer smile and gave Charlie the finger. "Very classy," she replied. "Sit on it and rotate, Chuckles."

Alis stepped down and recoiled to his dark corner of the room. Gwen resumed her position onstage. "Thanks, Alis. Is there anyone else who wants to read anything?" she asked. Charlie glanced to her left and then to her right. She hesitantly rose and approached the stage. Gwen smiled to her and said, "Thanks."

"No problem," Charlie replied.

"You gonna read some sad, goth poetry?" shouted a voice from the yuppie table.

"You gonna buy another latte with your Mom's credit card?" replied Charlie. Silence.

She began.

"Born with a silver spoon,
Gonna graduate college soon!
Wanna buy an SUV,
Live through my children vicariously,
Took my frustrations out on a geek,
Now," here Charlie moaned, "I'm about to hit my peak,
Just because he acts differently,
God…isn't it just great? Being me?"

Charlie curtsied to the sound of two people clapping. She returned to her seat and her notebook. Gwen grabbed the microphone stand from offstage and said, "I have a feeling that's it for tonight…the counter will be reopening for the last hour in about ten minutes. Thanks for coming out." She unplugged the microphone and walked over to Charlie's table. Without asking, she sat across from her.

"Jesus, you have a death wish or something?" she asked Charlie.

"No, just an intolerance for assholes. Sorry if I ruined the evening for anyone," said Charlie.

"Not at all," Gwen replied. "Earned yourself some enemies though."

"You mean them?" asked Charlie, nodding her head in the direction of the Future Leaders of America.

"Well, yes…" said Gwen.

"I'm not afraid of them," replied Charlie. "Let them riot. I don't give a shit."

"What about Alis?" asked Gwen.

"What about him? He's not one of them," said Charlie.

"But he wants to be," Gwen retorted. "He wants to fit in, and he wants that girl to choose him over some obviously cooler guy. He wants to wear their clothes and know their friends and be who they are…because he's miserable being who he is now. And they're not."

"But—" Charlie began.

"And he hates you right now," said Gwen. She reached across the table and took Charlie's soda. "May I?" Charlie nodded dumbly. Gwen sipped a long gulp through the straw and said, "Hmm…not bad."

"How do you know…he," said Charlie, a little lost for words.

"Alister?" Gwen asked. "You burst his bubble. You said it's better to be himself than them, which is true, but how does that saying go? The truth hurts."

Charlie disbelieved it. She turned to face Alis in his dark corner. His eyes darted into hers. She couldn't stand his gaze. She returned her attention to Gwen who raised her eyebrows once before leaving the table. Gwen reopened the bar and Charlie returned to her journal.

Charlie spent the next hour glaring at the would-be soccer moms and wannabe hipsters. When they finally hauled their H+M covered bodies out of Cool Beans, it was only open for another fifteen minutes. Charlie was doodling one of the members of the in crowd with his head severed when Gwen yelled a general, "Ten minutes!"

Charlie checked her watch. 9:50pm.

Gwen began to put the chairs atop the tables. Upon reaching Charlie's table, she cleared her throat.

"Oh, sorry," Charlie apologized.

"No problem. I just want to get out of here. Food service blows," Gwen replied.

"Yeah," Charlie nodded, thinking of her current waiting position. "Listen, this is going to sound odd, but do you want to hang out sometime? I just lost my best friend."

"God, I'm sorry," Gwen consoled her.

"Wait, no, not lost, dead. Lost, she moved away," Charlie reworded.

"Oh…then I'm still sorry, just to a lesser degree."

Charlie smiled. "Thanks."

"Anytime," Gwen returned.

"I'm Charlie, by the way. Gwen, is it?"

"Gwen it is."

A new friend at last.

"So, what are you doing tomorrow?" Gwen asked.

"Hmm?" Charlie responded.

"Tomorrow? You said you wanted to hang out sometime. How about tomorrow?" Gwen repeated.

"Oh. Tomorrow's cool. Uh, hold on a sec," said Charlie. She bent over and flipped through her journal. She found an empty page and scrawled out her name and phone number. She ripped it out of the book. "Here. Give me a call whenever it's convenient."

"Sounds good. I'll see you tomorrow then," Gwen said, taking the paper.

"See you tomorrow," Charlie waved and left the shop.

Gwen looked at the page. She started to fold it to put it away and realized there was something written on the back.

"Bad Driver"

Yesterday, I ran over a demon.

Wasn't much what I pictured a demon to look like, but a demon he was. Did you know they bounce on pavement?

I chuckled to myself when I saw it, then I put on my adult "I'm so sorry, I swear I didn't see you there" face.

He was relatively okay for the wear and tear of it, but God, did he bitch and moan.

"Do you know the severity of your actions?" this and "I could make it *very* bad for you in the underworld," that.

Then he threw in, "I know Satan, ya know. Just a word and like that," snapped a gnarled finger, "you're dust, my friend."

I guess I looked pretty unimpressed because he really started laying it on thick after that.

"What if I'd been seriously injured?" he asked. "There are rules about these things. I'd have had to stay with you. How could you have explained that?"

He gasped.

"What if I have internal bleeding? I've got a family to worry about. A succubus and three little hellions running around." And then I felt pretty bad.

Until this morning, when I ran over an angel.

The phone rang twice before Charlie answered.

"Hello?"

"Hi, is Charlie home?"

"This is she," Charlie replied.

"It's Gwen."

"Oh hey! How are you?" Charlie asked.

"I'm fine. Hey, you wrote your name and number on the back of what looks like a story or a poem or something. Did you need it for anything?" Gwen asked.

"Oh, um, I don't know. I didn't check the back of the page. What is it?" said Charlie.

"It's about a guy who runs over a demon."

"Oh, "Bad Driver." Nah, you can just throw it out," Charlie shrugged.

"Are you sure? It's pretty funny," Gwen said.

Charlie thought on that. "Keep it," she said.

"Really? You don't want it?" Gwen asked.

"Yeah. It's just a little short story. It's barely a page, handwritten. Besides, I'm no writer," said Charlie. "So, keep it."

"I'll display it proudly on my refrigerator," Gwen smiled.

"If you insist," said Charlie.

"I do. And just so we're even, since you've created something for me, I'll create something for you," said Gwen.

"Um, okay," Charlie said hesitantly.

"I'll explain everything when you get here. Do you know where The Greasy Spoon is?" Gwen asked.

"Know it? I keep the place in business," Charlie teased.

"Awesome. Meet me there in thirty minutes," said Gwen.

"I'll see you then," said Charlie.

"Okay…hey, wait," said Gwen.

"Yeah?"

"Wear something you won't mind getting dirty," Gwen warned.

Stephen's apartment was a five-minute walk from the dive restaurant affectionately known as The Greasy Spoon. Charlie journaled a bit before leaving. She wrote a mock dossier for Gwen.

Name: Gwen, the barista
DOB: Unknown
Description: Approx. 5'4", blonde hair, blue eyes, athletic build
Likes: Oscar Wilde, coffee houses, "Bad Driver"
Dislikes: People who don't tip

Charlie checked the clock. She had fifteen minutes. She snapped her notebook shut, donned some grubby clothing and locked the door behind her.

Gwen eyed Charlie's black Chucks, faded jeans and worn-out T-shirt.

"Thrift store?" she asked. Charlie nodded. "Girl after my own heart."

They took Gwen's car to her mystery location.

"You didn't drive?" Gwen asked along the way.

"Nope. I can't drive," Charlie replied. "I don't know how."

"Shit. Really?" said Gwen.

"Really. I've only driven once and I hated it."

"How do you get around?"

"I walk. That's why Darwin invented legs," Charlie teased.

"Darwin invented legs?" Gwen looked at her skeptically.

"Well, if I believed in God, which I don't, I would've said, 'That's why God gave us legs.' And since the only alternative atheists have to Creation idioms are references to Darwin, I might as well say that Darwin invented everything. It's more plausible than blaming the invisible man in the sky. At least we can go and see where Darwin is buried."

Gwen nodded. "We're here."

They parked outside a modest white building with no sign. Charlie followed Gwen to the front door.

"Go ahead in," Gwen instructed.

The room glowed from the midday sun pouring through the floor to ceiling windows. The walls had been painted an orange hue giving the room a warm aura. There were two long tables and twenty chairs. Signs covered the walls spouting warnings and sayings like, "Empty the wax jar!" and "A clean studio is a happy studio! J"

"It looks like a classroom," said Charlie.

"You're half right," Gwen replied. "It's part of the community college. Ceramics classes are taught here quarterly." Gwen walked toward the wall farthest from the entrance and retrieved a key from her pocket.

"This lets me into the assistant's room," Gwen told Charlie with an air of false arrogance.

"Do you know the assistant?" Charlie asked.

"You're looking at her." Gwen ushered Charlie into the room. She pointed to a six-foot tall backless bookshelf. Vases and mugs and sculptures and things in various stages of progression filled the shelves. "That shelf's mine," said Gwen, motioning to the second to last shelf. Charlie picked up a frame with a woman's face in the corner. It was a light pink.

"This is really pretty," said Charlie, replacing it on the shelf.

"Thanks. I'm thinking it'll be a mirror," Gwen replied.

"Why is all this stuff locked up?" Charlie asked.

"What do you mean?"

"Well, what if someone wanted to work on their piece on their own time?"

"They could ask. I mean, that'd be fine. I think the pieces are safer back here. This way, nothing is stolen, broken, or confused."

"And if it is," Charlie smiled, "they can blame you."

"Precisely," Gwen grinned. "So…ready for the fun stuff?"

"Fun stuff?" Charlie asked.

"Yeah. We're going to make something," said Gwen.

"I can't make anything," Charlie replied. "The last sculpture I made was a stick figure of Playdoh that my brother smashed with a plastic hammer."

"Good, then you have experience." Gwen rolled up her sleeves. "Go grab an apron." On the end of the bookshelf were two hooks. Six aprons hung between the two. Charlie hesitantly donned a denim apron and slid her hands in the stiff front pockets. They didn't move. The front had been caked in clay so often, the denim was permanently fixed to that pose.

"After you," said Gwen. They returned to the classroom. "Okay, this," Gwen explained, standing beside a large machine which Charlie envisioned created souls, "is a mixer." She grabbed the handle which jutted out from the middle of the top of the machine and yanked it upward. It flipped open to reveal a large metal spiral. She pressed a switch against the side and a low hum erupted from the mixer. The spiral spun. "Now," said Gwen, yelling over the din. "The mixer gets the lumps out of the clay. Reach into that bucket. The one next to your left foot." Charlie did. She pulled out two mounds of wet, mushy gray clay. "Throw them in. Okay, get more." Charlie threw in two more handfuls. Gwen closed the top of the mixer and instructed Charlie to follow her.

They stood in front of what looked like bowling seats without backs with overturned stools on them. Gwen quickly dismantled her bowling seat, pulling the stool off to reveal a flat circle guarded by two semi-circle pieces of plastic. In the middle was a long cord wrapped into a coil. Gwen plugged it in. "This is the wheel. This is what I'm going to use to make your…whatever. I could make you a handbuild, but that would take forever."

"What's a handbuild?" Charlie asked.

"It's something that's not thrown on the wheel. That frame you saw earlier. Obviously a handbuild."

"Oh," said Charlie. She turned the stool right side up and sat down. She caught sight of the mixer.

"Can I take a picture of that?" Charlie teased.

"What?" asked Gwen.

Charlie pointed to the end of the mixer. A limp log of clay hung crookedly waiting for Charlie to comment.

"Oh, that." Gwen smirked. "I don't even remember it's on sometimes." She turned off the mixer. The hum subsided. She grabbed the log and broke it in half. She handed one part to Charlie and kept the rest for herself. "Now, slap it all around until it's basically spherical."

Charlie and Gwen busied themselves whapping the clay with their open palms. Charlie started to giggle. "It sounds like sex."

"I know," said Gwen grinning. "Isn't it charming?" She walked back over to the wheels. Charlie followed. Gwen bent and slapped her clay smack dab in the middle of the wheel.

"Ooh, not sure I can do that," said Charlie, still shaping her clay.

"Sure you can," said Gwen. "Just smack it down."

"Yeah, but you got it directly in the middle. I'd be at least two percent to the left or something—"

"Oh, just throw the Goddamned thing," said Gwen. Charlie did.

Pause.

"Oh my God, did I fuck that up," said Charlie.

"Two percent, my ass," said Gwen, snickering. "But we can fix it." Gwen pulled from her apron a thin, malleable piece of stainless steel with a three-inch wooden handle on either end. "Affectionately known to ceramists everywhere as a wire. Used for removing clay from the wheel."

"So, basically, for fuck-ups?" Charlie asked.

"Well, in your case, yes," Gwen teased. She knelt beside the wheel and leveled the wire flat against it while pulling it across the length of the clay. The sound of her pulling the mound off the surface was wet and thick. "Now, you want to attempt to start with the clay as close to the middle of the wheel as possible." Gwen slapped it down in the middle. "That way, it's easier for centering." Charlie raised an eyebrow. "Centering it on the wheel. The wheel is the reason why pottery is symmetrical."

"Oh."

"Now, rest your foot on that pedal," Gwen instructed. Charlie did. Gwen covered the clay with her palms on either side and her thumbs on top. "Push down on the pedal." Charlie did. "Too fast! Too fast! Stop!"

When Charlie pressed her foot on the pedal, she held it down as hard as she could, spinning the wheel full force. The speed caused the clay to flatten to the shape of an overturned plate. "I suppose it's a good thing you don't drive," Gwen quipped. She scooped some water onto the clay and reshaped it. She returned it to the wheel. Bracing it on both sides and top, she told Charlie, "Now, slowly, push down on the pedal."

Charlie did.

An hour later, Charlie watched as Gwen put what was to be her mug in a locker to dry.

"Tomorrow, you can come back and put the handle on with some slip clay."

"Jesus, I wish I could do stuff like this all the time," said Charlie.

"Ceramics? You can. You could take a class at the college," Gwen replied.

"Don't have any money. Besides, I'm kind of anti-college. I was never one to buy into the whole you-need-college-to-survive thing, so I'm basically completely against it," said Charlie.

"That's a bit extreme," said Gwen.

"Yeah. I'll probably end up working retail," Charlie joked and couldn't help thinking of Abby.

"What about the writing thing?" Gwen asked.

"Oh, that's just something I do for kicks. Keeps me sane, ya know? I keep a journal. But I find making things up is more interesting."

"So you write little stories about men running over demons and things," Gwen finished.

"Basically, yeah." Charlie smiled. "Do you go to college?"

"Night classes," Gwen replied. "Liberal arts degree."

"Ahh…" Charlie nodded. "What do you want to do?"

"For a living? This. But it doesn't pay the bills. So I sling yuppy hash," Gwen grimaced.

"Could be worse," said Charlie.

"Yeah," Gwen's voice trailed off. "Hey, thanks for hanging out. This was fun."

"Thanks for inviting me. I feel like I actually did something today."

"No problem. This is the stuff that keeps me sane. Some days, I just want to burn Cool Beans to the ground," Gwen muttered.

"Well, if you ever need a match, let me know," Charlie offered.

"I'll do that," Gwen grinned.

Stephen loved tattooing. He was the main artist at Inky Doodles. There were two binders which featured his work in the shop and a good portion of the left wall had samples of his art. He had started drawing when he was about eleven years old. Normal little kid drawings. Superheroes. Aliens. People with completely distorted features. Thankfully, an art teacher showed him a book featuring photorealistic drawings and during his time in college, Stephen decided to minor in art. But when people asked him why he settled on tattoo artistry, Stephen's response was usually, "It's easy work and the tattoos are free." That was only partially true. The tattoos were indeed free and the work was easy. When Stephen was tattooing, he was in the proverbial zone. But the reason he did it was for the joy of it. If he had one gripe, it would be the commissioned work. He was sometimes commissioned to draw an original, which he really disliked because he didn't like being told what to do. Not by anyone, for any reason. And certainly not by some girl.

It had been over a year and Charlie's novelty was beginning to wear off. When she'd asked to move in, he said, sure, no problem. Yes, it made things easier with the rent money every month, but that also meant that she would be underfoot all the time. The last thing Stephen needed was an additional nineteen-year-old shaped appendage to account for. She was always there. That and she called all the time. At least twice a day for stupid reasons. Just to see how he was doing, to say she missed him or, even worse yet, that she loved him. Like he needed to hear that. Sometimes, he didn't feel like being nice about it either.

"Hey, it's Charlie," she'd say.

"What," he'd reply.

"What's wrong?" she'd ask.

"You just keep calling. Jesus Christ."

"I just wanted to ask you something," she'd comment, not understanding the bitterness in his tone.

"What."

"Forget it. I'll just see you later," she'd say. He wouldn't reply. "I'll try not to call again." And her last words were never spiteful or even meant to bring on guilt, she just didn't know what she'd done to anger him. She'd hang up the phone and call Gwen.

"What's he done now?" Gwen would ask.

"Nothing. That's just it. I would be thrilled just sitting and watching him draw. Just the comfort of being with him. That's all I want. And I keep calling him because it makes me feel better to hear his voice and know he's there," Charlie would say. "I guess I have to figure out how to care less."

Charlie's face lit up when she saw the ad in the paper requesting "promising young actors for an independent film." She ran to the phone to call Stephen. His machine picked up. "Hey! Guess what! They're casting for an independent film downtown and I'm gonna go. I'll be home about nine, so see you then. Oh, this is Charlie, by the way. See you later."

At the end of her shift at the restaurant, Charlie ran to Gwen's apartment. Gwen closed the book she'd been reading and answered the door. In between gasps of breath, Charlie spat out, "Open…casting call…need…ride…please?"

"Let me get you some water," said Gwen, turning to go to the kitchen.

"No…time," wheezed Charlie. "Get…keys."

"Give yourself a second to breathe. Think you can tell me where we're going?" asked Gwen.

Charlie nodded and walked to the car.

The casting call was being held at a bar downtown. Charlie wasn't twenty-one yet, but she looked about twenty-three, so she went in and acted like she belonged there. She expected there to be a crowd. There was, instead, a woman standing next to a table with a sheet of paper on it. She wore a sticker which said, "HELLO. My name is Helen, and I'd love to help you today." Her face did not coincide with the sticker. Her white roots were growing out and were a foil to the cherry chestnut hue of the rest of her hair. Her sticky purple lipstick was gooey on the end of her cigarette.

"That's what I want to look like when I grow up," Gwen whispered to Charlie. Charlie suppressed a giggle and approached Helen.

"Hi. I'm here for the audition," Charlie said hesitantly.

"Sign up there, mark which dates you're available for," Helen replied oh-so-cordially. Her accent smacked of the Southern states.

Charlie picked up the pen and read over the paper. The top said *Extra Sign-up Sheet*. "This is for extra work?" asked Charlie. She thought it would be an actual audition for main or at least speaking roles.

"That's right," Helen told her. Charlie wrote her name and specified that she was available for four of the ten dates. She had to work the rest.

"Uh, thanks," Charlie said to Helen.

"Yup. You have a good day," Helen said and smiled a smile that didn't reach her eyes.

Charlie caught the bus downtown for the first two days. It was early spring, but she wanted to be there early, so decided not to walk. Turned out she didn't have to be there at all. An indie favorite had been cast as the female lead and she was having problems with the lighting. And the costumes. And the dialogue. So, the first two scenes for which the extras were needed were cut. Finally, on day three, Charlie walked to the restaurant where the shooting was scheduled. As she walked in, a skinny guy, covered in freckles, wearing an *American Cinematographer* shirt pointed her in the direction of a sign-up sheet. He told her to find a seat and they'd let her know when she was needed. Charlie had thought ahead and brought a book.

No sooner than she had reached the crux of the plot, the cinematographer said, "Miss? We're setting up for the next scene now." She saved her page, put her book in her bag and walked over to the little space where the other extras had congregated. In the middle of the group was a short, balding man who Charlie could only assume was the director. He wore his hair cut practically to the scalp to hide his diminishing hairline.

He was assigning them certain spaces to stand, "to make the shot more artistic." He put Charlie at a table across from a girl who talked more than Charlie felt she should have. "So...what do you do? Oh, I'm a flight attendant," she babbled.

"Oh...why are you here then?" Charlie thought to ask.

"Luke's my brother," the girl replied.

"Who's Luke?" asked Charlie, hoping the loquacious girl's name was not Leia.

"The director," she said. Charlie's mouth felt dry and foul in that she'd been lumped together with the director's sister for a movie. The word talentless echoed in her head, if it was indeed a word.

They did a couple takes of the same scene and Charlie and Luke's sister made quiet conversation. The female lead then decided she needed a break. Luke yelled that everyone would get a five-minute break. His sister decided to leave at this point, Charlie figured, to have a smoke or go to the bathroom. At the end of the five minutes, she had yet to return. Charlie looked around and saw that Luke was ready to begin again.

Okay...

So there was a yell for quiet and then action. Charlie had no action to perform. So she glanced around without moving her head. She checked her watch, also done without moving. They got done with the first take. They did it again. At the end of the second take, Luke decided to go around to all the tables and gab with the extras. He hit on a couple of the girls. Charlie wanted to spew on his balding head. He got to her table, turned around and said, "Okay, we're ready for another take, people," Luke shouted. "Quiet, please! And...action."

In the middle of this take, Luke yelled for cut, ran to Charlie's table, leaned close to her face and said, "Relax." He ran back to his chair, which he didn't use. He just squatted in front of it. For the rest of the day, Charlie debated on whether or not she wanted to leave. She sat it out and decided to ditch her last scheduled day. As she was signing out on the attendance sheet, the freckled guy from earlier thanked her for showing up. "No," she replied with emphasis and a forced smile, "thank *you*."

Stephen saw light emanating under the door at end of the hallway. His room. Charlie.

"Fuck," he thought. He walked to the phone and dialed. "Hey. No. Not tonight. All right. I'll talk to you later. Yeah. Okay. Bye."

Charlie heard his heavy gait. She smiled. It was the boots he wore. He walked noiselessly barefoot. "Stephen?" she called.

"Yeah."

She appeared in the kitchen. He was looking through the cabinets.

"Hey," she said. She hugged him from behind. He squeezed her wrist and then moved away. "How was your day?"

"Fine."

"Are you mad at me?" she asked.

"No."

"You seem mad," Charlie ventured. She wished he would talk to her.

"I'm not mad," he said.

She didn't want to argue with him, but she didn't want to let it go. "Can I ask you something?"

"What?"

"I'm only asking because it's been a year," she said. "Well, over a year now... I think it's blatant that I love you, but most times, it seems like you're, umm... bored? And I was just wondering if you were."

"Bored?" Stephen asked.

"Yeah." After a while, he shrugged. "What does that mean for me?" she asked. He sighed.

"Charlie, listen. I never said that we were going to get married or anything, did I? I didn't say I wanted you to move in here. Extenuating circumstances brought you to live here, it's not because we came to a mutual decision because we wanted to further our relationship. You basically didn't have a place to go and I don't have a problem with morning sex."

The tears formed immediately. "Is that all I am to you? Just a fuck?" Charlie sobbed. Stephen looked at her as if to say, "You already know the answer."

She wiped her face with her sleeve. She was almost ashamed of her emotion. "So, now what?"

"Now," said Stephen calmly, "you stay here until you find your own place. We avoid each other and you sleep on the floor."

"That's it?" she stammered.

"Well, no. You can sleep on the couch if you want to," Stephen said, gesturing to the living room. Charlie couldn't believe what was happening. Stephen looked at her haplessly and raised his eyebrows. He returned to the phone and hit redial. "Hey, it's me. Change of plans. Yeah. Cool, see you in a few." He hung up and turned to Charlie. "A friend of mine is coming over. I suggest the couch for tonight."

Charlie's face fell. "You're going to fuck someone else while I'm here?" she asked.

"Yeah. It is my apartment," Stephen reminded her. "I'll move your clothes to the linen closet," he called from his room.

Charlie sank to the floor. She fell asleep with her head against the wall.

Four hours later, Derek stood over Charlie, shaking her awake.

"Hey...hey...c'mon..." he said. Charlie just barely opened her eyes. They were swollen from her crying.

"Derek?" she murmured.

"Yeah. C'mon." He offered her his hand. Wobbly, with his aid, she got to her feet. "You okay?" he asked.

Charlie tried to respond, but tears sprang to her eyes and she just wearily shook her head. She put her chin to her chest and tried to will back her pain. "I'm…sorry," she said shakily.

"What happened?" he asked.

"I guess I wore out my welcome," she said, pointing to the hall toward Stephen's room.

"What do you mean?"

"He told me I have to find a new place. He broke up with me," Charlie sluggishly made her way to the sofa and fell back against it.

Derek tightened his jaw. "Charlie, I'm sorry," he said. "I know this is no consolation and he is my friend, but, honestly, you could do so much better. Really."

Charlie just laughed. "The sad thing is, I don't want to do better. I want him to care about me." Derek sat down next to her. "And he won't." She started to cry again.

"Hey…it's okay." He put an arm around her. "Why don't you get some rest? You'll feel better in the morning."

"I doubt it," said Charlie. She leaned against one armrest.

"Want me to get you a blanket?" he offered.

"Okay," she mumbled.

"Okay." He went to the linen closet. When he saw all her clothes in there, he wanted to lay into Stephen. He pulled an afghan off the top shelf and unfolded it. He returned to the living room and Charlie was in the fetal position. She looked despondent. He felt helpless.

"Here we go," he said and spread the blanket out over her. She looked at him with only her eyes. They were glassy from the tears.

"Thanks, Derek," she said.

"No problem. Goodnight."

"G'nite."

Charlie slept unwell. She woke every couple hours and wept herself back to sleep. When the sun finally rose, she felt awful. Her sinuses ached. A tremendous headache kept her where she was for at least another hour. Within that hour, everything unraveled.

Charlie heard a giggle echo through the apartment as the door at the end of the hallway opened. A tall girl with purple hair strolled out of Stephen's room. Stephen followed. They spoke in hushed tones, but Charlie could imagine the conversation. They could get matching T-shirts. SHE'S MY HOLE HE'S MY POLE.

Stephen walked her to the door. They shared a quick embrace. "Tuesday?" Charlie heard the girl ask.

"That's what? Five days?" Stephen replied. "That should be good."

"Okay. See you then," Charlie could hear her smile.

"Bye."

Charlie heard the front door open and then close. Stephen turned to walk back to his room.

"Morning," she said. Her voice stopped him. He looked at her.

"Hello."

"How was your evening? Did you have a nice time?" Charlie asked, malice in her voice.

"As a matter of fact—"

"Oh, I'm so glad. She seemed such a nice girl." Charlie sat up. She was angry now. She didn't want to see him with someone else. Not yet. Not this soon.

"I'm so glad you think so," Stephen replied calmly. He would not be shaken by her brazenness. "I have a request, if it's not too much trouble."

"Yes?" Charlie asked icily.

"Could you find somewhere else to stay until you get your own place?" he asked.

Charlie squinted her eyes and furrowed her brow. She was out of tears for the moment. "Why." She didn't ask it. She said it.

"I kind of have someone else moving in and your being here would make things…awkward."

Stephen's apartment was small and Derek had the lesser of the two bedrooms, so the only place another person could have stayed was in Stephen's room. As this registered in Charlie's mind, her expression deadened. She quietly stood and walked to the adjoining room. Stephen heard numbers being dialed on a phone.

"Hey. Yeah. What's up? I have a favor to ask of you. It's an emergency. Can I crash on your couch for a few weeks? Okay. Yeah, I'll meet you there. Okay, thanks."

She returned to the living room and wordlessly started to fold the afghan Derek had gotten for her last night. Stephen watched her, waiting for an explanation.

"Well?"

"I'll be out by tomorrow."

Nothing more was said.

"Excuse me, miss?" a woman with three rowdy children flagged Charlie down as she passed their table.

"Yes, ma'am?" Charlie asked.

"We're ready to order."

You're not my table.

"Um, let me see if I can find your server…" Charlie said, looking around.

"Well, can't you take our order and then give it to her?" the woman asked, impatiently.

Are you intending on tipping both of us?

"Uh, sure," Charlie replied and retrieved her tab.

"Okay, I'd like three grilled cheese sandwiches, the crusts cut off of them, one with ketchup, two without. On wheat bread." Charlie scribbled at a hurried pace the order which she knew would be dissected and smeared all over the table, booth, and window. But, she did it with a smile because:

You're not my fucking table.

"I want a peanut butter sandwich!" proclaimed one of the woman's precious demon spawn.

"Not today, honey," she cooed.

"And for you, ma'am?"

"I'd like a chef salad, please," said the woman, rounding up the menus.

"I wanna chef salad!"

"No, sweetie, not today."

"What kind of dressing?" Charlie asked.

"Balsamic vinaigrette, if you have it."

"We do," Charlie said simply.

"I wanna doll sammy bin a gret!"

"You can have one when we get home," the mother lied.

"I'll get this to your server," said Charlie. She waltzed into the kitchen, handed the tab to Marcy, and sang, "Not my fucking table."

"Oh God," Marcy replied.

"And look at that, my shift's over," Charlie looked in mock amazement at the clock.

"You suck," Marcy groaned.

"I don't even want to hear it. I had to kiss ass for eight hours to get," Charlie paused as she counted out her tips for the day. "Thirty-two dollars. If my rent were higher, I'd apply for welfare."

"Shit, you could apply now," Marcy said, tying her apron around her waist. "But then you'd have to shop at stores and be all like, 'How many slices of cheese can I get for...this many stamps?" Marcy held up five fingers between both hands, two on her left and three on her right.

"Dude, you're fucked up," said Charlie. "I'll see you later."

"Have a good night."

Charlie got in about a half an hour later and hit the play button to hear her messages. One from Gwen. Charlie called her back. "Hey, I got your message," she told her.

"I was wondering what you were doing later," said Gwen.

"I'm unfortunately busy," Charlie replied.

"Doing what?"

"Ya know. Stuff," Charlie dodged the question.

"I haven't seen you for nearly two weeks. What have you been doing?" Gwen asked.

"More like who..." Charlie grinned.

"Oh, Jesus, the melodrama that is your life," Gwen rolled her eyes. "Who is he?"

"You have to promise not to lecture me if I tell you," said Charlie.

"Whoever it is, it's got to be an improvement over Stephen," Gwen commented. Charlie held her breath. "Charlie? Tell me it's not Stephen."

"It's Stephen," Charlie said.

"Oh my God."

"But it's better. Kind of," Charlie interrupted.

"What does that mean?" Gwen asked. "Kind of?"

"Ya know, we just hang out and I have my own place now..." said Charlie.

"Which you need four part time jobs to afford."

"But it's cool. The only thing is I'm not allowed to sleep next to him."

"What?" Gwen asked.

"He said the bed's not big enough and it's not like we're together, so…"

"So, you're his fuck buddy," said Gwen.

"That is such an ugly term."

"Charlie, he kicked you out," said Gwen. "You stayed at my place. He fucked someone else while you were still in the apartment. Have you forgotten all of this?"

"No," said Charlie. "I haven't. Seriously though, it's fine. I think he knows that I'm less needy now and won't be right there all the time, so ya know…it's better."

Gwen sighed. "Whatever. I have to ask. How did this occur?"

"I went to give my key back and he asked me inside. We sat talking for a little while and one thing led to another… Gwen, honestly. I'm fine with it."

"If he hurts you again, I'm going to have to hold my tongue when I want to scream through a megaphone that I told you so," said Gwen.

"Won't even be necessary."

"We'll see."

Derek and Stephen were on the balcony overlooking their parking lot. Derek crouched at the door, hand on the knob. Stephen held a can of hairspray and a lighter. He stood erect and alert, ready for battle. A few moments passed in silence. Then,

"There's one!" Derek screeched. "On the railing!" Stephen saw it and equipped the hairspray. With the lighter, which had a long neck as to allow you to light a grill or keep distance from your prey, he doused it in flame. Upon death, its legs shriveled and burned. Derek spat toward its charred remains.

They were killing spiders.

"So," Derek began in between spying for eight legged vermin. "Where's Charlie been?"

Stephen shrugged. "I don't know. Around."

"There's one." Derek pointed to Stephen's foot. A small spider ran idly by.

Spray.

Torch.

Dead.

"That's fucked up."

"What're you talking about?" Stephen asked.

"You've been with her almost two years—"

"Off and on," Stephen clarified.

"And you're still pulling your typical bullshit," Derek continued. "Girl on your arm for show, but have her display any affection and you send her on her way."

"I just don't need that. It's like having a wife," Stephen dismissed him.

"There's one near your right hand," said Derek.

Shh went the spray.

Click went the lighter.

R.I.P.

"I could understand you not wanting her around if she were one of your normal fuck 'em and forget 'em deals. But she's not," said Derek. "You kicked her out for Bethany, which I didn't understand because she looks ten times better than Bethany does, and then, when she forgave you and started sucking your dick again, you made her sleep on the floor. That's harsh. You need to look at what you have or end it and let her go, because if you don't—"

Stephen held the can of hairspray inches from Derek's face, finger on the nozzle. He held it down. Derek screwed his eyes shut. At the last possible instant, Stephen's hand moved to the right of Derek's head. Upon hearing the lighter and what he thought was a small shriek, Derek opened his left eye. He couldn't bear to look.

"Open your other eye," Stephen commanded.

Hesitantly, he obeyed. Less than a foot away, Stephen held, by one charred leg, a spider carcass. It was the size of a thumbnail. Derek barely found the courage to scream like a little girl before running into the apartment and slamming the door behind him.

After sixteen hours of work, Charlie went to Stephen's, hoping for a friendly face. He wasn't home, so she collapsed in his room and fell asleep. She awoke to muffled thumping and laughing. She had desecrated a sacred vow. She had fallen asleep in Stephen's bed. She sat up and shifted to the floor in hopes that he wouldn't notice.

"Ooh, is she for me?" Charlie heard a girl ask.

Stephen smiled wickedly. "Go ahead." Charlie's eyes had barely focused when the girl was upon her, shoving her tongue in Charlie's mouth. She tasted metal. The girl, whose name was Danielle, had a pierced tongue. Charlie had to admit, it was a great kiss. Danielle held her close and made her feel wanted. She started to take off Charlie's pants. Charlie pulled up the back of Danielle's shirt.

What am I doing?

By the time Danielle had her naked from the waist down, Charlie was still fumbling with the back of Danielle's bra. Releasing the clasp, she clumsily palmed Danielle's breast.

Charlie gasped. Danielle had shoved three fingers inside her. She fell on her back. Charlie wanted to tell her to stop. It hurt so much. She felt wrong. She opened her eyes and looked to Stephen for help. He was sitting on his bed watching. Danielle was pounding Charlie now, fast and hard. Charlie reached down and pushed her hand away. Danielle replaced it with her tongue. Charlie almost screamed. The girl's tongue ring was freezing. It warmed as she went deeper. Charlie clawed at the back of Danielle's head. This wasn't the sex she was used to. It was quicker, more chaotic. Charlie found herself clenching all the muscles below her abdomen. Danielle licked her at a furious pace. Finally, violently, Charlie came. She wanted it to go on for as long as possible, but it lingered briefly and then ceased.

Danielle didn't stop licking. Charlie couldn't handle it. She pushed back with her feet.

"No…stop. Please," she said. Danielle looked up, smiling. Stephen grabbed her arm and pulled her to him.

Charlie heard her say, "Your girlfriend's fun."

"She's not my girlfriend," Stephen replied.

"Your loss," Danielle moaned.

Charlie watched Stephen fuck her on the bed.

Charlie stood in the lobby of her old high school, leaning on a mop. Her calves ached and she was sick of the sideways glances her former teachers had been paying her. Since the evening with Danielle, Charlie had tried to stay away from Stephen, but had acquiesced to loneliness a few times. Their sex felt strained. She was trying for the both of them, but it wasn't enough.

This is a complete compromise of my integrity. All I want is for him to care about me as much as care about him. At this point, I would settle for half.

The afternoon was bleak. Clouds were gathering and she saw a flash of lightning on the horizon. On her break, she headed for the roof of the gymnasium.

Charlie sniffed the air. It hung stagnantly all around her. Rain was imminent. She could smell it. It was early May and she had just reached the rooftop as the first clap of thunder rolled across the sky. She watched as lightning illuminated patches of clouds. Not a drop of rain had fallen. The wind tucked up its skirts and ran across Charlie's face. She squinted, blurring her view of the lightning. It flitted through the sky as though carried by a breeze. It took great care not to fall, not yet. The thunder rushed in behind it, throwing its weight here and there. Charlie sat and waited.

The lightning was suddenly about her. The thunder was directly overhead. She closed her eyes. Wind whipped her hair against her face and neck. She saw the light through her eyelids, saw the pinks and reds. Thunder roared. She smiled.

Then—she heard it before she felt it—a dull thud on her left shoulder, a smattering of drops against her right hand. She opened her eyes and saw the rain falling before her.

Charlie had no easy time sleeping that night. She got home around nine, ate half a bowl of soup and tossed and turned for a few hours. With an exasperated sigh, she rose and redressed. She pulled on her boots and headed for Stephen's place. As usual, he wasn't there. She went to his room and retired to the floor for rest.

Stephen stumbled in around one-thirty and stepped over her to get into bed. He didn't even take off his shoes. She listened as his heavy breathing became steady and then lulled to a soft snore. Slowly, and silently, she stood. His face was blurry in the pale light leaking from the street lamps through the blinds. Her gaze moved over his sleeping body.

Why do I care about you? I'm not even good enough to sleep next to you in your stupid, fucking bed.

With this, she kicked the box spring with her bare foot, and even though her toes were arched upward when she did it, she struggled to suppress a yell. Stephen didn't even move. Charlie had initially feared waking him, but now she wanted him awake. She wanted him sleep-deprived as she was. She leapt on him, pounding his back with her fists. She said nothing, but continued her pummeling.

Stephen leapt awake. "Jesus Christ!" He put an arm up to shield the onslaught. "What the fuck is wrong with you?" He grabbed her forearms tightly. Charlie wriggled beneath his grasp, but she could not move. Finally she stopped and he released her.

Sitting up and fixing her hair, she said casually, "Oh. You're up."

"Yes, I'm fucking *up*," he replied grumpily. "What was so Goddamn important?"

"I feel terrible," Charlie said.

"And?" he scoffed.

"And it's your fault, you jackass! You make me sleep on the Goddamn floor. You fuck me when it's convenient, and I love you like an idiot…and then you have the audacity to remind me that we're not together to make me feel like a fucking whore. I hate this! I hate feeling this way and it's your fault!" Charlie was yelling. It felt great.

"Charlie, this is hardly the time…" Stephen said detachedly.

"That's too fucking bad, Stephen. Don't tell me we'll talk about it later, because we never do. You're out hanging out with your friends and I'm always at your beck and call in case you need to shoot your load."

"Are you through?" Stephen asked wearily. "I'd like to go back to sleep."

"We're done." Charlie replied. "I'm leaving." She crawled over him to get her shoes. As she was lacing up her boots, she was mumbling to herself. "I can't believe I fucked you after you practically fucking kicked me out for that twat. And then I went on loving you. You fucking jerk. I hope you wake up tomorrow to find your dick shoved up your ass."

Stephen rolled back over and said, "When you're done talking to yourself, don't forget to leave the key before you go." Charlie looked at him steely. She walked over to Stephen's dresser and lifted Red's bowl. "Charlie, put my fucking fish down."

"Something to remember me by," she said and emptied the contents on his head. As she was walking down the stairs later, she wondered whether or not she should tell him she already put Red in the aquarium and watched her eat Thing One and Thing Two.

Chapter Four – The Book or the Movie?

Spot sat on the counter in The Book End. He sipped at a lukewarm diet soda. Charlie sat backwards on a chair with her eyebrows pushed together. After a while, she said, "*Rosemary's Baby.*"

"Eek," said Spot. "That's almost unfair."

"Don't be a baby," she replied.

"This coming from the girl who cried during *The Usual Suspects,*" said Spot.

"Hey. It was during the featurette, okay?" said Charlie. Spot held his hands up in a cease-fire fashion. "Fine, I'll pick something else."

"No, don't," he said. "We'll go with *Rosemary's Baby.*"

They were playing Spot's favorite game. They happened upon it one night while drinking. They called it, "The Book or the Movie?" To play, two or more people choose a film which was based on a book and discuss and debate which was better. Charlie decided early on that novelizations wouldn't be part of the game because they're never any good. Spot was usually an advocate for the film being better because films allow people who didn't necessarily read the book to be introduced to the story and characters. Charlie, being a purist and self-proclaimed book elitist, normally disagreed. "*Rosemary's Baby,*" she said. "Which is better? The book or the movie?"

"If I had to pick, and it's a really hard decision, I'd have to say movie," Spot decided after some hesitation.

"I'll refrain from commenting for now; why the movie?" Charlie asked.

"For casting Mia Farrow alone. Those big blue eyes…the cropped hair.

Mm…just. Yeah."

"Granted," Charlie laughed.

"Also, you're adapting something by the Swiss watchmaker of suspense fiction and they pulled it off. I saw it when I was a kid, long before I read it, and it unnerved me. Kids should never watch *Rosemary's Baby*."

"You've said the same thing about *Ghostbusters*," Charlie reminded him.

"That first scene? The ghost in the library? Fucking terrifying. And the taxi driver?" Spot visibly shook.

"Let's get back to the game. I find your points valid, but I choose the book," she said.

"Of course you do." Charlie's expression deflated. "All right, tell me why."

"You already said it. We're talking about Ira Levin, here. The man did not mince words. He could unsettle you in under a page. Most writers can't achieve his level of scary in an entire book."

"Oh hey, speaking of, did you see The Stepford Wives remake?" Spot asked.

"No," Charlie said.

"It's terrible; you've gotta see it," Spot grinned.

"Ever see the first one?" Charlie asked.

"Mm, nope."

"You should. Next up: *Of Mice and Men*," said Charlie. "Which is better? The book or the movie?"

"That was the one with John Malkovich, right?"

"Malkovich, Malkovich," Charlie replied.

"Again, it's a toss-up," Spot told Charlie. "Directed by Gary Sinise—"

"Who also played a stellar George," Charlie pointed out.

"That he did. And surprisingly well. I don't say that because he's a bad actor, but while a lot of directors will give themselves non-speaking roles or brief cameos, Sinese was onscreen for at least three quarters of the film. And the direction didn't suffer. Sinese was able to do both deftly. Plus the rest of the cast was brilliant."

"I assume that's a vote for the movie," Charlie reasoned.

"Your assumption is correct."

"I," here Charlie paused. Spot leaned forward expectantly. "Am undecided," she finished. "I love Steinbeck; for that alone, I want to choose the book. But all your points are correct, not to mention I cry over the ending every time. Even the first time I watched it, when I knew Lennie was going to die, I cried. I'm not sure I could choose between the two."

"Does that mean I win?" Spot asked.

"I didn't know we were keeping score," said Charlie.

"I'm not sure we ever do. What's next?"

"Um…*Ghost World*."

"Okay," said Spot. "Which was better? The book or the movie?"

"The movie, hands down," Charlie replied.

"Agreed."

"It kept the essential core of the comic, but gave it a believable, funny script," she commented.

"And Doug was awesome," said Spot. "Some of the funniest things I've ever seen are the outtakes of Doug in the parking lot. There's the difference; the movie was just really funny. Any humor that was in the comic was very dark. That's just the way Clowes is."

Charlie nodded. "The entire cast was perfect; Steve Buscemi is the fucking man," said Charlie. "And almost every character could've walked out of a Clowes drawing."

"I love the actor who plays Enid's dad," said Spot.

"I know!"

They nodded happily.

"Did you read *Fight Club?*" Spot asked.

"Yeah."

"Book or the movie?" he said.

"The book," said Charlie.

"I don't know," said Spot. "The book had some great parts that didn't make it into the movie. Like Marla chasing the main character around the kitchen and slipping on the fat. Or her stories about her ex-boyfriends. But there was something about watching it. Ed Norton was amazing. And the little blips of Tyler before he was introduced into the story were pretty clever."

"The movie was incredible, I don't deny that," Charlie said. "But the ending completely ruined the whole point."

"I wouldn't go that far," he replied.

"I would and I do. He wasn't supposed to end up with Marla. That's so wrong. He was supposed to have that evil jack-o-lantern thing going on with his face and he was supposed to end up in the hospital. He was supposed to have become just as bad as everything he despised. That's a fucking ending, not some contrived pseudo-happy ending," Charlie spouted.

"That's so depressing," said Spot.

"Exactly," Charlie smiled.

"At least they got to blow up all the buildings," Spot reasoned.

"Yeah, that didn't happen so much in the book."

"And they left it open-ended. You don't know what happens from there. I vote for the movie," said Spot.

"There's a shock."

"Anyway…how about *Fear and Loathing in Las Vegas?*" he asked.

"Book is the movie is the book," she said.

"So true."

"We could do *Requiem for a Dream,*" she said.

"I'm not sure which was more painful. The movie or the novel."

"Truth be told," said Charlie, "I didn't finish the book. I could barely read it."

"I can understand that. But if you could get past the dialogue, the narration was okay and the story is essentially the same. But seeing it in your head is almost a little kinder than watching the last thirty minutes of the film," said Spot.

"I think I would still choose the movie. I mean, there are entertaining ways to pull off regional dialect. Think Mark Twain. Think *Trainspotting.*"

"There's another great book/movie combination."

"A lot more happened in the book though," said Charlie.

"Yeah, but it was already a pretty long film. They couldn't put everything in."

"No, I suppose not. But my point is, it was leagues ahead of *Requiem* and definitely made for a movie you actually want to watch more than once."

"I will cede you that point."

"Should we do one more?" Charlie asked. Spot nodded. "*Adaptation.*"

"Which was that again?" Spot asked.

"The Spike Jonze movie based on *The Orchid Thief*," Charlie reminded him.

"Oh, right, right… The movie, definitely. Jesus," he said emphatically.

"What the hell's the matter with you?"

"What?" he asked innocently.

"The movie was ridiculous," said Charlie.

"The movie was outstanding," Spot disagreed. "It poked fun at screenwriting, pretentious and otherwise. It satirized elitism—"

"No. Wrong. It was completely formulaic and the ending was terrible."

"You're just mad because you thought you had it all figured out and you ended up being wrong," said Spot.

"Oh, shut up."

"'Charles and Donald are one person,' and 'This is how Donald would've finished the movie,'" Spot mocked her. "You just wanted to be right."

"That is completely untrue," said Charlie. Spot pouted at her. "What? What is that?"

"That's you. That's you doing your, 'I don't wanna play this game anymore' face." Followed by more pouting.

Charlie laughed, "I don't look like that."

"You look exactly like that," said Spot. "I totally win. Heavyweight champion of The Book End!" He took a victory lap through the store with his arms in the air.

Footnotes

Charlie approached the information desk at the center of the store. A lanky young man with dusty blonde hair and dark roots was behind the counter. He was in a heated discussion with a short woman whose pink, jagged haircut left her looking harsh.

"I don't have time for your bullshit right now," he said to her in hushed tones.

"You have no idea what this is like for me, Jay. You're not even there half the time. You don't know what it's like to have to deal with you," she hissed back at him.

"Then don't fucking deal with me!" he snapped.

She slapped him across the face. Without looking, she turned and walked right into Charlie. She muttered something about the mother of fucking Christ and kept walking.

Charlie made eye contact with the guy behind the counter and he said, "Sorry about that. If she weren't so self-enamored, she would've apologized herself."

"That's all right. She'll probably go sit in the parking lot and cry. Are you hiring right now?" Charlie asked without pausing between statements.

"She's not the crying type. And yes, we are hiring," he handed her a legal sized slip of gray paper covered with black ink. "Need a pen?"

"No, I've got one, thanks." She smiled and went to find a seat to fill out the application. When she returned, he was still there. She handed the paper back to him and said, "We have to stop meeting like this."

He laughed. "I'm Spot."

"Charlie."

They shook hands. "You okay?" she asked. "Your cheek's still red."

"Yeah, I'll live." She wanted to ask more about the situation, but didn't want to pry.

"So, is there anyone I should call?" asked Charlie.

"Hmm?" he replied.

"About the application?"

"Oh, yeah," he said. "In a few days, just call back and ask for Perry. He's the general manager but since our HR manager is on vacation all this week, he's taking her calls."

"Okay, thanks."

"Sure."

Charlie hadn't slept well. Her blankets, which usually enveloped her in a womb, felt like a wet, sticky bandage. Her eyes, still heavy from slumber, simply would not open. She blinked and rubbed them until they adjusted to the light. Charlie dragged herself to the bathroom.

She pissed as if she were emptying a bottle. It felt good to have an empty bladder. When she looked in the mirror, her stomach fell a little lower in her abdomen. She had cut off the black leaves a few months earlier and her hair had grown long enough to have a shaggy bedhead look. Dark circles had appeared under her eyes.

"God, when did I get so old?"

She was twenty.

Charlie sighed defeatedly and forced herself into the shower stall.

She had to be at work in an hour and it was twenty minutes away. She worked for a chain bookstore: the kind of bookstore that didn't so much sell books as they did DVDs and CDs and videos and coffee.

She quickly washed, rinsed and did a cursory shave. More rinsing and she was done. She patted herself dry and brushed her teeth.

Charlie reached for her jeans, black T-shirt, bra and boots. She ran some water wax through her hair, grabbed her bag and a coat, stepped over the boxes in her living room and out the door.

Charlie didn't drive. She'd tried it a few times and abhorred it. She hated all the drivers with their my-destination-is-more-important-than-yours-is attitudes. She really did enjoy walking. Good for the cardiovascular system. Prevented osteoporosis. Brought her closer to nature. That and she couldn't afford a car.

Charlie arrived at work just in time to sit through the mandatory shift meeting.

Charlie's general manager, Perry, held the meeting binder. He addressed the group assembled in the employee lounge. "Good morning, everyone."

Among them was the assistant manager, a thirty-five year old hippie going by the name of Blossom. Rumor had it her real name was Ann, or something similarly plain. Also, there was an employee from the music department whose name was Jason, but whom everyone referred to as Spot. Rounding out the group were one of the nondescript, interchangeable café baristas and Charlie.

"We have about fifteen minutes before we open," said Perry, "and I just wanted to touch on a few things before we get started." He rubbed his hands together and smiled uneasily, if not unsteadily. Obviously a gesture one is taught in the retail management "How to Look Approachable" seminar. Perry opened the binder and removed the previous day's sales sheet.

"Now, yesterday, we made $9,346. I know that sounds like quite a sum, but we're down from last year by about $1,300. I know we can do better than that. We need to make sure we are the first store people think of when they want a book, CD, or movie. Not an alternative if someone else doesn't have it, but the first. We need to let the customers know that we have everything they want and they don't need to shop anywhere else. Okay?" Blossom nodded emphatically.

"It's a very exciting time to be a bookseller," Perry continued. "What with Oprah's book club and all. Celebrities are reading, folks. That means the little people will soon follow the trend. And we want to make sure they come here first. Sure, they could go to amazon.com and have the book delivered, but we need to create an atmosphere that'll keep them coming back." At this point, Blossom looked like a dashboard doll.

"This leads us into our next topic. Our return policy. I know it's printed on our receipts that you need your sales slip and it needs to be within thirty days, but, in all actuality, we don't really have a return policy," said Perry, grinning sheepishly.

"If a customer comes in with a copy of yesterday's paper and complains loudly enough, we will redeem their money. I know it says in our return policy that we don't return periodicals, but the customer is always right. If a customer brings a CD back and the seal is broken, and the reason they give for returning it is because they don't like it, even though it's against our return policy, if they make a really big stink about it, by all means, take the merchandise back. According to our return policy, we are not to return any CDs if they have been opened, but we want return customers. We don't really have a concrete policy. All we want is for them to return to the store again and again. They'll buy something eventually," said Perry.

"Uh, Perry?" Spot interjected.

"Yes?"

"What if a customer comes in and wants to return something which we've never carried and is clearly used and they're basically fucking us over?" Perry's face registered nothing. "What then?"

"Spot. It's not in our place to question." Spot pressed his lips together and nodded once. Charlie's head ached. "Okay, gang, I think it's time to open. Remember, big smiles today and don't forget: we're here to have fun."

Charlie looked around the table. Perry was making small talk with Blossom, the café girl smiled and looked vacant, and Spot made eye contact with Charlie, and raised his eyebrows to say, "Let's make a break for it."

Charlie smiled and nodded to say, "I'm right behind you." She went to unlock the door. Spot followed.

A bitter wind sifted the powdery snow across the parking lot. The thermometer inside the unheated lobby read 12 degrees Fahrenheit. The sun was just coming up. Charlie moved the deadbolt and held the door open for the two lunatics who'd, no doubt, been waiting for at least twenty minutes to be let inside.

Charlie whispered to Spot, "What the fuck are these people doing here? If I didn't have to work, I'd still be asleep. Even if I were awake right now, I'd be wrapped in a blanket and still in bed."

"If any of these people leave without buying something," said Spot, "I'm going to follow them out to the parking lot and beat them to death with a lead pipe."

Charlie laughed and said, "What was with that speech our fearless leader gave?"

"Don't you know? We only have four hundred stores worldwide. Barnes & Noble is on the verge of shutting us down as we speak. Fucking drone," Spot muttered. "'We have to be the first store everyone goes to… Our very jobs and lives are at stake, surely you understand that.' What a tool."

"You should come to Wired tonight. My band's playing there," Spot told Charlie.

"Yeah? What kind of stuff do you play?" she asked.

"Well, we do a lot of covers. Metal," replied Spot.

"Oh." It wasn't exactly Charlie's taste, but she found herself longing for male companionship. Not sexually, she just missed males. She got directions from Spot. The venue wasn't far from the bookstore.

She tried to find tasks to occupy herself with until the end of her shift. By the last hour, she was talking to herself. "Fuck, man. Closing shift sucks." She was almost done when she saw a woman sitting in the café. Charlie walked over to her and said, "Ma'am, we're closing now."

"What?! It's only eleven o'clock! I thought you were open until midnight," the customer sputtered.

"No, ma'am." Charlie knew she'd heard the four closing announcements so had no problem telling her, "Only until eleven."

"Well, you should be open later! I have to use your restroom before I leave," the woman announced, rising from her chair and stamping off to the bathroom.

Charlie let the girl in the café know she could close up now and told the manager they had one customer left. Twenty minutes later, the customer resurfaced and waltzed out the front door. Charlie checked the bathrooms for any additional stragglers. All she found was a used tampon stuffed in one of the toilets.

"Aw, why would you do that?" Charlie muttered. She covered both her hands heavily with toilet paper and withdrew the tampon. "Eww, eww, eww, eww! Goddammit!" She ran and threw it in the garbage, then went to the sink to scour the skin off her hands. She used all the coarse, non-effective soap and turned the water on as hot as she could stand it. Before leaving, she said to her manager, "The ladies' room is out of soap."

Wired wasn't known for its ambiance. The stage was stripped bare of tile and a black, gritty coat of dirt had been stomped into the floor. The lights were dim and the air was smoky. The slightly under 21-ers who frequented the establishment were your basic group of kids. A few preps, a healthy number of goths, some potheads, and a nice sized group of wannabe punks sporting the Johnny Rotten safety pins on the crotch look. Wanting so badly to gain acceptance and rebel at the same time. When Charlie arrived, a few eyes passed over her briefly before returning to what they were doing. Staring, squinting, trying not to make too much contact.

The majority of the crowd wasn't there for the music. Nor were they there for the company. They were wretched…or at least they tried to be. They had "nothing to live for" and they hung at Wired to whine about it. If there were ever something to actually do, they'd whine about that too.

Bored eyes gazed, two by two, at the stage. Spot strolled onto the scene toting his guitar. A scrawny, pale guy with a vague expression affixed himself behind the drums and an individual Charlie guessed was male, she couldn't be sure since his hair had completely obliterated his face, shuffled in on bass. Classical Gas had entered stage right. Charlie lonely clapped.

Spot leaned to the microphone and said, "We're Classical Gas, we'll be playing a few songs for you tonight. None of them are originals, but that's kind of the point."

The drummer counted off. Spot played the intro to Dance of the Sugar Plum Fairy. It then changed into a quicker, louder, heavier version. Charlie's mouth hung open in a stupefied grin. They played the overture to *HMS Pinafore* and Beethoven's *Symphony no. 9* before they were done. Charlie yelled and clapped and laughed. Spot smiled and said into the mic, "Thanks. We're Classical Gas." He stepped off the stage and went to meet Charlie.

"Hey, you showed up," he said.

"Yeah. I was afraid I was going to miss it. This crazy woman was holed up in the café and just would not leave. It was insane," she replied.

"Oh no…did she complain about us not being open until midnight?" asked Spot.

"Yeah," Charlie answered. "Why?"

"And did she spend about twenty minutes in the bathroom before leaving?"

"Yeah…who is she?" said Charlie.

"Oh my God, it's the tampon sniffer lady," he said with a shudder.

"What are you talking about?" asked Charlie.

"She's this lunatic who hangs out in the café all day. She never buys anything. She just sits at a table, reading all the magazines and orders a cup of hot water. We never thought anything of it until she started staying late. It was ridiculous. One night, one of the café girls was so pissed, she followed her into the bathroom. Big mistake. She caught her sniffing a used tampon. She ran out of the bathroom screaming," said Spot.

"No wonder she orders the hot water," said Charlie.

"Why?"

"She uses the tampons to make tea," replied Charlie.

Spot covered his mouth and laughed into it. "Oh my God, she probably does! That's fucked up," he said.

Charlie laughed and shrugged. "I aims to please."

"There's going to be a party at the drummer's place in about an hour, you should come," Spot told Charlie.

"I don't know...I don't think this is exactly my kind of crowd. And I won't know anyone there," she said.

"You'll know me. C'mon, it'll be fun," said Spot. He leaned his head onto her shoulder. "Pweeze?"

She arched an eyebrow and smiled at him. "Can I catch a ride with you?" she asked.

"But of course," he replied.

Charlie was hard pressed finding something to do for an hour while Spot tended to the enthusiastic crowd. She counted fourteen girls wearing accessories with little skulls on them, two guys with spider tattoos on their shaved heads, and five girls that weren't wearing dog collars. She was in the middle of counting how many people were wearing too much eyeliner when Spot approached her.

"Hey, you ready?" he asked.

"Yeah...I'm cross-eyed with excitement," she said.

"Aw, don't be like that."

"Sorry, this place reminds me of what I used to be like and it's always embarrassing thinking about what you used to be like if you're not like that anymore. It's like looking at old pictures from the eighties. You know you went through the period, but you don't want to relive it."

"Charlie, you were, what? Ten, at the oldest, in the eighties?" Spot asked.

"Yeah, around there, but you know what I mean," she said.

"Yeah, big frosted hair. Acid wash jeans. Scary," he replied. "C'mon." He motioned for her to follow him. After getting out of the club, the night almost seemed garishly bright. And it was a new moon.

"I feel like I just left a black hole," Charlie said.

"Not the best place to be after a long day at work, I know," said Spot.

"That and I think I'm now addicted to cloves," she quipped. She did her parking lot routine. Not driving and not knowing which car was Spot's nor where he parked, she hesitantly followed him and hoped not to look too foolish if she stopped at the wrong car. They stopped at a black Dodge.

"This one's mine," he said, motioning to the car. He unlocked her side and they got in. "I have to call Andy and let him know you're coming."

"Okay." Spot opened the glove compartment and removed a cell phone. He punched through an index of names and pressed the call button. "Andy, hey, what's up? We still on for tomorrow? You've got a date? She Asian? You're changing. Listen, I'm bringing someone to the after party. No, I work with her. No, you can't. What? Oh, that's a great book." He put the phone to his shoulder and said to Charlie, "*Harold and the Purple Crayon.*" He put the phone back up to his ear again. He laughed. To Charlie, "He's telling me the plot." She smiled. To Andy, "Okay, I'll read it when I get there. About five minutes. No. No. Yeah, bye." He hit the off button, threw the phone in the glove compartment and pushed it shut.

"Why did you keep saying no?" Charlie asked.

"He wanted to know if we were fucking," Spot replied.

"Ahh…he didn't believe you?"

"After I told him no, he wanted to know if he could," he responded.

"Fuck me or you?" Charlie asked.

Spot stopped and looked as if in deep thought. "Ya know, I don't know. I didn't ask. I assumed he meant you."

"It's okay, I'm kidding," she said.

"We'll be there in about five minutes. You can ask him then if you'd like."

"Tempting. But no," she replied. Charlie looked at Spot's dashboard. There were dents across it and scratches on the vents. She glanced up the doorframe. More slashes.

"Uh, Spot?" said Charlie, pointing to the damage.

"Oh, that's from Dave," Spot said, with more than a little disgust in his tone. "He's our drummer."

"Skinny, pale guy?" said Charlie.

"Aren't they all?" Spot asked.

She laughed. "So, what did he do to the car?"

"He carries his sticks wherever he goes. And we were playing Weezer one day while he was in the passenger seat. 'Only in Dreams' came on. It played once through. He put it on repeat and pummeled the shit out of my dashboard," said Spot as he parallel parked. "I forbade him to ever call shotgun again."

"Nice," said Charlie.

"We're here."

They were in the door less than five minutes when a girl vaguely familiar to Charlie approached Spot.

"Hello," she said icily.

"Jenn," he replied.

"Thanks for calling me back," spat the girl.

"No problem. If you'll excuse us. Charlie?" Spot said and took Charlie's hand. Charlie tossed a confused look to the girl and followed Spot. Once out of earshot, Charlie asked:

"What was that about?"

"Sorry," Spot responded. "That's my newly exed girlfriend, Jenn. She was the one who slapped me when you and I first met."

"That's why she looked familiar," Charlie reflected. "I'm surprised you remembered that."

"What? Her slapping me? I had the welt as a reminder," he said.

"No," she smiled. "I meant meeting me."

"Hard to forget," he grinned. Charlie smiled and turned her cheek. "Ahh, you're blushing." She laughed.

"I don't blush," Charlie replied.

"Eh, fair-skinned girls are overrated. You want a drink?" he asked.

"Long as it's not a date rape drink, sure." He tried to make it to the kitchen, but was stopped at arm's length.

"You'll have to let go of my hand," he said.

"Oh, fine," she played it off.

Idiot.

Charlie watched the partygoers drift by. It was a tremendous house. She wondered idly what this Andy did for a living. Spot returned with a beer. "There you are, then."

"Thanks," she knocked back a gulp, hoping it wasn't dark draught. It was. She felt the skin around her eyes seize up and smiled to cover. She would have to nurse this one for a while.

"I'm going to try to find Andy," Spot said. "Feel free to wander."

"Okay," Charlie smiled. She watched Spot walk away. Yes, it felt good to have a male friend again.

She moseyed through a few rooms. There was a room from which music was blaring and Charlie saw the drummer from Classical Gas, Dave, dancing with a despondent looking girl. Next to them was a couple sitting on a sofa. The girl was either blowing him or hyperventilating into his lap. With her hair covering her face and the sound of her breathing, it could viably have been the latter.

In the adjoining room, there was a group of guys watching TV. Charlie stopped at the precipice and waited to see what was playing. Once the music started, she knew it was pornography. She thought of her brother and smiled wistfully. She lingered to see if it was anything that she recognized. It was a lesbian leather flick. Her curiosity was piqued. There were two blondes, both wearing too much lip liner and mascara. Blonde Number One grabbed Two by the hips and pushed her face into her crotch. The guys cheered. Charlie found it both erotic and shameful. It reminded her of Danielle. She left the room.

She went out to the patio. It was empty and the night was clear. Despite the new moon, there was a sky full of stars. Charlie leaned back to look at them. She knew nothing about constellations; she merely found them comforting. She spun around to see the stars behind her and in mid-rotation saw Spot join her on the patio. A scrawny guy followed behind him.

"Hey," said Spot.

"Hey," Charlie replied. "Just looking at the stars."

He looked up as well. "Hmm," he grunted. The guy behind Spot gazed at the sky behind Charlie with his eyes only.

"I know nothing about the stars. Can't tell the North Star from Polaris," he said.

"Andy, this is my friend, Charlie. Charlie, this is Andy," said Spot.

"Nice to meet you," said Andy, extending his hand.

Charlie switched her beer to her left hand and met Andy's grip with her right. "Quite a place you've got here."

"Yeah…" said Andy, looking up like a small child admiring museum artwork.

"It's his Mom's," said Spot.

"Ahh," said Charlie. "That makes more sense."

"Andy…" a girl cooed from the glass sliding door. She poked her head outside and shot Andy a come hither gaze.

"Spot, Charlie, if you'll excuse me…" Andy turned with a grin. He reentered the house and, upon the girl turning around, Charlie recognized her as the oral sex darling from earlier. Charlie smiled and turned to Spot.

"So, how go things with the ex?" she asked.

"Things with Jenn are…complicated. We met a couple years ago and there were…" Spot looked at Charlie and saw that she was actually paying attention. "Ya know what? I don't want to talk about it. Let's talk about something else. Did you like the show?"

"I did, very much," Charlie replied. "Sorry if I overstepped my boundaries just now."

"No, don't worry about it," Spot waved it away. "It's just a sore subject. The relationship went stale long ago and neither of us wanted to admit it and she's having trouble letting go and it's just a big mess." Spot drank the last of his beer. "What about you? Are you drowning in that manic depressive sea we call love?"

Stephen.

"You could say that," Charlie replied. "It's unrequited. I'm trying to move on and… It's just tedious right now. I'd heard people talk about love when I was younger and I just thought that it would be all hearts and flowers. And it's not. Love is, at the same time, the pinnacle and the nadir of your emotions. And that's where I am right now. Nostalgic over the former and miserable over the latter. It's fucking with me pretty badly."

"Love is a many splendid thing," said Spot, tipping his empty bottle to clink the air.

"Splendored," Charlie corrected.

"Hmm?"

"The quote is, 'Love is a many splendored thing.' Splendored, not splendid." Spot thought on this. "I knew that."

"Uh-huh," grinned Charlie.

"Hey," said Spot, quasi-serious for a moment, "do you have a pen and paper?"

"Uh, yeah, just a sec," Charlie responded, digging through her canvas bag. She exchanged her notebook, open to a clean page, and a pen for his empty beer bottle. She watched as he doodled tipsily. He stopped every few second and siphoned in the air with his index finger. After a few minutes of this, he happily examined the paper and handed it back to Charlie. She returned his bottle and walked to the door, closer to the light.

"I'm not fucking tan! Hoots R hot, G," she read aloud. "Uh, Spot, how much have you had to drink?" She squinted at him.

"It's not because of the alcohol," he said, shaking his head. "This," he pointed to her notebook, "is a test. It's a secret code." He smiled at her proudly.

"A code?" she laughed. "What's that about?"

"You're the writer. You tell me. What does it say?" he teased gently.

"What do you mean?" she asked, confused. "I'm not a writer."

"I see you scribbling in that notebook all the time. You write. You're a writer. So…what does it say?" he asked again.

She arched an eyebrow but played along. She smiled at the challenge. "A code, huh? Like each letter is represented by a different specific letter?" she asked.

"No…fuck, man. I couldn't do that when I'm drunk. It's simply a scrambled message. The letters are all there, I just fucked with them and tried to make coherent sentences. I've yet to make one that actually made sense and didn't substitute letters for words," he mused.

"Like *R* instead of *a-r-e?*" she asked.

"Exactly. So…what does it say?" he said, leaning forward excitedly.

She studied the paper. "How many words?" she asked.

Spot counted on his fingers. "Five."

"One sentence?"

"Yup."

"Okay," she said. She read and reread the two phrases. She laughed to herself.

"What?" Spot asked. "Did you get it?"

"No, I was just wondering…is the second sentence a sly breast remark?" she asked, grinning.

"What? Let me see that." He took the paper from her. "Oh," he laughed. "No."

"Five words…" she whispered. She jotted down several notes on the page, crossing out letters, scratching out potential words. She mumbled to herself.

"And…" said Spot, "time's up. What've you got?"

"Nothing with just five words that makes sense," Charlie sighed. "Tom thinks rain oft…oh, forget it. Just tell me." Spot smiled.

"It said, thanks for coming out tonight," said Spot.

"Oh." Charlie returned to her paper and matched up the letters. "I guess it does." She looked up at him. "Sorry I failed your test."

"Nah…it's like the Matrix. Everyone always falls on the first jump," Spot said. "It wasn't really a test. It was just easier than saying it."

Charlie smiled shyly and felt self-conscious all of a sudden. "Well, thanks for inviting me." She checked her watch. "Think you're okay to drive?" she asked.

Spot stuck his finger in his mouth and looked at the tip as though checking a gauge. "Looks like my alcohol content has returned to normal," he said. She looked at him skeptically. "Close enough."

"Would it be all right if we took off then? I've never been much of a party girl. Besides, I have to return to the magical land of retail tomorrow. Whee…"

"Your chariot awaits," said Spot, ushering her back through the house.

Once in the car, Charlie felt the effects of the evening hit her. She sighed softly.

"What's up?" Spot asked.

"Just weary, that's all," she replied.

"Oh, good. I was hoping I hadn't depressed you back there," he said.

"Hmm?" Charlie looked at him.

"With talk of your ex…" Spot trailed off.

"Oh. Stephen. It's just hard to think about him sometimes. A lot of the time, actually. I'd never met anyone like him before." She half-laughed. "I suppose that's a good thing seeing as how he fucked me over."

"If you don't want to talk about it, that's okay…but, if you don't mind my asking, what happened?" Spot asked gently.

Charlie hesitated before answering. After a while, "I met him when I was young. Well, *younger.*" She smiled. "I don't want to say it was lust at first sight."

"But it was?"

"In a way, yeah. He was older than me and had this bad boy thing going."

"Oh no…" Spot teased.

"I know. I fell victim to a stereotype. Again, I was young—"

"—er," Spot finished.

"Yes," she grinned. "But he really was rebellious. He loved to piss off his parents. Lots of piercings. And though he wasn't covered in them, he had about twenty tattoos."

"Any terribly cheesy ones?" Spot asked.

"Hmm…he had a few skulls, but nothing gaudy." They fell silent. "Oh wait! There were the firey things on his ankles…" she said. "They went around his entire leg right above his ankles to almost the middle of his shins."

"Quite the martyr. Burned at the stake and all," Spot mused.

"It's funny; I don't think it was a pretentious thing. He could be very intimidating when he wanted to," said Charlie.

"Eh, he sounds like a dick," said Spot.

"Yeah, he was definitely that. I mean, he knew I was in love with him, so he broke it off. But we were still fucking after that."

"Like a fuck buddy thing?" Spot asked.

"No. Not for me, anyway," said Charlie. "Once we started again, I was at his place a lot anyway. I had a key to his apartment, so I'd spend the night just to be near him. It was no easy task either. I got about five jobs to get my own place which is roughly the size of a bird feeder, and I barely slept there because I would be over at Stephen's. But I didn't leave his place until he really pushed me over the edge. So now it's just me and my hole in the wall."

"Why not get a bigger place?" he asked.

"Can't afford it. I mean, look at where I work," she winked.

"True. Get a roommate."

"Everybody I know has a place already." Spot nodded. "Besides, there are perks to my place. The previous tenant had stained glass windows installed and they ripped up the carpet and refinished the hardwood floor. So, what it lacks in space, it makes up for in aesthetics," she said.

"That reminds me," said Spot.

"Yeah?"

"I've just been driving around in circles for about the last thirty minutes. I don't know where you live," he said.

"I was wondering if we'd really passed five different post offices," Charlie commented.

"Yeah," he smiled.

"I live on Fairmont Street," said Charlie. "It's about a twenty minute walk from the book store."

"Okay…I'll drive to the store and you just direct me from there," he said.

"Deal."

Before getting out of the car, Charlie leaned over and hugged Spot. "Thanks for listening to my sob story," she said. "You didn't have to and I appreciate that."

"No problem. It only cost me a quarter of a tank of gas," he replied.

"Yeah, sorry about that," she said with chagrin.

"Hey, you didn't twist my arm," he said. "But listen, about Pyre…"

"Pyre?" Charlie asked.

"Yeah, your ex."

"Stephen?" she laughed.

"Yeah, whatever. He has flame tattoos. His new name is Pyre. Anyway, don't give him a second thought. You're better than that."

Charlie smiled wryly. "I'll keep that in mind."

"Okay. Have a good night."

"You too. And thanks again."

Spot arrived at work the next day. In his mailbox was a note. It said: *Got head? Chain liar to time, lad. *sigh**

He smiled, grabbed a pen and wrote on the reverse side: *Glad you had a good time. See you soon. – Spot*

Chapter Five – Reproduction is Hell

Charlie and Gwen shelved books while Spot trained Mark at the counter. An earsplitting wail pierced the air.

Charlie bolted upright. "What the hell is that?"

"Charlie, it's just a kid crying, relax," Gwen tried to defuse the situation.

"Oh, I know what it is," Charlie said.

"Please don't," Gwen begged.

Charlie tilted her head to find the origin of the wail. From the business section, she could see the little towheaded grub's mouth was open like a tunnel, emitting the shrill discord that his mother could so easily ignore. "There's the little miscreant," Charlie muttered.

"I'm asking you as a friend, don't," Gwen pleaded.

"Rules are rules." She made her way toward the child. "Hello," she said, towering above him. He looked up and cried louder. "Where's your mother?" The sobbing persisted. "Well, I'll go make sure she's not trapped under some bookshelf." Making haste to peruse the rest of the store, Charlie found there was only one other customer. She was in the self-help section. Charlie approached her.

"Excuse me, ma'am, are you here with your child?" Charlie asked politely.

"Oh, yes, he's around here somewhere," she replied, not taking her eyes off the book she held by Dr. Phil.

"Mm-hmm. If you would be so kind as to direct your attention," said Charlie, clapping the book shut and depositing it under her own arm, "to the resounding chaos discharging from your son's lungs, I'm sure you'll notice he doesn't want to be here." Charlie led the woman to the business section. "First of all," Charlie yelled over the din. "When the child is *screaming*! That's not a good sign. Secondly, children are not allowed in this store."

"Says who?" the woman demanded.

"Says the sign placed directly to your left when you walk in the door. It clearly states, and I quote, 'This is not a children's bookstore. No children shall be allowed on the premises.' That includes yours. If you'd like, I can direct you to a bookstore with a cafe attached where your evil spawn can spill your freshly purchased latte all over the merchandise." Charlie did not attempt to smile. She was dead serious.

The customer took her bemoaned child's hand and exited the store, shooting every employee a dirty look on her way. Charlie returned to shelving books with Gwen.

"I can't believe you have to do that every time," Gwen chided.

"If I didn't do it every time, it would seem like I was showing favoritism. Should I have told her to have a nice day? Did I commit some mortal sin by telling her to fuck off?" Charlie asked, not so much of Gwen, but of anyone willing to listen.

"If you would simply have taken my advice," Spot yelled from the counter, "and called it, The Book End: An Adult Bookstore, you wouldn't have this problem."

Halloween

Charlie rapped the back of her knuckles against Spot's door thrice. She twirled her skirt absent-mindedly while she waited. Shadows danced against the bay window. Charlie watched them flit across the glass. Her face itched. She didn't scratch it for fear of smearing the make-up. She was about to knock again when the door creaked open…slowly. The interior of the house was neither light nor dark, but a dim, pale neutral which Charlie couldn't describe. She looked from left to right, absorbing the atmosphere and letting out a low whistle.

"Spot?" she said.

"Yeah!" he yelled from the next room. "In here!"

She followed his voice to the adjoining room. Spot sat in the middle of the dining room table, surrounded by little bags for trick-or-treaters which have generic salutations printed on them like "Happy Halloween!" or "Fright Fest!" or some other contrived seasonal greeting. "I'll be done in just a second," Spot told Charlie, without looking up.

"Okay," she replied. She watched as he finished his task. He was cycling through each bag, adding an equal number of lollipops, candy bars, and the part which amused Charlie the most, mucus. Spot would clear his throat, loudly, and then bring up a mouthful of phlegm and deposit it in each bag. "Dare I ask?" said Charlie.

Again without looking up, Spot replied, "We're going out. So, there's no one here to give out candy, thus we have to leave a basket of candy on the porch. But, in doing so, there's a certain amount of trust we'll be giving these little bastards to only take one bag of candy. There's a punishment for taking more than one."

"What about the kids who only take one?" Charlie asked.

"All children are dishonest. All of them," answered Spot.

"There's an exception to every rule," reasoned Charlie.

"Yeah, but," said Spot, finishing his task, "I hate kids." He looked up. His jaw dropped. "Jesus Christ!" Charlie stood before him in a blonde wig and white sleeveless dress showcasing her sternum. Her face was done up in 1950's style make-up complete with doe eyes and blood red lips. A birth mark had been added to her cheek. With her recent loss of baby fat and the cut of the skirt, her figure had become an hourglass and if she'd been a bit shorter, she may well have passed for Marilyn Monroe.

"Do I look fat?" she asked.

"I refuse to answer that. But I will tell you I prefer your regular garb to this; it suits your personality better," said Spot.

"Good. Then I did my job adequately," commented Charlie looking at her arm and hand.

"I don't follow," Spot replied.

"Gwen, the girl whose party we're attending, and I decided to go as each other for Halloween. She, I'm sure will be donned all in black and have a tear painted on her cheek. Whenever she talks, she sounds like Marilyn Monroe," said Charlie. "I think it's pretty clever, no?"

"We'll see. Let me get my costume ready and we'll be off."

Spot went as the same thing every Halloween. An over-the-hill alcoholic goth. He had a shoulder length black wig for just such an occasion. He wore a black gauze shirt with black pants which laced up the sides and he topped off his attire with a pack of cloves and an Udjat Eye pendant.

Charlie laughed when she saw him. "Very nice," she said.

"I know. You'd think I were going as you in high school," he teased.

"In that case, you forgot to paint your nails and you need more eyeliner," Charlie chided.

"Mea culpa," said Spot loftily.

She gave him the directions to Gwen and Gregory's place.

A tall, strapping man in lederhosen answered the door when they arrived. He yodeled a hello and beckoned them in. All the lights were off except strings of green and purple lights lining the walls. There were fake spider webs in every doorway and cauldrons full of alcohol dotted each room. All of this could barely be seen through all the guests. "Spot, this is Gregory," Charlie introduced the yodeler. "Gregory, this is my friend, Spot."

The two shook hands.

"Where's Gwen?" Charlie asked.

"Still getting dressed, I think," he replied. A knock came from the door. "Sorry," Gregory excused himself. "It was nice to meet you, Spot."

"You too." Spot looked at Charlie. "I somehow keep forgetting it's Halloween until I see someone dressed like that."

Charlie laughed. "Yeah. Not something you see everyday."

"Nope," he agreed.

A masked figure appeared behind Charlie. Clearly female, she wore a black leotard and an antiquated mask with a mouth that was both a smile and a frown. She leaned her face next to Charlie's left shoulder. She tilted her head near Charlie's ear. "Boo," she whispered. Charlie froze. She continued facing forward but looked as far as she could to her left with wide eyes.

"You fucking bitch," Charlie breathed. "You scared the shit out of me."

Gwen laughed and blew her a kiss. "Do you see the resemblance?" she asked through the mask.

"Very nice. It's like looking in a mirror...but not."

"Yeah, because your interpretation was so clever," Gwen teased.

"What can I say? I'm a clever bastard," Charlie smirked.

"But you're not a writer," said Gwen.

"Hush. Gwen, this is Spot. Spot, this is Gwen," Charlie introduced the two.

Gwen pushed her mask up to the top of her head and extended her hand. "Hi, I've heard a lot about you."

"Likewise. Some place you've got here," he said.

"Yeah. We just moved in. It's all," said Gwen, striking a dramatic pose, "*very sudden.*"

"Are you mocking me?" Charlie asked.

"Maybe. Seriously though, Gregory and I have only been together for four months. We're apparently either rushing for disaster or falling headlong into china patterns and baby showers," she shrugged.

"Sounds like every relationship I've ever had," said Spot.

"You were debating wedlock with Jenn?" Charlie asked.

"No, that was a case of rushing for disaster," Spot corrected. "But she was convinced otherwise. Luckily for me, I used my patented Girl Be-Gone and she was gone in seven months flat."

"For the members of our audience not in the know," said Charlie to Gwen, "Jenn is Spot's ex-girlfriend."

"So I surmised, but Girl Be-Gone? You'll have to tell me about that," Gwen told Spot.

"Eh, I just told her I had the clap."

A smile played on Gwen's lips. "Charming." She leaned over to Charlie to feign subtlety, but said loudly enough for Spot to overhear, "Where did you dig this one up?"

"I work with Spot," Charlie said.

"Yeah, I have 9,000 hours of community service left before I have to go out and find a *real* job," Spot joked.

"Some days, I think I'd prefer community service over the bullshit we have to deal with," Charlie said. "But, fuck it. I don't want to think about work right now."

"I'll drink to that...except I don't have a drink," said Spot and wandered off to find one.

"Grab me a beer!" said Charlie.

He gave a thumbs up and waded through the madding crowd.

"He seems nice," Gwen said to Charlie. Or was it Charlie to Gwen?

"Yeah," Charlie nodded. "The place does look good."

"Thanks," Gwen replied. "Gregory's been great about moving things around. I keep changing my mind as to where I want everything."

"Speaking of Gregory...what's with the outfit?"

"He's always been a *Sound of Music* fan. His yodeling getup is a sort of homage, I suppose."

"Ahh," Charlie nodded.

"Know what's sick though?" Gwen asked, scrunching up her face.

"Hmm?"

"I'm kind of digging it," she said with a mischievous grin.

"You're right. That is sick."

Gwen giggled. "I know. So, you completely avoided the unspoken question in reference to your coworker. No interest?"

"I don't know, Gwen. I'm completely fucked up. Any time I think about having sex again, I just get depressed. I don't want to think about it."

"I can guarantee you'll get over that. Desperation will take hold and you'll start humping the first available warm body."

Spot returned with drinks. He doled them out.

Charlie leaned over to Gwen and clinked her glass. "May I never get to that point."

Chapter Six – The Newcomer

Mark saw Charlie sitting on a bench right outside The Book End. She was reading what looked like a daunting task of a book. A cigarette hung out of the corner of her mouth, but there was no smoke. As he approached, he realized it had not yet been lit. She didn't look up when he approached. He cleared his throat. When she paid him no attention, he opted for speech.

"Um…hi," he said.

Without moving her head, she glanced at his shoes and said, "Hello, Mark."

"May I join you?" he asked.

"You may." Again, she did not look up.

He noticed the cigarette again. "You got a light?" asked Mark.

With great pain, she put a photograph in her book to save her place and finally made eye contact. There was a heavy silence and she squinted before answering. "No. I don't smoke."

"But you have a…um…" said Mark, pointing to her cigarette and feeling incredibly foolish.

"Yeah. When some kids grow up, they want to be doctors or lawyers. Me? I want mouth cancer," Charlie retorted. Mark laughed. Charlie didn't.

"Sometimes I can't tell if you're serious," Mark commented.

"It's a thespian thing. I feel like the whole world's my straight man. My parents were always telling me to grow up. I kept telling them I was only nine." He laughed again. "Yeah, they're dead now." He stopped. "No, it's no big deal. I didn't cut them up in their sleep or anything. Not that I never thought about it.

They just died. It was in a car accident." Mark tried to think of something to say. It didn't work out very well, so he remained silent. "It didn't really matter though," Charlie continued. "They weren't really there. Not like a negligence, they-weren't-physically-there thing, but more like a not-emotionally-present kind of thing. Anyway, after that, I went to live with my aunt, a severe disease of a person and the only thing I had to 'make things better' was acting, so I threw myself into that."

"Do you still get to do it?" Mark asked.

"Not really. I guess it was just a phase though because after I got out of school I saw what it would really be like. I have this weird inability to kiss people's ass and there's a lot of that apparently. Also, I don't exactly have the look for Hollywood. But I retained certain things from it. I can tell a joke over and over again and never laugh. I can deadpan pretty well. Other than that, I basically suck."

"Nothing wrong with that," Mark smiled and looked away.

"Yeah…"

"I heard you were a writer," Mark ventured.

"Yeah, something like that," Charlie returned.

"You're not?" Mark asked.

"I am…hesitantly." Mark looked puzzled. "It sort of happened by accident. Like I said, I wanted to be an actress. I guess I still do…kind of…a little bit…not really, actually, now that I think about it. Anyway, I write short stories mainly. Sometimes I'll write a little sketch or a play. I just get flashes of scenes in my head. And writing is a way to get them out. Maybe I'll be a real writer when I grow up."

"But until then, you own the bookshop."

"Yes…and on the side, I own the shop. And I write, occasionally," she mused, looking down at her book.

"So, what are you reading?" Mark asked.

"Oh no, I've killed the moment," said Charlie inhaling through clenched teeth to mimic pain. "We've resorted to the, 'Hey, you have a book, let's talk about that.' What a conversationalist I am."

"No, that's not…" Mark explained.

"Sorry. Over-projecting. Sorry about earlier, by the way. I just hate being interrupted when I'm reading. And it's like a magnet. I could be, literally, the last person alive. If I happened upon a book and started reading, I'd get mauled by a bear, or a swarm of wasps would descend on me." Charlie twirled her cigarette through her fingers, passed it from hand to hand, palmed it.

"Should I just not ask about the cigarette thing?" said Mark, half facetiously.

"It's a security blanket thing," Charlie answered. "For a long time, all my friends smoked, and I didn't. Everyone would ask if I wanted a cigarette, and I was so sick of saying, 'No, I don't smoke,' that I just took one. And I've had it ever since. I occasionally do that jackass thing of wearing it behind my ear. Sometimes, I try to be cool. It rarely works."

Mark shuffled from one foot to the other. Charlie looked at him and raised her eyebrows in a "Yes?" fashion.

"I don't mean to completely interrupt your reading, but would it be all right if I join you? I came out for a cigarette but that kind of fizzled…"

"Please," said Charlie, gesturing to her right. He sat down. "So, you're what?

Twenty-five? Twenty-six? Why did you decide to work here?"

"I like books," he replied with a shrug.

"Token response. Let me guess. You've read all the classics. James Joyce, Fitzgerald—that's F. Scott, not Penelope—Hemingway, Dostoyevsky, but your love of literature has left you wanting more. So, you decide to read some current authors." Through all this, she's gesticulating emphatically, cigarette clenched between her index and middle finger. "You read Amy Hempel, Vonnegut, Bret Easton Ellis... And then you hit a glitch...*Bridget Jones's Diary*. Your mind goes numb. Your motor skills cease to function. Let me tell you, it's sad when that day comes. So, I warn you now, should you read *The New York Times Book Review* and *Publisher's Weekly* religiously: Don't believe the hype. If it has a full page ad in *Harper's*, read the first five pages and *then* buy it." Had she actually smoked, she would've taken a long drag at this point. "Oh, and get yourself a library card, it'll save you a lot of money and heartbreak."

"Are you like this all the time or was that speech just for me?" Mark said when she'd finished.

Charlie nodded and smiled to herself, "I—" She sighed. "I'm sorry. I'm usually not much like this at all. I'm just punchy today, I guess." Mark nodded. "I'm not trying to scare you off, if that's what you're worried about."

"No," said Mark. "You don't seem the type. Managers who drive their employees to give notice usually travel through life blissfully unaware."

"Either that, or completely apathetic," Charlie said.

"That was the case with my last job," Mark confided.

"Oh, there's a story in there somewhere," Charlie mused.

"Not so, actually," said Mark. "I had a thing with my former boss."

"Incompatible personalities?"

"No. We were very compatible, actually."

"Oh," Charlie drew out the vowel. "Not a thing with your boss, but a thing, thing."

"Yeah."

"What happened?"

"We got along really well, spent a lot of extra curricular time together, I didn't agree with the way business was done, I said something I probably shouldn't have, my boss shut down emotionally and that was that."

"Wow. I'm really sorry."

"Don't be. Most relationships end when you find out the hard way that they wouldn't have withstood the test of time."

"That's one way of putting it," Charlie smiled again to herself. Mark saw this and couldn't help but grinning curiously. "I killed my ex's pets."

"Ouch. That's a little extreme."

"It wasn't, actually. They were fish and I just allowed one of them to eat the other two."

"Was the carnivore out of regular fish food?"

"Not that I know of." Mark shook his head. "What?"

"I think you should donate money to the SPCA or something."

Charlie nodded. "Yeah, probably. Karmic retribution dictates. Well," she said, standing, "I suppose it's back to the coal mines. Can't sit too long or my legs will give out."

"How old are you?" Mark asked.

"Younger than you by at least a year," Charlie replied.

"And you're afraid of your legs giving out?"

"If you had to walk four miles every day and then stand for eight hours and then on some days, turn around and walk four miles home, you'd be a little frightened of your legs giving out too."

"Can't you take the bus?"

"Yes, I *could*. But I don't. I hate mass transit. There's one bus that travels out near my place and it does so once every ninety minutes. It takes me less time to walk than it would if I were to ride the bus. Plus, I hate people. I can't stand strangers and if I'm around them long enough, one of them will generally start talking to me. It's an extension of the interruption whilst reading clause. Also, the one time I did take the bus, I wore headphones and that turned out disastrously."

"How so?" Mark asked.

"I'm one of those people who commit the cardinal sin of singing while wearing headphones."

"Oh my God. I think I hate you."

"Yeah," said Charlie. "I think I hate me too."

Post Stephen

Three years after Abby moved and what seemed like eons after Stephen, Charlie was ready to step up to the plate again. It was time to buy a vibrator.

She made a trip to her local sex shop, Grand Opening.

The varying sizes of artificial penises astounded her. Thinking back to her brief foray into self-violation, she decided to avoid anything requiring insertion. Owning that well over half the stock was comprised of dildos or tools for anal entry, that left her with few options. She found a section featuring an array of what looked like children's playthings. Rubber ducks, penguins, plastic flowers.

"Did you need any help?" a clerk asked Charlie.

"Sort of," Charlie confessed. She tried to think of a way to describe what she was looking for. "I have no idea what I want."

"That's okay," said the clerk. "Is it something just for you or would it be a shared toy?"

"Just me," said Charlie.

"All right. Would you prefer something manual or battery operated?"

"Umm...battery operated, I guess," said Charlie.

"Well, you've found our vibrators."

"Yes, I saw that. Do you have anything more...simplistic?"

With the aid of the plucky young clerk, Charlie found a wide, curved vibrator that looked friendly, but also a little dangerous. She liked both.

"Just so you know," the clerk said as she rung up Charlie's purchase, "your vibrator is also waterproof."

"Really?" Charlie raised her eyebrows.

Charlie ran a bath as soon as she got home. She disrobed and took her new parcel into the bathroom. It clicked on and moved at three different speeds.

Charlie stepped into the water, turned the faucet to make the water hotter and submerged as deeply as she could.

Very much to her surprise, in the throes of her bath, Charlie found herself thinking about girls.

It didn't feel unnatural or wrong. She didn't even question it until she had finished. She sat up in her tub, completely sober following the afterglow of her climax. She imagined a naked woman.

She felt nothing.

She imagined a naked man.

Still nothing.

She exited her bath, toweled off and told herself that next time, she would try to think of men.

The next time arrived and the only men she could think of were ones she knew in the non-biblical sense.

After that, she promised herself that she would try to think of nothing at all. Barring that, she would purchase some pornography.

It was on a not-so-special day at work when Charlie met Ray.

Ray was short for Rachel. She wore her hair in tight braids which flowed from under a bandana. The very front hung loose. Her hair, at the time they met, reached the middle of her back. She wore a nose ring which matched her silver eyes.

"Do you have *The Man Who Was Thursday?*" Ray asked Charlie, whose hands were full of books. A more striking girl, Charlie had never seen. A light dusting of freckles lay across her nose. High cheekbones. Delicate features with a strong jaw. Kissable mouth.

"Uh…" Charlie stopped herself from staring. "Let me check." She put the books down and made her way to a computer. "By Chesterton?"

"Yeah, you ever read it?" asked Ray.

"No. No, I haven't," replied Charlie.

"My first girlfriend said it was great," said Ray, not so subtly. "Guess I should've read it while we were still together."

"Hindsight is 20/20. Especially when it comes to exes," said Charlie.

"Ex screw you over?" asked Ray.

"Ex boyfriend, actually," said Charlie.

"Oh."

"Not that I have anything against having a girlfriend," Charlie quickly countered.

"Oh," said Ray again, in a completely different tone.

"I've just never had the opportunity," said Charlie.

Ray nodded and smiled in a manner that Charlie wouldn't describe as warm, but certainly wasn't unfriendly. Charlie returned the favor. Ray was about to make her move when Charlie said, "So…we should have that book over in lit."

Charlie grabbed the book off the top shelf, exposing her midriff. "Paperback okay?" she asked.

"Yeah, that's great. Thanks," Ray grinned. Charlie found herself staring at Ray's mouth. She averted her eyes, but her gaze fell on Ray's chest.

"So," said Charlie, a little too loudly, "let me know what you think of the book."

"Sure," said Ray, still grinning.

"If you need anything else, let me know."

"I'll do that," Ray replied. There was an awkward silence before Charlie shuffled off to shelve.

"Well, bye," said Charlie.

"See you around," Ray replied.

Charlie had all but forgotten about the interaction when a copy of *The Man Who Was Thursday* found its way into her mailbox. There was no note, but when she opened it, Charlie saw someone had written on the first page.

The book was fantastic!
Please read it and let me know what you think.
It was nice meeting you.
Ray – 203-839-2954

Charlie smiled at the thought of this cute girl going out of her way to be nice to her. "Most guys don't even do that," she thought. As an afterthought, she wondered whom Ray got to put the book in her mailbox, seeing that she didn't ask her name.

Charlie took the book home and read it that night. Ray was right, it was incredible. She checked the clock. It was 11:30 PM. She decided to chance it. She dialed the number in the front of her book.

"Yeah?" said a voice after a few rings.

"Hi. Is Ray there, please?" asked Charlie trepidatiously.

"Who's this?" asked the voice sternly.

"Uh, it's Charlie. I have her book," she replied.

"Just a sec," the voice told Charlie. She heard him call Ray to the phone. "Hello?" said Ray.

"Um, hi. I'm sorry to call so late. This is Charlie. I have your book."

"Oh! Hey…just a sec," she said and called to the other room, "Mike, I have it! Hang up the phone!" A click was heard through the receiver. "Hey, you still there?"

"Yeah," Charlie replied.

"Sorry about that. That was my brother. I think he might've been asleep. Either that or drunk," said Ray, laughing. "So, did you like the book?"

"I did, very much. Thanks. I can drop it off to you, I just need to know where," said Charlie.

"No, that one's yours. I bought an extra copy just in case you never called me back," replied Ray.

"Oh." Charlie was taken aback. "Um, thanks. Did I seem like the kind of person who'd take your book?" Charlie asked.

"That's not it, I just pictured you getting the book and being all like, 'Okay, some lesbian just gave me a book and her number. Hmm...' Ya know?" she asked.

"I don't think I could do that. Take somebody's stuff, I mean. Even if I were a narrow minded bigot," said Charlie. Ray laughed.

"Well, good to know that you're not, and even if you were, you're a nice, polite, hypothetical hate monger," Ray joked.

"Yeah..."

Ray sensed the silence approaching, so she bit the bullet, "Do you want to hang out some time?"

"Umm..." Charlie faltered.

"Just friends," said Ray.

The thought of seeing Ray again appealed to Charlie. So much, it surprised her, in fact. "Yeah, definitely," she said.

"Awesome. What're you doing tomorrow?" asked Ray.

"I work until five," Charlie replied.

"I'll swing by and pick you up if that's okay," Ray offered.

"Cool. See you then."

Five o'clock arrived with neither haste nor torpidity. Charlie found herself anxious and impatient for the evening to commence. She distracted herself from waiting by grazing the new hardcover fiction.

Charlie, against proverbial advice, couldn't help being taken in by a book's cover. Had she any talent for designing things, she would adore the occupation of dressing and clothing books.

She plucked up a copy of Seamus Heaney's translation of *Beowulf* and opened to a random page. Fine font choice. Adequate margin space. She held it to her nose and breathed deeply. It had a hearty, fresh, pulpy scent.

Someone cleared his throat from the other side of the book. Charlie looked up to see a squat, elderly man regarding her harshly.

"Yes?" she said.

"Are you through with that? I'd like to see it," he demanded huffily.

Charlie glanced down at the book in her hands and her eyes flitted back to the man. "No, actually, I'm not done with it."

"You aren't even reading it," he sighed.

"Well, no, not yet," Charlie began. "I usually like to lick the endpages before deciding if I want to purchase it. If you give me just a second." Charlie ran her tongue across the black paper preceding the copyright page. "Nope, a bit too salty for me." She offered the book to him. "You can have it if you want."

The man went seven shades of red. He stomped away, Charlie assumed, to pester someone else.

"Do you do that to all the customers?"

Charlie turned to see Ray smiling at her. Charlie felt a little sheepish for having been caught.

"I actually wasn't just being weird. He started it."

"I know; I saw. I've been here since four," said Ray.

"Why didn't you say something to me?" Charlie asked.

"I didn't want to get you in trouble. I used to work at one of these soul-sucking chains and every time I go back there to see an old friend or something, one of the managers gets on their ass about it," Ray replied. "They're just pissed because I got out and they didn't."

"Oh," said Charlie. "So…what do you want to do?"

"I don't know. You hungry?" Ray asked.

"Not really, I had a late lunch," Charlie replied.

"Okay…umm, what do you usually do when you get out of work?" Charlie thought on that. When she worked for Abby, she was already home after work. And then they would just sit around doing whatever they wanted. The memory made Charlie smile. "What?" Ray asked.

"Just thinking of an old friend," Charlie answered. An idea struck. "Do you like to play pool?" she asked Ray.

"I have no aversions to playing pool."

"Pool it is, then," said Charlie. "I just have to buy this book before we go," Charlie gestured to the semi-soiled *Beowulf*.

She gave Ray directions to a pool hall downtown called Chalky Balls. "Nice name," Ray commented.

"I know. I love it," Charlie smiled mischievously.

It had been a while since Charlie had been to the pool hall. They'd revamped the outside completely with a new parking lot and a new sign. "Jesus, has it been that long since I was last here?" she thought aloud when exiting the car.

"I don't know. When was the last time you were here?" Ray asked.

"I was with my brother, so…about seven years ago."

"Wow, I wish it had been that long since I'd seen my brother," Ray said.

"It's not that great actually. He just moved out and I haven't seen him or heard from him since. Sometimes I wonder whether or not he's okay. Not considerate enough to make a fucking phone call," said Charlie.

"I'm sure he's okay," Ray said. Charlie tried to shake her worries off.

"You're probably right," she said. "Wanna head in?"

"Sure."

Charlie found her once adequate pool skills to be lacking. The stick felt awkward in her hands and her follow-through was weak. Ray, on the other hand, was like a painter rediscovering her art. She wiped the floor with Charlie in the first game and even shook her hand afterward.

"Damn, I suck," Charlie said. "I think my ego needs a break before we play again."

"Well, there's a jukebox in the corner," said Ray. "We could see if it'll play anything worthwhile."

"As long as it stays away from the top 40, I'm game."

"Girl after my own heart."

They wandered over to the jukebox and found such wonderful classics as "My Woman Left Me and My Hound Dog's Dead", "I'm Stranded in My Pick Up on I-85", and "After Mama Beat Me, I Up'd and Porked Aunt Lou." That last one piqued Charlie's curiosity.

"I have to play that one," she said. She inserted a dollar which allowed three songs. So, she played it three times.

"Oh God, they're gonna kick us out," said Ray giggling.

"It's their song. Maybe the guy who wrote it comes in here. Wouldn't that fill his heart with joy?" asked Charlie, smiling at Ray like they shared a secret. "'Aunt Lou,' he'd say when he got home, 'You won't believe it! They were playing our song at the pool hall!' And she'd come rushing out from the kitchen to make sure she knew which song he meant. 'Our song?' she'd start to well up. 'That's right, baby. I wrote that song for you.'" Charlie grinned and nodded slowly and lecherously.

Ray laughed while looking away, "I'm not sure which is worse. Your voice or the face you're making. Either way, I can't look at you right now." She laughed until Charlie shushed her.

"The song's coming on, shh! Listen!"

When the song played the first time, Charlie thought it sounded familiar. "I think they made an instrumental muzak version of this for easy listening stations," she said.

"That's obviously censorship," said Ray. "I want to hear him say it..." About a minute and a half into the song, the singer was about to say the titular line. Ray and Charlie held their breaths.

"After Mama beat me...I up'd and _____ Aunt Lou!" the singer twanged. They listened to the rest of the song. It came out like that each time. The word had been blatantly deleted from the song completely.

"What the fuck was that?" Ray demanded.

"I have no idea," said Charlie, shocked.

"That's worse than using a really good song in a commercial," said Ray.

"What's wrong with that?" Charlie asked.

"Are you serious?" Ray looked at her in disbelief. Charlie nodded slightly and gave half a shrug. "Don't you think it's sad that some people have to hear their favorite song bastardized by some advertising fuck because the album said song was on didn't go platinum enough so it was sold to the highest bidder in order to sell airline tickets or potato chips or something else that has nothing to do with music?"

"I'm not following," said Charlie.

"Placebo sold out to Nissan, Lenny Kravitz sold out to an airline company, I'm not even sure which one anymore, and trite little punk songs are used every day to hock chips and dip," said Ray. "It's disgusting. Don't they make enough money touring and selling CDs? Need we sell every last idea to corporate America?" Charlie kept silent. "Sorry. I just wish being a successful musician only meant writing and performing music."

"No, don't worry about it. I see the same things, but in a different way. I see out-of-work actors selling contact lenses and hemorrhoid cream and you're right. It is sad."

"Yeah it is," said Ray. "So, what now?"

Charlie shrugged. "We boycott products that ruin music?"

Ray chuckled. "I meant what do you want to do now?"

"Oh," said Charlie. "Wanna get a beer?"

"I thought you weren't twenty-one yet," Ray said.

"I won't tell if you won't," Charlie smiled.

"Okay. I know a place we can get you in," said Ray.

She took Charlie through an array of back streets and alleys until they arrived at Shooter's. It looked like a tavern except you couldn't see in any of the windows.

"And you're sure they'll serve me here?" Charlie asked Ray on their way in.

"Yes, so long as you don't ask me that when we're ordering," she replied.

Once inside, Charlie saw there were two parts to the bar. To the left was the actual bar surrounded on all sides by bar stools. To the right were some tables and what Charlie assumed was a dance floor.

"I'll grab us a booth," she said.

Ray nodded and asked, "I'll order you a…?"

"Um, whiskey sour?"

"Coming up," said Ray and headed for the bar.

Charlie slid into a booth and took in the atmosphere. There was a jukebox behind her and two pool tables in front of her. A group of girls sat in a crowded booth across the dance floor. Charlie glanced over. She caught the eye of one of the girls and smiled politely. The girl glared back and her and then the entire table turned to look.

Okay…

Charlie looked at all of them and didn't see anyone she recognized. She decided to ignore them. Ray returned with her drink.

"Thanks. What do I owe you?" Charlie asked.

"Nothing. It's on the house," Ray replied.

"No, really. How much was it?" Charlie insisted.

"No, really. It was on the house," said Ray.

"Why?" Charlie asked.

"Because when I'm not lurking in bookstores or writing songs, I tend bar," Ray replied.

"Oh. In that case, do you know any of the people in that booth over there?" Charlie asked and motioned with her head. Ray looked over.

"Aww, Christ. They saw me look. They're coming over," she warned Charlie.

Too late. They were at the head of the table. The shortest one among them—the one who had first stared at Charlie—spoke to two others. There were five in all. "Cindy, Paula, go get a round and some food for everyone." She handed them money and smiled a little too graciously for Charlie's taste. The girl took a seat next to Ray and her other friends pushed Charlie in to make room for themselves. The shortest put her arm around Ray and said, "Rachel…it's been such a long time. Aren't you going to introduce me to your friend?"

Ray removed the girl's arm and placed it away from herself. "Monica, this is Charlie. Charlie, this is my ex-girlfriend, Monica."

"I wish I could say it was nice to meet you, but thus far, it's not," said Charlie.

"That's not very friendly of you," said Monica.

"No, it's not. I'd appreciate it if you left," Charlie said flatly.

"Oh, the food's not even here yet," Monica pouted in an attempt at disappointment.

"I don't want your food nor do I want your company," said Charlie. She looked to the other two girls whose names she had not yet learned. "Excuse me, please. I'm leaving." The girls remained immobile. "Fine." Charlie stood on the seat of the booth and stepped over the back, exiting through the booth behind her. She walked around and stuck her head next to Ray's ear. "I thank you for the game of pool and the drink, but I'm not putting up with this shit. Are you staying or going?" She put out her hand. Ray grabbed it and Charlie helped her over the back and out of the booth. They stood at the end of the table.

"Monica," said Ray, "as always, I wish you'd drop dead."

"Adequately put," said Charlie. "Goodnight, all."

Out in the parking lot, Ray threw her arms around Charlie. "That was fucking great! You're amazing! I wish I could've seen Monica's face clearly. Jesus, let's go back in and do it again!"

"Ray," said Charlie. "Please let me go."

"Oh," Ray said, letting go. "Sorry. I just thought…"

"I had a good time with you tonight and I like you, really. But a little head's up would have been nice. Something like, 'Hey, we're going to the gay bar where I work and my ex might be there and turn into a succubus when she sees you.' Just a little warning," said Charlie. "Something." Charlie tried not to yell. She was tired of yelling.

Ray couldn't help smiling.

"What?" said Charlie.

"Nothing. It's just…well, a few things actually. You called Monica a succubus. That's great because she really is one. Two, when you get angry, you're articulate and that's incredible. And, forgive the cliché, but you're cute when you're mad," said Ray.

Charlie sighed a little.

"What?" said Ray.

"It's just… My buttons are easily pushed, I guess." Ray wanted to apologize, but she wasn't sure it would help. A silence lingered between them. "Seeing that there's no way to top what just occurred in there, I guess I should head home," said Charlie.

Ray nodded, not without a look of disappointment. "Before we go though… you might want to glance toward the door." Charlie looked. Five heads disappeared from sight. She smiled and got in the car.

Outside of Charlie's apartment, there was a moment that wasn't quite awkward, but far from light and breezy.

"About the bar thing," said Ray. "I'm really sorry."

"It's okay. You didn't know," Charlie said.

"I know, but—" Ray started to say.

"No 'buts.' Don't worry about it. I'll live," said Charlie. "I'm going to head inside, but I would like to hang out again. Don't think that you're rid of me or that things are 'weird,' because they're not." She turned to leave.

"Charlie?"

"Yeah?"

"Can I hug you goodnight?"

Charlie hadn't been looking at Ray when she asked. She was almost overwhelmed by the kindness of the gesture. When she looked back, Ray was centered in her field of vision. Arms outstretched, Charlie walked back toward her. Ray felt warm and small in her arms. Charlie closed her eyes and took in her scent.

She released her then. "Goodnight," Charlie said.

"G'nite," Ray said. "And thanks...for the hug."

Charlie nodded and backed toward her apartment.

"Can you tell me when John Grissam's next book is going to be out?" a customer asked Charlie. She was at the information desk. It had been a trying day. Charlie had woken up late and had run to work. She arrived sweaty and faint only to find she was working the middle shift, not the morning shift. When she finally caught her breath, she decided to go outside and relax. Upon sitting on a metal bench, she found it was incredibly cold—colder than it should have been. She ripped her pants when she was running to work. She then decided to go back to the bookstore to read a book. She was about two blocks away when a car made an illegal right turn at a red light, colliding with Charlie who was standing in the crosswalk. The driver looked up, gasped and sped off. Charlie stood in the middle of the intersection laughing at her astounding misfortune. By six o'clock, she was staring down a woman who wanted a book by an author whose name she couldn't even pronounce. She typed *john grisham* into the inventory computer. Seventy-three results appeared on the screen. They appeared in chronological order, the most current being listed first. And the date of the first book had already passed.

"Ma'am, his most current title is *The Brethren*. And it came out in February." It was March then. "He has yet to announce the release date of his next novel," said Charlie.

The woman took a short, quick breath in and spat it out again. "No. Wrong," she said. "I just read about it in *The Oxford Literary Journal*. They mentioned the title, but I can't remember what it is. All I know is it's to be Grissam's next book."

"Well, let me check Books In Print," said Charlie. She did. "No, the most current title is still *The Brethren*."

"No, it's not," the customer insisted.

"Well, ma'am, I'm afraid I'm not able to find the title you want. My inventory doesn't have his next title listed."

"I cannot believe this store doesn't know what Grissam's next novel is. It was in *The Oxford Literary Journal*!"

Charlie removed the periodicals binder from its dusty position atop the information desk's CD player and flipped through it. There was no listing for anything closely or remotely resembling *The Oxford Literary Journal*. "Well, I don't see that we carry that particular periodical..." said Charlie.

"Well, a store like this one should clearly carry every magazine pertinent to literature!" spouted the customer.

"I can leave a note with the periodicals clerk," Charlie offered.

"Well, that doesn't help me today, now does it?" snapped the woman. "This is why you're losing customers to online services! Maybe, if the staff of this store were more knowledgeable, I would be able to get a copy of Grissam's next book. I suppose I'll have to take my business elsewhere!" She aimed her purse in front of her and marched out the door.

Spot, who was then the periodicals clerk, walked behind the information desk to relieve Charlie of her shift. "What up, girlfriend?" he said, pursing his lips and looking her up and down. "Honey, you know you gots a rip in dem pants?"

Charlie made a mental count to ten. "Yeah. I know. Customer left a note for you. Wants us to carry *Oxford Literary Journal* or some such shit."

"Never heard of it. She probably made it up," said Spot.

"Who knows? She was a fucking idiot. She wanted the next John Grisham novel, which has no set date," Charlie sighed.

"He just put out *The Brethren*," replied Spot.

"Yeah, that's what I said," said Charlie. "That's not what she wanted. And she couldn't even pronounce his fucking name correctly. She kept saying 'Grissssssssssam.' I wanted to find a hardcover copy of *War & Peace* and beat her with it."

"Sounds charming," said Spot.

"I just hate people sometimes."

"Did I ever tell you about the five of nine guy?" Spot asked.

"No. Tell me."

"Well, I'm working the holiday shift, so I start at five in the morning and get out at two in the afternoon," Spot began.

"Nice."

"Yeah," he said. "So, I'm really fucking tired because I've been working this shift for three weeks and I've been up since four and it's about time to open the doors. So, I start wheeling the bargain tables toward the door and this guy is banging on the window. I look up and he walks over to the front door. He starts banging there. He points to his watch. Now, I have little to no tolerance for assholes with no patience, especially assholes with nothing better to do than hassle me about opening the door so they can sit on the newspaper ledge while I'm doing the morning papers. I look at my watch. It says 8:55. So, I open the doors to the lobby, push the carts out there, and then I walk away."

"Did he cry?" Charlie asked.

"Oh, I'll get to it. So, I go to the bathroom. And I wait. And I wait. And I pee, and then I wait some more. I check my watch. 8:59. I casually stroll up to the register, get the doorstops, and go to unlock the door. Of course, the dickhead's still there. So, I open the door and push out the tables and the carts. He comes right up to me and gets in my face. He says, the store opens at nine. And I said, yes, it does. And when you arrived at the door, it was five of nine. He starts yelling that five of nine is nine and that he can't believe what an inconvenience it had been and I look at him and say, sir, when last I checked, five of nine is 8:55. And I went inside to do the papers."

"I swear, lunatics gravitate toward bookstores," said Charlie.

"It's true. So, this Oxford Literary Journal woman," Spot said while flipping through the periodicals binder. "Think she meant *Oxford American*?"

"I don't know, what is that?" Charlie asked.

"'The magazine of good southern writing,' according to Grisham, actually. It's a literary magazine, of sorts, that only publishes fiction having to do with the south."

"Ahh…" said Charlie as though it all suddenly made sense.

"Mind watching the counter a bit longer?" Spot asked and headed for the magazines.

"Why not? A few more minutes won't kill me."

"Heh. It's not you getting killed that I worry about," Spot joked.

"Ha ha."

He returned moments later with the most recent issue of *Oxford American*.

"Yeah, so John Grisham's next novel will be serialized in the upcoming issues of *Oxford American* and then published as a full-length novel."

Charlie sighed slowly and loudly.

"Yeah. I know. You hate people," Spot translated her thoughts.

"Mm-hmm, basically," Charlie replied quietly.

"So," said Charlie, "can I ask you a question?" She and Ray were getting water ice outside the record store Ray had been name-dropping non-stop.

"Personal question?" asked Ray.

"Yeah," Charlie replied shyly.

"Ooh, my favorite kind. Proceed."

Charlie laughed and said, "Okay. Hmm…" she hesitated. "How do I go about this?"

"With difficult questions, it's best to approach them bluntly and directly," answered Ray.

"Right. Um, why do you like girls?" Charlie wrinkled up her nose, regretting that her curiosity had gotten the best of her. Ray's lip curled up on one side and a dimple appeared in her cheek.

"Well. I wasn't expecting that one. I have one condition upon answering your question. If I succeed in sharing a private little piece of myself, you have to do the same. Deal?"

Uh-oh.

Charlie nodded. "Deal."

"Okay," Ray said, leading the way into the record shop. "When I was younger, I liked boys. I found them to be cute and endearing and, by far, easily the cruelest creatures on the earth. I had a crush on a boy who tormented me. I was different and thus the target of my classmates' hatred. Rodgers and Hammerstein were wrong. You don't have to be taught to hate another human being. You merely need an arrogant feeling of superiority. And children know nothing better. So, guarding my little heart as best I could, I told no one of this infatuation with the most popular asshole in school. I held on to the hope that one day he'd come to his senses and see that I was what he wanted. I held out for about seven years. By the time I was in ninth grade, life had wiped the floor with me—different story altogether—and I was on my little journey to self-discovery. I had, at that point, made it my mission in life to befriend any poor soul the popular kids had chosen to systematically destroy. A new girl had transferred from a different school.

"Her name was Audra. She had long, wavy strawberry blonde hair, a face full of freckles and big blue eyes. She wore tons of black make-up and black and white checked tights. I was immediately enamored. Well, obviously, all the other kids had a strong distaste for her. But she didn't care. She walked around like things only existed when she looked at them. She looked at me. She liked me; she liked *me*. We bonded immediately. She knew all this stuff that I had no clue about: books and music and things that were actually important, instead of the stupid high school bullshit that everyone else was involved with at the time.

"Well, one day we were at her house up in her room. Her parents didn't come home until after seven and it wasn't even four yet. We had one of those relationships where you feel like you know the person forever from the very first day. She told me on this afternoon that there was a certain person she'd set her sights on, but she didn't know how to approach them. I was crushed. Until she reached out and touched my hand. She leaned toward me and she was so close, I could smell her hair. She smelled…outstanding. We just kissed for hours." Ray closed her eyes and took a deep breath. She opened her eyes and said, "Anyway, we still hung out after that, but never touched again. She moved to a different school at the end of the year. Then I met the Chesterton fan about six months later. But, I hope that answered your question. Audra's the reason I like girls."

"You never saw her again?" Charlie asked.

"Nope. Not even in passing. It was sad, really. I still think about her sometimes. I wonder what she's doing and whether or not she's happy. Stupid shit like that."

"That's not stupid," said Charlie. "It's kinda sweet…"

"Yeah, I guess."

"Well, I have nothing on par with that unless you count the several times I called Stephen after he hung up on me in the middle of a sentence. God, I was such an idiot," Charlie mumbled.

"You're definitely right about that," Ray chided. "But you do have to say something. We had a deal that you have to share a private story about yourself," said Ray, smiling widely.

"Okay. What do you want to know?" asked Charlie.

Ray just barely hesitated before asking, "Why do *you* like girls?"

Charlie stuttered, "I—no, it's not like…I mean, I have nothing against…"

"You don't want to talk about this in public, do you?" said Ray.

Charlie looked around the store and expected every eye to be on her. But no one, except Ray, was actually looking at her. She felt the air instantly become stagnant and found it hard to breathe. "I think I need to go outside."

They walked back to Charlie's apartment in silence. The wind was warm and it felt good to get into the air-conditioned apartment. "You hungry?" asked Charlie once they were inside.

"Sure," said Ray, following her into the kitchen. Charlie was looking through the cabinets when Ray said, "Listen, I'm sorry about earlier. I just thought…"

"It's okay. I didn't know how to take it, that's all. I don't dismiss the idea. I just…for the most part, I think I like guys."

Ray sighed silently and nodded.

"But I think I might like you," Charlie said with her eyes shut. Nothing moved. If asked, Charlie would say that she tangibly felt nothing happen. She opened her eyes and saw Ray looking at her. "Oh my God, this is so embarrassing."

"No, it's actually pretty nice," said Ray.

Charlie covered her face with her hands and shook her head. She couldn't say anything. Ray crossed the room to her. She tried to move her hands, but Charlie wouldn't let her. They were both giggling.

"C'mon…let go," Ray laughed.

"I can't," Charlie smiled. "I feel like an idiot."

"Well, you are an idiot. But that's all right. I like you anyway," said Ray.

Charlie stopped shaking her head. She peeked one eye out between her fingers. "Yeah?" she asked.

"Yeah," Ray replied. She stepped closer. Charlie put her arms around Ray's waist. She tucked her head over Ray's shoulder. She breathed against her neck. Ray pulled her to the floor. Ray put a hand under her T-shirt but then stopped.

"Is this okay?" Ray asked. "That we're, I mean?"

"No, yeah. I mean, yeah," Charlie nodded. "I'll be fine."

Ray stopped and looked at Charlie. "What do you like?" Her voice had become smoky.

"It's funny you should ask that," Charlie half-laughed. "I don't exactly know."

"You don't know? Really?"

"Well, not that I don't know," Charlie backpedaled. "I'm just not really sure."

Ray focused on a point in the distance. "There's something I didn't expect."

"See, the only person I ever had sex with was Stephen, and he didn't really care… That's not true, actually. He asked once. I just didn't know what to say. So we kept having sex and there was this one night that he brought this girl home—"

"Really?" Ray's curiosity was piqued.

"It wasn't like that. I mean, it ended up being like that. I was half asleep and she pounced on me…and, well, anyway… I never really found out what I liked. One way or the other…"

"Girls or boys, you mean?"

"Well, no, not even that. I mean, do I prefer penetration or no. What about clitoral stimulation? Do breasts come in to play?"

"Yours or mine?" Ray quipped.

"I'm serious. These are questions I would ask myself, but I've been single for a while and not exactly comfortable with doing it myself, so…"

"You don't even masturbate? Ever?"

"Not often. I did buy a vibrator though."

"Well, that's a start."

"Yup."

Silence.

"So," Charlie said, "I have a big kitchen."

"I can help you figure stuff out," Ray offered. "Ya know, if you want…"

Charlie became silent. "What's wrong?"

"Nothing. I just don't want this if it's out of pity."

"It would definitely not be out of pity," Ray insisted.

"It's not off-putting?" Charlie asked. "That you'd have to teach me stuff?"

"Everybody's got to learn sometime," Ray grinned.

"You have a beautiful smile," Charlie told her.

"Thanks," she returned. "I floss."

Charlie laughed. Ray took this opportunity to put her tongue in Charlie's mouth. Charlie stopped laughing. She gasped through her nose. She grabbed the back of Ray's head and pulled her closer. This went on for several minutes. Finally, Ray broke for air.

"So we can say you like kissing."

"That doesn't count," Charlie said. "Everyone likes kissing."

"Not true," Ray insisted. "Monica didn't. Except she used to say this really annoying thing before she'd go down on me. She'd look me right in the eye and whisper, 'I want to make out with your clit.'"

"Tell me you're kidding," Charlie said.

"I wish I were. It was novel the first few times she said it, but I had a hard time not laughing after that. It was ridiculous."

"Was she good at it?" Charlie asked.

Ray nodded. "But even good sex can't save a relationship that's doomed." Charlie gave the sympathetic head tilt. She leaned closer to rest her forehead against Ray's. They moved their noses toward each other. Then their chins touched, then their mouths.

Their kissing became more. Ray pushed Charlie on her back and straddled her. She took off her own shirt and bra. Ray pulled against Charlie's shirt. Charlie was nervous about being naked in front of Ray. But, Ray was taking her clothes off and it was too late.

"God, you're gorgeous," whispered Ray.

"No," said Charlie, looking away.

Ray pushed her jaw back to force Charlie to meet her eye, "Yes. You are." She stood and slid off her remaining clothes. Charlie stared up at her. Her pubic hair was shaved to a thin line. Ray kissed up Charlie's legs and put her tongue against her labia. Charlie tried not to think about Danielle. Ray stopped to breathe. Charlie took that moment to speak.

"Ray?"

"Yeah?"

"I'm not really sure I know what to do. I mean, I never really got the hang of sex, not that I had a great partner, but this is so foreign. There was that one time but I didn't even know her and while it wasn't unpleasant, I'm not quite sure I can—"

"Charlie?" Ray interrupted.

"Hmm?"

"Don't worry about it."

Charlie tried to be mentally present at all times. Her sex with Stephen had been so disassociative, she would think about something else until it was over. Her encounter with Danielle was far more manic. Sex with Ray was a happy medium, a severely happy medium.

Ray rolled over on her side and hummed tunelessly. Charlie's mind focused enough to register her presence. Ray kissed her cheek. "You okay?" she asked.

"Mm-hmm," Charlie replied, turning to lie on her stomach. Upon seeing her back, Ray said, "Hey, nice tattoo." she asked.

"Thanks."

"Does it mean something?"

"Don't they all?" replied Charlie. "When I got it, I was feeling very unloved and misunderstood and mediocre. I explained it to the tattoo artist and he branded me with this." She'd said all this without turning around.

"Oh," said Ray. She sat up and stretched. She admired Charlie's backside.

"What about yours?" asked Charlie, in reference to the scarlet lip print on Ray's neck.

"I think that should be fairly obvious," Ray smirked. "Cry of a young lesbian."

"Cry for help?" Charlie teased.

"More like, 'Look at me!'" Ray winced. "Only certain people see it though because I usually wear my hair down."

"Even in the summer?"

"No. Then it's just to ward off young boys who want to stare at my boobs or my ass or whatever else is on display because it's too hot to cover."

Charlie giggled.

"What?" Ray said innocently. Then it hit her. "Wait, no. I didn't mean it that way. Too warm to cover. Too *warm*, not hot." But it was too late. Charlie was in hysterics.

Charlie was helping a customer when she heard the security gates trigger. She didn't give it a second thought. They were always going off. It was usually due to a child wandering too close to the doors while holding a CD which contained a theft prevention device. Charlie walked her customer to the display where the movie he wanted was and she heard raised voices. Like the alarm, they were coming from the front of the store.

"Get a good look at my face! Look at me! I could be a wanted felon!" A man was pointing at his own face and berating Spot about having to check his merchandise at the door. Spot had been the closest employee when the gates had been set off. He went through the motions and apologized to the man about having to demagnetize his bags, but this was protocol. The customer was outraged that, after having spent almost one hundred dollars in the store, he would be accused of shoplifting. Spot repeated that this was normal, but the man would hear nothing of it.

"Why don't you just have someone take my picture?" the man shouted.

"Sir, this is just standard procedure," Spot said.

"No, I understand, I could be a murderer!" he spouted.

Spot, finished with the bags, returned the merchandise to the man and, with no emotion in his voice, said, "Here, sir. Have a good day."

The customer handed the bags back to Spot and said, "No, after all that, I want you to take them out to my car. Take them out to my car!"

Spot shut his eyes and inhaled deeply. He opened his eyes, handed the bags back to him, and said, "Go to hell." The customer, too shocked to respond, took that as his cue to be silent. Spot snapped his lanyard off his neck, tossed it on the counter and walked out the door.

Charlie wanted to clap and cheer.

Chapter Seven – Hot Days, Caustic Afternoons

"I can't believe how warm it is out here," Gwen complained to Charlie. It was August in West Hartford, the time of year when the sight of strip malls and row homes are distorted by the intense heat rising from the pavement. They were arranging books outside for the sidewalk sale at The Book End.

"Don't worry," Charlie reassured her friend. "Once we get inside, away from the sun, it'll be cooler."

"I know. I just hate summer. I couldn't even bear wearing a bra today. I'm wearing band-aids."

Charlie ceased all action save breathing. "Are you serious?" she asked Gwen. Gwen nodded. "Dude. I'd have to wear an ace bandage."

"You'd have to wear two."

"Yeah," Charlie crossed her arms over her chest.

Ring, ring...

"I'll be right back," said Charlie. "I think I hear the phone."

"Okay," Gwen replied.

"Book End, this is Charlie."

"Hello," said a jovial voice on the other end. "I'd like to know if you have any books about Custer's last stand."

"Just a second," she put him on hold and did a search. She returned to line one. "Thanks for holding. It seems we're out of everything we normally stock involving Custer. Are you looking for a specific title?"

"Um…" The man was unsure.

"If you are," Charlie continued, "I can check the availability and see what I can order for you."

"Well, I don't know of any specific titles. I want a book because today," the man proclaimed as though he'd been personally involved, "is the 128th anniversary of the last stand." Gwen reentered the store and breathed a sigh of relief for the fully functioning air conditioner.

"That a fact?" said Charlie. She beckoned Gwen to her and rolled her eyes, mouthing the words, "Help me."

"Just a little trivia for you," the man on the phone said joyfully.

"I'll jot that right down," Charlie sneered and mimed shooting herself with her free hand. Thinking she was serious, the man went on to talk about Custer for the next fifteen minutes. Charlie brushed her leg against Gwen and motioned for the box cutter. She pretended to drag it across her wrist. Gwen took it from her, shaking her head, no. Gwen proceeded to gesticulate cutting her wrists up and down rather than across.

"More effective," she whispered.

Charlie curled her index finger at Gwen and handed her the phone. She put her finger to her lips and they both kept quiet.

"So when Custer arrived there…" the man yammered on.

Gwen and Charlie passed the phone back and forth and laughed noiselessly. Periodically, Charlie would throw in a, "Yeah? Wow." She held the phone down near her thigh. "Riveting, isn't it?" she said to Gwen.

"Biggest thrill I've had all week."

After they'd finished with the Custer customer, Charlie turned to Gwen and asked, "Why do people do that?"

"I have no idea," Gwen replied. "Loneliness?"

"I guess." After a while, she said, "Hey, have I ever told you about my favorite customer ever?"

"When you say favorite, are we talking that you actually *liked* this person?" Charlie looked at Gwen through lowered lids. "Oh, right, what was I thinking? Right, so your favorite customer."

"Well, I was manning the information booth at the store which shall remain nameless—"

"Yeah…" Gwen said in an attempt to push Charlie's story forward. She didn't want to get her started.

"So, this guy comes up to the counter and is completely stoned. So, I'm waiting for him to say something because I don't want to encourage him if he's only there to gaze wistfully at the coffee beans or the newest Deftones CD. Finally, he locates his voice and says, 'Hey…I'm uh, looking for…uh…uh…'" As Charlie spoke, she slurred her words and slowed her speech. "'I'm, uh, lookin' for a…' And finally, I said, 'You're looking for a book?' And he gets really excited and practically opens his eyes, even. Practically. And he goes, 'Yeah! And it's, uh, it's got, uh… Uh…' And I just want to physically rip the sentence from his mouth. At this point, he's poking his index finger against the desk, trying to figure out what he wants and he goes back to, 'It's got…uh…' And I offer, 'Words in it?' And he's all like, 'Yeah!' And that was all he could tell me about the book."

"You're kidding."

"I swear to God," Charlie insisted.

"You're an atheist," said Gwen.

"Okay, I swear to Darwin."

"Fair enough," Gwen shrugged.

"People are just so stupid sometimes though. There are some people who don't know what they want when they come in because they just want to browse and I get that. But then there are the people who think they know what they want and whatever you find isn't it and they're so dead set on being right. It's ridiculous."

"They can't all be that bad," said Gwen.

"Oh, they're not. I mean, there are some people who are just scared to ask for what they want."

"What do you mean?" Gwen asked.

"This couple came in one time and they looked sort of lost, so I asked if they needed help. And the man said, 'Yes, where's your self-improvement section?' And I had no idea what he meant, so I asked, 'Are you looking for a specific title, sir?' And he said, 'I think we'd just like to browse.' And I still didn't know what he wanted, so I said, 'Well, I don't think we have a self-improvement section, sir.' At this point, his wife or girlfriend or whatever said, 'It's more like a self-help section.' And I said, 'That we have.' So I led them to the psychology section of which self-help was a subcategory. And he looked at the big psychology sign and said, 'Uh, I don't think this is what we want.' And I just wanted to ask, 'Well, what do you want?' But his wife slash girlfriend person thing took over again and said, 'Where is your sex section?' And I'm sure my facial expression gave away everything. Luckily enough, it was still in the psychology section and I just pointed it out and said if they needed anything else, to just ask. But was it really funny. It wasn't annoying, they were just kind of shy."

Later, Charlie looked over the day's sales.

"How'd we do?" Gwen asked.

"Well, with the money we lost putting the books on sale at cost, but with the money we got from regular priced merchandise sold…" she tallied the figures at the bottom of her tablet. "We made…about $400 more than I thought we would."

"That's great!" said Gwen, hugging her. "Isn't it?"

"Financially, yes. That is great. I'll be able to pay my wonderful employees with that money," she lightly pinched Gwen's cheek.

"And otherwise?" Gwen asked.

"Well, I'll probably break even this month and scrape by, paying my rent and utilities and all the rest, as usual." Charlie rested her fingers over her eyes, a telltale sign she had a headache. "I can't help but think about how much easier it is to split the bills with someone. When you live alone, you live *alone*." She scratched her scalp and ran her fingers through her hair. "That…and I just miss her." Charlie bit back to urge to cry.

"It's hard to wake up alone," Gwen lamented.

"Christ, do I know it."

"I think it's time to close up shop for the evening, before you and I hurl ourselves from the roof," Gwen sighed.

"Sounds like a plan."

Holidays

Charlie's early years mainly consisted of blurry memories of Mom and Dad ignoring each other or following Lee when he disappeared for hours. The holidays were no exception. There just happened to be some ornamentation present. Like a tree in the background. Or Charlie and Lee would be dressed in their tried-and-true Bonnie and Clyde outfits. Thanksgiving was the worst. Charlie remembered feeling the suffocating tension. They'd go around the table and say what they were thankful for. Their last year together, the tradition was forgone. No one knew what to do. The food sat in festive clumps, steaming but not touching, on their respective plates. Mother eyed Father who looked to Lee who just stared blankly forward. Charlie focused on her plate. It was then she realized that her parents were the children and, by some cruel hoax, she and her brother wore the helm of responsibility. Hesitantly, Charlie lifted her fork. She looked to her mother and arched her eyebrows, urging her to follow suit. Soon, everyone had utensils. Like automatons, they ate. No sudden movements. Little eye contact. After twenty minutes of silence, their mother asked, "So, how's school?"

"It's okay," one of them replied. Holidays became routine. The children would finish eating or opening presents or sifting through candy and then they'd go wander off to play video games or, in Charlie's case, read or watch old movies. Mother and Father would linger in the room, not wanting to move and abandon the other, instead sitting and secretly hating each other.

After Lee left, Charlie still spent the holidays in her room reading or watching old movies. Eventually, she'd leave to visit Abby and when she got the house, Charlie went to see her there.

The past few years, she'd had to work on holidays, so that had saved her from any one-sided emotional scenes with Stephen.

The November after she'd started seeing Ray, Charlie started wondering about holiday protocol. She liked Ray and Ray seemed to like her. She didn't know how to broach the subject. Fortunately, she didn't have to.

"My parents want you to join us for Thanksgiving," Ray said over dinner one night. Charlie had trouble swallowing her food.

"Um," she said, her mouth full of food, "do they know about…ya know, that we?"

"Yeah, that's why they want to meet you, goof," Ray said.

"Oh." Charlie chewed and chewed and chewed. "And they're okay with us…ya know?"

"Yes, dear. They're okay with you licking my bush." Sometimes Charlie didn't know how to take Ray's bluntness.

"So, are we supposed to bring anything?" Charlie asked Ray.

"I was just told to bring you. Mom usually makes turkey, mashed potatoes, mixed vegetables, dinner rolls, cranberry sauce, stuffing, gravy, broccoli cheddar salad, soup, and, of course, pumpkin pie," Ray replied.

"Jesus, why that much?" Charlie asked.

"She cooks for thirty. My brother eats like twenty-five."

Charlie ended up spending Thanksgiving and Christmas with Ray and her family. The idea had originally jarred Charlie. She thought Ray's parents would disapprove of their relationship. But if ever there had been any laid-back, understanding parents, they were Ray's. A few years later, Charlie would remember Jim and Diane, as she was told to call them, and feel pangs of guilt.

Another matter was Ray's brother, Michael. He was, for lack of a better term, a loner. Charlie always laughed at that word. It reminded her of James Dean, someone beautiful and tragic. But it fit Michael. He spoke rarely and quietly. He was perpetually dwelling on something not at hand. He was the kind of man who, when angered, was silent and distant. Ray forewarned Charlie about Michael.

"He'll seem cold and despondent, but that's just how he is. It's a cliché, but: it's not you. It's him."

"So how will I know if he just didn't like me?" Charlie replied.

"Impossible. Even if he didn't like you, none of us would know."

Charlie had been reading a book when she felt her bladder twinge. *Right at the end of this chapter*, she thought. She glanced at the bathroom. It was vacant. *Two pages left.* She shifted in her seat.

"What's your problem?" Ray asked, poking her leg.

"I've gotta pee," Charlie replied.

"So go, stupid."

"I can't. I have to finish this chapter."

"You're so fanatical," said Ray.

One page to go and Charlie heard footsteps.

Pad, pad, pad to the bathroom. The door closed. Michael.

Charlie groaned into her book. She finished the chapter and put the book down. She stared at the door, willing him to come out. She looked at the clock. One fifteen. "Is there a gas station around here?" Charlie asked Ray.

"Closest public restroom is the mall three miles away," Ray answered.

"Aw, fuck." She lay down and tried to sleep, keeping one ear open just in case. She couldn't sleep. She looked at the clock again. One-thirty. She closed her eyes. Behind the door, the sound of a toilet flushing was heard. Charlie opened one eye and saw Michael leave the bathroom. He walked across the hall to his room. She got off the sofa and started for the bathroom. Michael reemerged from his room with a towel, went into the bathroom and closed the door. Charlie stopped and almost wet her pants right there. Ray came up behind her and shook car keys next to her ear.

"C'mon, I'll drive you to the mall."

"Oh my God, thank you so much, you're the best," said Charlie.

Charlie came out of the bathroom reborn. She put her arms up and rejoiced, "Empty bladder!"

Ray laughed. "You're so silly."

"So, what do you want to do now?" Charlie asked.

"Get the hell out of here. I hate the mall," said Ray with more than a little tone of disgust. "It's a fucking holiday, but God forbid the mall would be closed and lose half a day of business. Greedy motherfuckers. These people don't want to be working. They want a Goddamn day off."

"You'd think they'd get a day off considering tomorrow," Charlie said as they made their way to the parking lot.

"Black Friday is for losers. And the thing is, people eat that shit up. 'Can't go shopping before Black Friday.' I hope they all go to a hell where nothing's on sale," said Ray.

"If only such a place existed."

"Last year, I had to shop on Black Friday with Monica."

"Lucky you," Charlie groaned.

"That wasn't as bad as when she met my grandfather. Over Thanksgiving dinner, he informed her that she was on the path to hell. That what we were doing was immoral and a desecration of our God-given bodies. She thanked him for the information and said she would see him there."

"Ha!"

"Yeah," Ray mused. "Grandpa died a few months later."

"Oh, I'm sorry."

"It's okay. He thought I was a lousy sinner anyway. When Monica forbade me from attending the funeral, I broke it off."

"She's insane."

"That's a word for it."

"May I see your ID, please?" the waiter asked Charlie when she ordered a bottle of wine for Ray and herself.

She retrieved her state-issued identification card from her bag. He checked the picture's features against Charlie's and handed it back to her. "Happy belated," he said. "I'll be right back with your wine."

"Thank you," Charlie and Ray chorused. Charlie leaned over the table so her voice would be audible only to her companion.

"Do I not look 21, or do you think it was the outfit?" she asked in hushed tones. Charlie's hair had grown out even further and you could see several inches of brown roots seeping toward the black. She wore a red tank top with a pink taffeta skirt and white evening gloves that stopped past her elbow.

"I think it's his job to check," Ray smiled.

"Oh...I guess you're right. I mean, you would know."

"I still think you should've worn the false eyelashes. That would've looked fucking hysterical," Ray teased.

"I would've looked like the love child of Tammy Faye Baker and Miss Piggy," Charlie replied.

"Only if you wore a crucifix," Ray finished.

Charlie giggled. The waiter returned with their wine. He popped the cork and handed it to Charlie to smell. She did and nodded. She had no idea what she was supposed to be sniffing for...perhaps poison. That reminded her of *The Princess Bride* and she smiled. She tasted the small amount of wine he had poured for her and said, "That's fine, thank you." He poured some for Ray and left the bottle.

"Your appetizers should be out momentarily," he said and left them alone.

"Wow, that's quick," Ray commented.

"Yeah, I love this place." Charlie looked around the room. There was a crystal chandelier in the lobby with over twenty non-electric candles on it. A red velvet curtain hid the coatroom. The waiters—there were no waitresses—wore red dinner jackets with starched white dress shirts and black cummerbunds. Instrumental opera music was broadcast through the entire restaurant. The food was affordable, which Charlie preferred.

"Charlie, do you have your notebook?" Ray asked and snapped Charlie out of her fog.

"Uh, yeah," she replied.

"May I have it for a second?" Ray inquired. "And a pen?"

"Um, sure." She sifted through her bag for the book and a pen. She opened it to a clean page and slid it across the table. "Here you go."

Ray took the pen in her hand and scribbled on the first line. She handed the book and the pen back to Charlie.

Ray had written: *I'm gonna tell you something.*

Charlie smiled gently and wrote back:

You're pregnant?

No...but it is important.

Okay, lay it on me.

Alright...but it's a secret.

Are you sure you can trust me? Maybe you should keep it to yourself.

It's burdening my soul. If I don't tell you, I may well explode and then we'll have to pay to have this place repainted. You don't want that, do you?

It's that mushy-gushy-touch-my-tushy stuff, isn't it?

Most certainly not.

Good. I'd hate to have you touch my tushy...you don't know where it's been.

That's nasty. I hate you.

But only loooooooooove must be spread throughout the world!

You've uncovered my secret. I lied. I don't hate you. Only your breath. Here, have a life saver.

Here, Ray drew a little picture of a life preserver. On it, she wrote *SS Charlie.* She handed it back to Charlie. Charlie laughed and wrote back:

Aye, it's been a lonely life out at sea. I smell.

It's okay, I still love you.

Charlie looked at the notebook for a long time, but said nothing. That worried Ray. "Charlie? Are you okay?"

The waiter arrived with their food. "Thanks," said Ray. Charlie didn't look up until he had left. When she turned toward Ray, Charlie's eyes were teary. "Are you sure?" she managed to squeak out. "About the thing at the end?"

"Your breath? Yes, it's awful," Ray joked. Charlie managed a smile and tears streamed down her cheeks. Ray took her hand. "Yes, I'm sure."

Charlie dabbed her face with a napkin. "Goddammit, I'm so ugly when I cry."

Ray took her hand. "I know."

"Oh hush," said Charlie. "You made me cry in my soup."

"Soup is always salty anyway," Ray replied. "No harm, no foul."

They ate their appetizers in silence. Once she was calmer and her breathing was a little easier, Charlie said, "I love you too, you big oaf."

Ray gasped in mock horror. "You're bigger than I am!"

"That doesn't make you small," said Charlie.

That night was their eight month anniversary.

Heat from unnecessary florescent lights. Clicking from the register tape. Monotone announcements of totals, sub-totals, the amount saved with coupon, discount, promotion, no, sir, your organization is not tax exempt. Okay, fine, you have to fill out these forms, yes, the same information on both...because one is for the discount and one is because you claim to be tax exempt. No, sir, I'm not calling you a liar. Yes, sir, you have a good day.

I fucking hate people.

"I can help the next person down here, please!" Charlie bellowed from the last register in a line of five. It was a busy Saturday. She tried not to look at the clock. She tried not to think of being home. She failed on both counts.

A doe-eyed woman in her mid-forties wandered down to Charlie's end of the counter looking a little flighty. She plopped down five remaindered copies of The Rules II. Charlie snickered, but regained composure quickly.

"Hi, did you find everything you were looking for today, ma'am?" Charlie asked blandly. She practically said it in her sleep.

"Oh yes, this book is wonderful," the woman responded overzealously. "I'm buying it for all the single women I know."

Charlie nodded indifferently.

After a pause:

"I notice you're not wearing a wedding band," the customer said and leaned in towards Charlie until she was almost an obscene distance from her face. "You're unmarried?"

"Yes, ma'am," Charlie responded. "Single, as charged."

"Have you heard of *The Rules*?" the woman asked like she was hard selling Amway.

"I'm familiar with the premise, yes," Charlie answered. She looked at the line snaking at least ten people deep.

Don't have time for this bullshit...

"Oh, it's wonderful..."

"So I heard," said Charlie.

"Would you like a copy?" the woman offered. "I plan on buying several more."

Charlie's mouth hung open in half-shocked grin.

"Oh, I couldn't, really," said Charlie, attempting to sound flattered.

"Are you sure?" the woman asked with concern. "You don't want to grow old and embittered alone, do you?"

Smiling widely, Charlie cheerily replied, "Oh, but I do! In fact, I live for moments like these—interactions with persons such as yourself—to brighten the dark spot that is my existence."

"Are you being facetious?" the customer asked, aghast.

"Why, no, ma'am! Your total is $19.95 and please don't rush so I may linger a bit longer in your presence."

The woman huffily paid as Charlie joyously yelled and waved.

"Have a nice day! Do come back and visit us again, you poor excuse for a compassionate being."

The other customers and her co-workers stared. She looked at them as though nothing happened.

"Next."

Charlie rarely suffered from insomnia. But when she did, it was unbearable. She would toss and turn. Any slight sound would be deafening. She tried warm milk and hot baths. Chamomile tea and soothing music. Only one thing really worked. She'd wait until Ray was sleeping on her side, facing away from Charlie. She would curl up behind Ray and let her wrist fall against Ray's arm. When she was in a deep sleep, it was as if Ray's entire torso was beating. Charlie would strain to hear her own heartbeat. The breathing always came first. She'd feel herself inhale, then exhale, again and again. It was difficult getting past Ray's heartbeat and her own breathing. And then—like waking—it was there. For a few brief instances, their hearts would beat together. In that time, Charlie would fall into a sound, peaceful sleep.

Ray showed up at the bookstore right before Charlie was about to take her break.

"Well, this is unexpected," Charlie said.

"I'm not allowed to visit?" Ray asked innocently.

"I didn't say that. Seeing as how you hate this place though, I'm just shocked to see you here."

"I keep coming back for the customer service," Ray flirted.

"Is that what the kids are calling it these days?" Charlie teased. "Let me go punch out."

They took a walk.

"To what do I owe the pleasure?" Charlie asked.

"I guess you wouldn't buy it that I was just in the neighborhood," Ray offered. Charlie shook her head.

"I know better than that. This place is completely out of your way."

"Yeah," Ray confessed.

"So, do I have to drag it out of you?" asked Charlie.

"I got a phone call the other day," Ray began.

"Uh-oh. That sounds ominous," Charlie interrupted.

"Nothing serious. Just an old friend who I haven't seen in a while. And she was speaking for a large group of friends whom I haven't seen in a while and she was wondering what we were doing next week," Ray explained. Charlie visibly winced.

"I take it you wouldn't be surprised if I weren't overjoyed about meeting your friends," said Charlie.

"No, but I was hoping that you would put all self-doubt out of your mind and try a little. For me?" Ray ventured. Charlie's face seemed impassible. "I haven't seen them in almost a year. They'd really like to meet you. But, more importantly, I'd really like you to meet them."

Charlie sighed. "You don't make these things easy for me."

"Nope. Not part of the package," said Ray.

Charlie saw that this was important to Ray. "Honey, I'm sorry. I just don't want to be that wannabe gay girl to them. Or, worse yet, a wannabe gay grrrl."

"Oh my God. Promise me you'll never say that again," said Ray.

"Sorry. I was overtaken," Charlie grinned.

"At least I've got you smiling," Ray said.

Charlie amicably groaned. "What night next week?" she asked.

"Really?? You'll go?" Ray beamed.

"Yes, I'll really go," said Charlie.

"Awesome! I told Deanna Thursday at eight."

"Wait, what if I had said no?" Charlie questioned.

"You underestimate my powers of persuasion," Ray smiled.

Thursday night, eight PM.

Charlie crawled through her closet. She passed by her black pants which zipped from the crack of her ass to her navel. She pondered her see-through nylon shirt before vetoing it along with the low-cut shirt she stole from Ray, her parachute strap top and the red vinyl pants with a handprint on each cheek. Finally, she settled on gray corduroy pants, black boots and a red T-shirt.

First impressions are, after all, very important.

She should have known better.

She arrived at Ray's place at a fashionably late eight-fifteen. Michael let her in and showed her to the dining room. Everyone was already there. Sitting with Ray's parents around the table were Ray, a couple of guys holding hands, two girls Charlie saw from the back and an androgynous looking figure wearing baggy cutoff shorts, a backwards baseball cap and a jersey that identified the wearer as 5, with the last name SLUT.

Jim and Diane stood up from the table and hugged Charlie each in their turn. "Well," said Jim, "if you'll excuse us. We're going to spend a delightful evening upstairs."

"You crazy kids," said the indeterminate member of the bunch. Diane laughed giddily and followed her husband up the stairs.

"Charlie, this is Jeremy, Cain, Deanna, Rhonda, and Mackenzie, also known as Mack," said Ray, hissing the nickname. She pointed clockwise around the table ending with the figure in the hat. "Everyone, this is Charlie."

Charlie held up a hand and waved, once, stiffly. No one got up, no one shook hands. There was a collective hello from everyone.

The girl who Charlie remembered was tagged Deanna spoke first. "So, we hear that you're making an honest man out of Ray," she said. "I, for one, am enthralled to hear it."

Charlie wondered what dishonesty lurked in Ray's past and why her friends were so eager to marry her off.

"Charlie…isn't that a masculine name?" asked Mackenzie. Her voice gave away her gender. "You have a guy's name."

You have a guy's face.

"I was born with the name," Charlie replied flatly. "What's your excuse?"

"Jeremy," said Ray, quickly changing the subject, "Deanna and Rhonda told me you and Cain went to Provincetown. I am so jealous."

"Well, it was beautiful. We took the convertible and the weather was lovely…" Charlie sat and heard about biking and backpacking and the beaches and bars; tanning nude on the patio and grilling salmon that tasted just fabulous.

Ray looked at Charlie and smiled, "Can we go to the beach, honey?"

"You'd be on your own there, I'm afraid," Charlie replied. "I'm not a beach person and there's no way in hell you're getting me in a swimsuit." Ray pinched Charlie's side. "Leave my fat alone."

Rhonda laughed and said, "Aww, women are supposed to be soft."

Two hours and several backhanded compliments later, Mack decided she wanted to go to the bar. "Okay, you lush," said Deanna. "Are you two coming?" Ray glanced at Charlie. She took Ray's hand and squeezed it tightly.

"Another time," said Ray. "It really was good to see you guys. I think of you often." She hugged everyone but Mack. "Mackenzie. Enjoy your alcohol."

Mack replied by putting a cigarette in her mouth and lighting it. "Not in the house," Ray scolded and pointed to the door. Mackenzie took a long drag and puffed it in Ray's direction.

"It was nice to meet you," she said as she walked out the door.

"She has such a stick up her ass," said Cain. Charlie laughed internally over his sibilant S.

Ray's friends exchanged niceties with Charlie and then filed out the door.

"What the fuck was that?" Charlie asked after they'd gone.

"I'm sorry about Mackenzie," Ray apologized. "I didn't know she was coming. There's some...stuff that happened between us."

"That's rather apparent," Charlie replied.

"We all went out one night and she got drunk and made a pass at me. I told her no. She didn't take it well and has been a twat about it ever since," Ray explained.

"That explains her hostility."

"I really am sorry," Ray repeated.

"I know. It's not your fault," said Charlie. "She was just such a bitch. Or maybe not...would I be correct in calling Mackenzie a bitch? Is she a she? I couldn't really tell."

"Be nice. That's the way some of us are." Charlie inhaled to speak but then decided against it. "What?" said Ray.

"That's just the thing. I'm not one of you. I'm something else entirely," said Charlie.

"But you're wrong. Being the way you are makes you one of us," said Ray.

"I'm not so sure," said Charlie.

"Trust me." Ray smiled at her. Charlie did trust her. She just felt uncomfortable. And wrong. She didn't fit in among misfits.

Once Charlie had calmed down, she and Ray sat together on the couch. The room was dim save a snowy TV.

"Can I ask you a question?" Charlie prompted.

"Go ahead," Ray replied.

"I hope you don't take offense to this, but do you have any straight friends?" Charlie asked.

"Just you," Ray answered.

"I don't really count seeing that you've fucked me," Charlie pointed out.

"My point is that you're the closest I get," said Ray. "Did we creep you out tonight?"

"No, that's not it. It's just different for me, that's all. I grew up around heterosexual people and while I have no problem with any deviation from the norm, it's just new. That, and..." She said something which Ray didn't hear.

"What?" Ray said.

"Some of your friends are...overly gay," said Charlie.

"Okay..."

"And, well, I can kind of see why certain stereotypes exist about gay people," said Charlie.

"I think you're going to have to expand on that because I'm having a hard time not being offended," said Ray.

"Okay…you know how most religious sects will shove their beliefs down your throat because they're convinced that they're right and everyone else should agree with them and it gets really annoying?" Charlie asked.

"Yeah…" Ray followed.

"It's like that with Mackenzie and her don't-fuck-with-me-because-I'm-a-butch-dyke attitude. Like that's really necessary…" said Charlie.

"I think that was just bullshit posturing to intimidate you," said Ray.

"Regardless, she was just reinforcing a stereotype. Same thing with Jeremy and Cain. They spent the entire evening talking about the pride parade and getting rainbow license plates and their very homosexual trip to Provincetown. It's just… overkill."

"Compared to what?" Ray asked.

"Well, don't they have something else to talk about? Aren't there other aspects of their personalities? Jobs? Hobbies? Something? I got that they were gay from the lisp, they didn't have to hit me over the head with it," said Charlie.

"Wow," was all Ray could stammer.

"What?" Charlie asked.

"Don't you think that gay people get sick of hearing how some guy saw this chick he wanted to screw?"

"I guess… I don't know. I just think that sexual orientation doesn't have to be like a shirt you wear. It doesn't have to be underlined," said Charlie.

"For us, if it's not underlined, it's not addressed," said Ray. "Jeremy and Cain talked about their vacation and their license plates to us because they felt comfortable in doing so. Because it's not something they can talk about with their parents or at work. It's a topic that's open for discussion with us because we're not judgmental and we don't care that there happened to be fellatio involved. Yes, they are gay, and yes, they are flamboyant about it. Would you rather have them the way they are or would you prefer they were a couple of apathetic tattoo artists?"

Charlie turned her face from that.

Ray exhaled. "I'm sorry."

"I'm pretty sure I didn't deserve that," said Charlie quietly.

Ray put her arm over Charlie's shoulders. Charlie shrugged it away. She stood.

"I should get going."

"Don't leave like this," said Ray.

"I'm not mad at you. I shouldn't have brought it up," said Charlie. "I'll see you tomorrow."

"Charlie, wait."

But she was already out the door.

Charlie flopped on her bed with all her clothes on. Her room was dark. She didn't bother to reach for the light switch. In her peripheral vision, she saw a flashing red light. She lifted her head in its direction. It was the answering machine. She groaned as she sat up and shuffled over to the phone. There was one new message. With her index finger adamantly pointing downward, she pressed play.

"Uh…hi." It was Ray. "If you're home, pick up. Please? I guess you're not home. Listen, give me a call, okay? Bye."

If I call her, she'll only be upset. But if I don't call her, she'll be upset. So, I guess the question is, which will make her more upset?

"Dammit," Charlie said aloud. She picked up the phone and dialed Ray's number.

"Hello?" Ray answered quickly.

"Jesus, you didn't even let it ring," Charlie grinned.

"I was hoping you'd call," Ray said defensively.

"Here I am, calling."

"I know," Ray replied. "I'm glad."

"Ray, I'm—" Charlie began.

"Before you say anything, let me apologize," Ray interrupted. "I'm so used to jumping on my soapbox, I don't know when to give it a rest and I'm just really defensive about the sexual orientation thing. I know plenty of gay people who don't like other gay people because they're flaming or whatever and, basically, I'm sorry. I know you're not saying anything out of hatred or intolerance and I didn't mean to get all persnickety."

"It's all right. I'm sorry too. I guess I shouldn't have said anything," Charlie mused.

Pause.

"But…since I did…"

"Oh no," said Ray.

"No, just a sec. I was thinking to counter the, um…gaiety in the room? Can I invite some straight people to hang out with us?" Charlie asked.

"Ugh," Ray groaned melodramatically. "I guess. Ya know. If you have to."

Charlie could hear the smile in her voice. "Okay, good. I'll try to keep them from procreating on the table."

"Good. I hate it when that happens," said Ray.

"Gwen, hi!" Charlie had called her for the first time in almost ten months.

"Hey, I was wondering what you'd been up to. I haven't heard from you since Spot's go-to-hell debacle," said Gwen.

"Yeah…" Charlie replied. She wondered how he was.

"Did you hear he moved up to Stamford?" Gwen asked.

"No! Jesus, I can't even remember the last time I talked to him. He didn't even call to say he was moving."

"I think it was a hasty decision. Something went awry and it had to do with a certain redhead," Gwen trailed off.

"Not Jenn. I told him she suffered from brain hemorrhaging," Charlie quipped.

"All natural redheads do. That's where the color comes from," Gwen replied.

"I just hope he's okay," said Charlie. "So, how are things with you? How goes the pottery?"

"I'm muddling through, haven't sold anything in a while, but I've been spending a lot of time with Gregory, so I haven't made anything either. Not that

I'm complaining," Gwen replied. "What have you been up to? Still hocking the literature?"

"Yeah, I'm still there." Charlie tried to think of something that she could tell Gwen to lead up to Ray. Some bit of segue. "I met someone."

Nice job, slick.

"I was hoping you'd been MIA for a good reason. Is he cute? Do I know him?" Gwen asked eagerly.

"Um, no to both, but the first one only on a technicality," said Charlie. "He's a she." Charlie was hoping Gwen would immediately respond. She was instead left in silence.

"Well," said Gwen finally, "didn't see that one coming."

"Yeah…her name's Ray."

Another pause.

"I really fucked up the conversation by telling you this, didn't I?" said Charlie.

"Not at all. I'm just not sure how to react. I'm assuming that you're happy; that's a good sign," said Gwen.

"Yup," Charlie said.

"There's doubt in that response."

Charlie decided not to mention her recent disagreement with Ray, "It's hard to explain. I haven't been feeling quite myself lately. I feel out-of-sorts."

"Out-of-sorts is yourself," said Gwen.

"No, I mean it," Charlie insisted. "I just don't know where I stand."

"Regarding what?" Gwen asked.

"Regarding everything. Like the other day, this guy was talking to me. Nice, funny, cute…"

"And?"

"And I felt bad."

"Why?"

"Because I found him attractive. Don't I owe it to Ray not to flirt with guys anymore?" Charlie asked helplessly. "Shouldn't I go out of my way to avoid cute, funny males?"

"Has she ever told you to do that?" Gwen asked.

"Well, no, but…"

"Then no," Gwen retorted. "You're not having sex with these men. You're just talking, part of everyday interaction."

"Yeah, I guess. I just feel so foolish."

"You're not foolish, you're loyal. If you were to avoid contact with cute guys forever, you'd never see Spot again."

"Spot's not cute!" Charlie laughed. "He's…Spot."

"Fine, different example. Do you ever flirt with other girls?"

"Besides Ray?" Charlie asked.

"Yes," Gwen replied.

Charlie thought on that. "Not really, no."

"Let's say you did."

"Okay."

"If you go by the same guilt factor," Gwen began, "you shouldn't be talking to me."

"But I don't flirt with you," Charlie interrupted.

"But if you flirted with other girls, just talking to me would be wrong."

"Kind of, yeah," Charlie said.

"Don't you trust yourself?" Gwen asked.

"What do you mean?"

"You don't trust that you can talk to a guy without having sexual overtones be part of it?" Gwen asked.

"Well…"

"So you're guilty, not of talking to guys, but of flirting with them," Gwen said.

"Yes," Charlie replied.

"Why?"

"I don't know," said Charlie.

"I think you do."

"Who are you? Daniel Quinn?" Charlie stammered. "What the fuck does that mean?"

"Charlie—besides Ray, are you attracted to other girls?"

"Yes…well, not really…wait, in what sense are we talking?"

"Fucking," said Gwen. "Do you see a cute girl on the street and want to fuck her?"

"And this girl is not Ray?"

"This girl is not Ray," said Gwen.

"No, not exactly."

"Then therein lies your problem," Gwen stated.

"How does that pertain to flirting with cute guys?" Charlie asked.

"In a normal relationship," said Gwen, "and before you flip out, by normal, I mean the type of relationship you've had the most experience with, that being heterosexual, certain ground rules are laid. For example, you wouldn't be expected to spend a lot of time with a guy who was not your significant other.

"But in this instance, the rules have changed and thus you should not hang out with another girl more than you do with Ray. However, since you normally seek out male sexual companionship, you're left with a new set of rules. You're attracted to two groups of people: men and Ray. I'm not even sure that qualifies as bisexuality. It's more like Ray fetishism."

"You make her sound like a carpet," said Charlie. Gwen ignored this.

"Your problem is that you're still behaving like you would if Ray were male. You're doing what you're accustomed to. Being with, hanging around, and hitting on men."

"I could've told you that," Charlie laughed.

"But it's different because Ray is female," Gwen said. "It's new territory for you. You know the basic rule is still no fucking someone else, but you're not sure if the other half of the species is off limits."

"Yes, exactly, thank you," Charlie smiled. "So, how do I fix this?"

"There's nothing to fix," said Gwen. "Your guilt is completely self-inflicted, so your punishment would also be at your own hand. If you feel that you've actually done something wrong, you either have to break yourself of that habit, or admit that you're human and will still look at males as you always have."

"Well, you're no help," Charlie pouted.

"No help, she says. I just spelled out your problem in less than thirty minutes. Had I a degree, you'd owe me eighty dollars."

"Here's the thing though," said Charlie. "I don't really see anyone in a sexual light, not at first. I can admire both masculine and feminine beauty, but I've never seen a stranger and thought, 'Wow, I need to have sex with that person.' I just don't think that way."

"All right, then why do you flirt with men?"

"Because they're cute?"

"Babies are cute. You don't flirt with them."

"Well, no. I guess it's a personality thing. And I know that it's allowed."

"What's allowed?"

"Flirting with guys. Most guys are straight. Even if they're not, they don't mind being flattered by having a girl find them attractive."

"No one minds flattery," Gwen replied.

"Well, no, of course they don't," Charlie agreed. "But not everyone sees it that way. Most guys can't deal with having another guy find them attractive."

"Oh, I get it. So, wait, you don't flirt with girls because they might be homophobic?"

"I don't want to freak anyone out. That and there's this mental block in place, I guess. I obviously don't find every girl I've ever met to be attractive, but even if I did, I wouldn't even consider it because I assume they're straight. My mind doesn't even look at them as sexual beings."

"From that scenario, it still sounds like you're mostly straight."

"Yeah, probably. Not to mention that I would feel guilty checking out girls."

"Because of Ray?" Gwen asked.

"Because they're girls. They get ogled all the time. Men shout at them from cars, stare at them on the street, and masturbate to them in the privacy of their own homes. I don't want to be part of that. Women deserve to be respected and treated like people, not like meat."

"What a gentlemanly feminist you've become," said Gwen.

"See, that's my point. When did I get this way? My life has gotten so fucking odd."

"Are you happy?" Gwen asked.

Charlie thought about her lack of ambition and career goals. She thought about the friends who'd moved away and wondered about where her brother was. She thought about Ray. She thought about listening while Ray played piano. She thought about her smile and her body and her incredible ability to make things right. "Yes," she replied. "I'm happy."

"That's better than most," was Gwen's response.

Chapter Eight – Snow Days

Charlie had been in the bathtub for forty-five minutes. She was finished bathing, but the water was so warm, she didn't want to leave. Her hair was starting to dry and curl.

She checked her fingertips. Her skin resembled that of a drowning victim. Still, she hesitated. She glanced out the window. The sky was white. From her position, it looked like a gigantic cotton swab was cleansing the ozone. Charlie sighed painfully and got out of the tub. She shivered when the air hit her, changing her skin to gooseflesh. She flipped the drain switch down and watched the level of the dismal, filthy water decrease. She peered out her window and saw snow dancing in her parking lot. She grabbed a towel, covered herself and pressed her hands against the glass.

She wondered if they would stick, but they didn't. The condensation had moistened the window. Charlie yanked her socks on and made haste toward the phone.

"Spot! Look outside! What do you mean, 'so?' It's snowing! Come outside and play with me! Oh, c'mon, you work on that stupid shit everyday. No, I didn't mean it like that. Yes, I know how important your band is. Okay. Yeah, fine. No, I'll talk to you later. Okay, bye."

Charlie got dressed, found her cigarette and inserted it in between her middle finger and index finger at the knuckle. Her phone rang.

"Gwen, hey!" Charlie slid the cigarette behind her ear. "You know you want to play outside in the snow with me. Oh, right, you're at the shop today. What's up? Um, what time is it now? We do close in an hour anyway. Yeah, go ahead. Think you'll make it home okay? All right. Give me a call when you get in. Yeah. Bye." Charlie returned the phone to its base. She moved her cigarette from the left to right side of her mouth.

She dressed at mach five.

Bundled in her winter coat, scarf, hat, and gloves, Charlie stepped outside and breathed deeply until her lungs felt tight in her chest. The air was charged with snow. At least five inches had already fallen. Charlie set to work making a snow angel. When she was done, she drew on horns and added a pitchfork in its left hand.

"Angels have halos, not horns," said a voice behind her. She turned and saw Kaitlin, a blonde girl of about eight years. She lived in the apartment across from Charlie. Charlie did not like children. She did not like Kaitlin.

"At the soul of every angel is a devil," said Charlie.

"Why are you playing in the snow?" Kaitlin asked. "Grown-ups work, not play."

"Shows what you know," said Charlie, sculpting a snowball. The snow's texture was perfect for packing. She passed it from hand to hand. She held her arm back for the pre-emptive throw. Her hand came forward at a speed that would have whipped the ball hard enough to break the skin had she not dropped it first. The girl had closed her eyes and covered her face. When nothing came, she peeked through her fingers to see Charlie sitting on the ground, cigarette in mouth and smirking.

"Why are you out here alone?" asked Kaitlin.

"All my friends are busy," Charlie answered, poking holes in the snow with her gloved forefinger. "You?"

"I'm not alone."

Charlie feared looking around to find herself surrounded by children. Then she realized Kaitlin was talking about her and she nodded in an oh-I-get-it-now fashion.

"Do you want to build a snowman?" Kaitlin asked evenly.

"Yes," said Charlie immediately. "Yes, I do."

The pair worked quietly. Charlie rolled a small snowball and Kaitlin set to work padding it.

"Round it more at the top," Charlie instructed. Kaitlin did.

Kaitlin ran to find sticks for arms and rocks for eyes. Charlie didn't have any carrots, so she worked on the mid-sized snowball.

When Kaitlin returned and all the pieces were attached, with no nose or mouth, the snowman looked quizzical at best.

"You should give him your cigarette," Kaitlin told Charlie.

Charlie looked at Kaitlin as though she had suggested Charlie give the snowman her face.

"It's a really bad habit. Besides, you're not even smoking it," Kaitlin reasoned. Charlie looked at the cigarette while it was still between her lips. Cross-eyed, she removed it from her mouth and jabbed it in the region where one would expect a corncob pipe. She stomped back to her apartment and slammed the door.

"Hey Charlie!" Spot yelled to his employer who was in the back of the store. "The new radiator's here!" She was in the back reorganizing fiction.

"Just sign for it and I'll be right there!" she yelled in response. She stood up and dusted off her pants which suffered from chronic bookseller's knee. She arrived at the counter and saw a box the size of a coffin. "What's that?"

"That," replied Spot, "is your new radiator. Hopefully, there's a lot of packing in there." The previous heating unit had died the week prior and since the rate of the landlord's attention to problems stood somewhere in the realm of a week from never, Charlie opted to purchase a radiator.

"I guess it's better than freezing our asses off," she mused. "Help me get it out of the box."

By the time Gwen arrived at work, it was a little after noon. She stamped the snow off her shoes and went inside. "Jesus! It's warmer out there," she said upon entering the store.

"Thanks, we hadn't noticed," Spot said with his hands under his arms.

"The heating unit broke and we're trying to figure out where to put this fucking monstrosity until it's fixed," said Charlie.

"Why don't you put it below that ledge?" Gwen asked pointing to the current events display. The top of the radiator fell just under the ledge.

"Won't it catch the books on fire?" Spot asked.

"Set the books on fire..." Charlie corrected.

"No, books aren't flammable," said Gwen.

Spot and Charlie exchanged looks.

"Gwen, who told you that?" Charlie asked.

"No one," she replied. "I read it somewhere."

"*The Big Book of Lies?*" Spot interjected.

"No! It's true!" she protested. "Books are...what do you call it? Flame retarded."

Charlie laughed almost to hyperventilation. Spot practically spat his tea across the counter.

"What?" Gwen yelled. "It's true!"

A few hours after the radiator had been situated, Charlie approached Spot. "Yeah, so yesterday," she began, "I resorted to playing in the snow with a small child. A fucking infant."

"An infant? How old was he?" asked Spot skeptically.

"She. And eight, but that's not the point."

"Dude, you are so gay. Bitching about getting to play in the snow," said Spot. He was shelving books as he said it, so he didn't notice Charlie fuming. He looked up. "What?"

"I'm disappointed in your word choice," she said.

"Don't even start, you know what I meant," he said flippantly.

"Don't act like I shouldn't take offense to that."

"It's just a word, Charlie," Spot said.

"But you know where it started. Even if you're going to argue the figure of speech angle, I don't think you'd be so quick to speak if the phrase were 'That's so black.'"

"African-American," Spot corrected.

"My point exactly."

"It's not the same, Charlie and you know it."

"But it should be," she insisted.

He stopped shelving and looked her square in the face. "You're in favor of freedom of speech, yes?" She opened her mouth to protest. "Let me finish. By telling me not to use this flimsy three letter word, you're empowering it and making it more harmful than it has any right to be. Don't look at me like that," he said. "You know I'm right. Besides, you're not gay, you're bisexual, and if I had really meant to hurt your feelings, I'd have called you a fucking faggot."

"Jerk," she pouted.

"Fag."

City Life

Charlie was manning the information booth when a customer approached her. The woman was holding a jewel case for the most recent Secret Garden album.

"May I listen to this?" the customer asked.

"Certainly," replied Charlie, opening the portable CD player and handing the woman the headphones.

"Oh no, I don't like those. They flatten my hair," said the customer, palming down her copper helmet of hair. "Can you just play it in the store?" she asked.

Charlie looked at the CD. There was no parental advisory label. "Uh, sure," Charlie answered.

"Okay, I'll walk around and listen and come back if I want it," said the customer. Charlie opened the case, changed the CD and pressed play.

Charlie ran to grab all the copies off the shelf and when she returned, sure enough, there was a customer waiting for her. "Can you tell me what's playing now?" the woman asked.

"The latest Secret Garden," she replied. Two customers fell in line behind the first.

"Okay, I'd like to buy that," said the customer. Charlie smiled to herself. *I knew it.*

The customer handed Charlie her credit card.

"No, ma'am. This is only information. The registers are at the front of the store."

"Oh, thanks."

"Sure," said Charlie. "May I help you?" asked Charlie of the next customer. They both wanted the same Secret Garden album. She retrieved two more. A young man approached the booth.

"Is this the new Secret Garden?" he asked.

"Yes, it is," Charlie replied, putting one in his hand.

"Thanks."

The original customer appeared behind Charlie, CD in hand.

"I'm going to buy it," she said. "I'll take this one."

"Umm, okay," Charlie replied.

As Charlie was going to retrieve the first CD and reseal it in its original case, a woman asked, "Excuse me, what's playing right now?"

"Secret Garden's newest," answered Charlie.

"I'll take it."

"Okay." There were none left unopened. Charlie stopped the one which was playing and started to put it in the case.

"Wait, is that the only one you have?" asked the customer, taken aback.

"Yes, ma'am."

"Then it's used?" she asked.

"I was playing it for a customer who wanted to hear it," Charlie replied. "It's been on for less than five minutes."

"Well, I don't want a used CD," she said, adamantly.

"I can order you another one," Charlie offered.

"No, forget it," said the customer and walked away. Someone tapped Charlie's shoulder.

"Hi, do you work here?" said a middle-aged man.

"Yes, sir," said Charlie, who despised the blatant stupidity of the question, 'Do you work here?' especially when she was behind the counter.

"Could you tell me what was just playing?" he asked.

After a deep breath, and a sigh, she said, "The latest from Secret Garden."

"Do you have any left?" he asked.

"One," said Charlie, going to shut the case.

"Oh, it's *used*...never mind," he said, frowning. A woman appeared behind him.

"May I help you, ma'am?" Charlie asked, suppressing all the bile.

"Yes," she said curtly. "It is my understanding that your last copy of that compact disc is used."

Jesus Christ, people. It's not a fucking syringe.

"Ma'am, it was on for less than five minutes," Charlie replied.

The customer sighed, exasperated. "When will you be getting more in?"

"I can order one for you," Charlie said.

"No, no. When will you be getting more in?" she snapped.

Charlie clenched her jaw. "When we sell this one."

"Well, is there a discount for used merchandise?" asked the customer with a smarmy grin.

"No," said Charlie.

"Well, I suppose you won't be selling that one, now will you?" quipped the woman.

"Not to you, no," returned Charlie.

The woman stopped smiling. "This is certainly the last time I will shop here."

"Oh, my heart is breaking," muttered Charlie.

"What was that?" the woman demanded.

"I said," Charlie cleared her throat and annunciated each syllable, "Oh. My. Heart. Is. Breaking."

A look of concentrated fury flashed through the woman's eyes. Charlie heard her words before the customer spoke them. "I'd like to speak to your manager."

"Gladly," said Charlie, picking up the receiver. She dialed three numbers and her manager answered. "Hi Perry," said Charlie. "There's a woman out here who would like to speak to a manager. I think it's in regards to my lack of customer service skills. Okay." Charlie looked at the woman again. "He says he'll be right out."

Perry had a hushed conversation with the woman with their backs to Charlie. She overheard apologies being tendered and wanted to push a display over on both of them.

After the customer left, Perry said, "Charlie, I'd like to talk with you for a second." She followed him as far as the employee lounge when she said:

"Perry, are you about to fire me?"

"Well, I think I'm going to have to let you go."

She held up a hand. "Save your paperwork. I quit." Charlie handed him her name badge, punched out and emptied her locker. She had a manager check her bags at the door, exchanged a curt farewell, and promised herself she would never go back.

Charlie arrived at Shooter's to find Ray taking the chairs off the tables. She knocked on the glass. Ray looked up and went to unlock the front door. Smiling, she said, "Aww, you came to see me on your break. How sweet." She gave her a quick peck on the cheek and a voice yelled from a passing car,

"Dyke!"

Charlie gave him the finger with both hands and yelled, "Fuck you, you ignorant prick!"

Ray raised her eyebrows. "Oh my. Come in before they start to riot."

"I hate people so much," muttered Charlie.

"But we love you. You seem irritable. What's wrong?" asked Ray.

"I have some good news and some bad news," Charlie replied.

"Bad news first. Then the good news will buffer it," said Ray.

"I would usually comply, except the good news is the bad news," Charlie said. "I lost my job." Ray took a quick breath in, but thought better of saying something negative. She chose her words carefully.

"You were wasting your talent there anyway. If you're going to be forced to work retail, you might as well do it independently. It's better on the soul," she said.

"I'm scared though. I'm afraid I might not be able to pay rent this month. I get paid tomorrow, but half of that goes to bills. I need to find a new job soon. I'm not sure I have the strength at this point to go job searching," Charlie sighed. She hung her head backwards and yelled into her hands. "Goddammit! I'm such a fucking idiot."

"It's all right. We'll figure something out."

"Sometimes I wonder what the hell I'm doing with my life," Charlie sighed.

"Hey, you've got me, right?"

"Yeah," Charlie smiled and put her arm around Ray's shoulders. "Listen, I know you have to work. I'm going to pick up a paper and look through the classifieds." Ray kissed the side of her head.

"We'll figure this out."

Charlie nodded. She liked the pronoun choice.

Charlie sat at her thrift store kitchen table and scanned the want ads. Armed with a red pen, she circled all the hopefuls. After an hour or so, she woke to the phone ringing. She staggered to the phone.

"Hello?" she mumbled.

"Hey, were you sleeping?" Ray yelled over the background noise of the bar.

"Uh, yeah. I probably have newsprint on my face. What's up?"

"I wanted to make sure you'd still be up when I got out. I have an idea about how you can save money on rent." Charlie could hear the smile in Ray's voice.

"How?"

"I'll tell you when I see you. Will you be up?"

"Yeah, I'll just go back to sleep now. Give me a call when you're done with your shift."

Ray was smiling before Charlie even opened the door.

"Move in with me."

"Ray, you live with your parents."

"Not with my parents. We'll get our own place," Ray told her.

"I don't even have a job," Charlie countered.

"We'll get you one."

"Where? I've waited tables in every worthwhile hovel in this forgettable village," Charlie moped.

"That's why we'll look somewhere else," Ray said.

"What're you talking about?"

"Move to Hartford with me."

"Hartford?"

"C'mon, say yes. It's a big city. You could find a job there, do some acting on the side…"

"Hold on a second, okay?" Charlie said. "Have you ever even been to Hartford?"

"Sure! Once or twice," Ray trailed off.

"When?"

"I've driven through it…at night. C'mon, do this with me," Ray begged. "It'd be exciting. We could do whatever we wanted!"

Charlie looked into Ray's face. Ray saw so much potential in Charlie. The possibility of letting her down broke Charlie's heart.

"Stop arching you crazy eyebrows at me. I'll do it," Charlie said.

"You will?" Ray said, excited.

"Yes. I will," Charlie repeated.

Despite her smaller stature, Ray hugged Charlie to the ground. She held her there and rolled back and forth, beaming, "It's gonna be so great, you won't regret this, I promise, where do you want to go looking for things, nowhere too expensive, not IKEA or anything, maybe Goodwill for the furniture—"

"Honey?" Charlie interrupted. "Let's take care of the job first."

"Right. Good idea." She nuzzled into Charlie's neck. "You're so smart."

"I'm not as smart as you are cute," Charlie smiled at her. Ray shook her head and pulled her shirt up over her face. "Go ahead, just prove my point."

"Did you hear they're opening another McDonald's downtown?" Ray asked Charlie over boxing up books and picture frames.

"Jesus, what for? Aren't there two down there already? Not to mention the Burger King right across the street from them. I'm so glad we're leaving," Charlie replied. She finished a box and sat down for a break. Her hand went immediately for a small sheet of bubble wrap.

"It's not going to be anywhere near the others though. It's going to be right in the middle of a residential area. Around St. Elmo Street," said Ray.

"Oh." Charlie tried to remember why St. Elmo sounded familiar to her. She massaged the bubble wrap between her index fingers and thumbs.

Abby and I had lived on Northampton Avenue, and my apartment now is on Fairmont Street. Ray and I are moving to Church Street in Hartford...

Her hands slowly moved across the bubble wrap, flattening everything with her fingers.

Spot used to live on Birch Street and Gwen lives on Parker Lane.

Pop, pop, pop went the bubbles.

"Charlie, are you okay?" Ray asked. Charlie was staring intently at the stack of boxes right in front of her. In actuality, she didn't even see them. "Charlie?" Ray repeated. Still nothing. She nudged her shoulder.

"Hmm?" Charlie said distantly.

"Are you okay? You're staring a hole into that box and you're murdering the bubble wrap."

Charlie looked down at her hands. She stopped playing with the plastic. "Oh, yeah," she said. "I was just trying to place where St. Elmo Street is. It sounds so familiar to me."

"Well, there's a tattoo parlor closing and that's where the new McDonald's is going to be."

"Inky Doodles is closing?" said Charlie, snapping out of her fog.

"Apparently," Ray said. "I have to get more boxes, I'll be right back."

"Hey, listen, I'm gonna take a walk," Charlie yelled from the other room. "I'll be back in an hour, okay?"

"Where are you going?" asked Ray "I thought we were packing stuff."

Charlie already had her coat on and was looking for her keys. "We are. I just need to go do something. I'll be right back, okay? See you later." And she left.

Charlie debated running the whole way, but she was no athlete, so she alternated between a stiff power walk and a spastic jog. It always took her fifteen minutes at a leisurely pace, so she made the journey in less than ten. She stopped before entering just to see the window. It looked as it always had, save the "Going Out of Business" sign. She took in a short cold breath, swallowed her pride and went in. There was no one at the counter. Absentmindedly, she paged through the sample tattoo sketches mounted on the wall. She wasn't actually looking at them so she was startled when the proprietor asked her if she saw anything she liked. Her head snapped in his direction.

"Oh…I was just kind of browsing," she lied.

He nodded and smiled in a way that said, "I'm here should you need anything."

"Um…is Stephen still working here?" Charlie asked in a quiet almost regretful manner.

"Which Stephen?" he asked.

"Stephen Drucker? Long hair, blue sideburns? At one time, anyway…" Charlie trailed off.

"Yeah. Just a second." He disappeared into the back.

Oh fuck. I don't even know what to say. Why would I do this?

Charlie was halfway to the door when his voice stopped her.

"Charlie?"

Slowly, painfully, she turned to face him. "Hi Stephen."

"What are you doing here?" he asked. Not accusingly, not hurt, just out of curiosity and shock.

"I heard about the installation of a fry cooker and came to see if it was true. I guess it is," she gestured toward the sign in the window.

"Yeah. It's true. I heard you're with a girl."

"Yeah?" Charlie asked. "Who told you that?"

"Just people. Ya know…people talk," Stephen replied.

"This town really is too small," Charlie said, more to herself than Stephen.

His sideburns and hair had grown out red. He'd cut off his ponytail. She smiled at him. "What?"

"Nothing. Yes, it's true," said Charlie.

"And? How is it?" Stephen asked, leering ever so slightly.

"It's not about that."

"Sorry," he said. "I was just remembering you and Danielle."

"Yeah, because that was fair. I was half asleep and…forget it. It doesn't matter now."

"What's she like?" Stephen asked.

"Danielle?"

"Your girl," he replied.

"Oh. She's great," Charlie answered, smiling. "She's smart and funny…and really attractive. But it's more than that. It's more like what I felt…"

"Yeah..." He didn't cut her off because she wouldn't have finished. What he was about to say was difficult. Charlie could see it in his face. "I'm sorry for how things ended," Stephen said quietly. She didn't know what to say. To simply fill the silence, she said:

"That's good to hear." It was almost a whisper. She felt tears coming.

"No, really," he said.

"No, I know," she replied. She cleared her throat. "I meant that. It really is good to hear. I'm glad you're sorry," she said, smiling a little. "I loved you and..." Stephen looked in her eyes and saw she meant that. He nodded. "What'll you do when this place closes?"

"I don't know. I was thinking about going out west," he replied.

Charlie thought of Abby. "That's the trend. Where out west?"

"Who knows? The mystery's part of the fun. Maybe I'll go to Arizona or Cali. Maybe Seattle..." he gazed off dreamily.

"I hope that goes well for you," she said. "Honestly."

"Thanks."

They exchanged a warm smile they never knew before.

"Well," she said. "I should go."

"You sure we can't interest you in one of our fine array of tattoos? We're having a liquidation sale. Everything must go."

Charlie looked from the walls to the books to Stephen. She shook her head and told him, "No, I'm set. Thanks."

As she walked back home, she wondered what it would be like when there wasn't a building to remind her of Stephen. She realized it would be the same as moving away.

Charlie lounged on the sofa, reading. Well, she took the guise of reading. She was actually staring at the same page, rereading the same paragraph. She was lost in thought. Charlie wanted to love Hartford. She wanted it to be everything Linnmoore wasn't. She wanted it to be big and exciting and meaningful. It was certainly big. The downtown area was like an impenetrable concrete block. Most often, the streets were empty, which made for very lonely walking. But, she told herself, *I'll get used to it.*

She kept notes in her journal. *Hartford is very...art-oriented.*

And as much as Charlie supported promotion of the arts, it often depressed her to see the massive theater that housed the Hartford Stage Company. She could almost understand why her passion went out of acting, but she didn't comprehend why it wasn't replaced by something else.

Maybe I just need to try harder...

She was finally able to follow her dreams. She just didn't want to anymore.

"What are you doing?" Ray poked her head over Charlie's shoulder.

Charlie was lying on the couch, nosedeep in a book.

"Reading," Charlie replied. "A pastime from which I loathe being disturbed."

"I meant with your hand, brainiac," Ray corrected. "What are you doing with your hand?" Charlie had, in her left hand, a book. Her right arm was crossed over her midriff so her hand was lazing right underneath the waist of her pants, too shallow to be a masturbatory act, but deep enough to pique Ray's curiosity. "I mean, that book may be good, but…"

"Oh. I'm just…um…" Charlie looked down. She'd been gripping the strap on the left side of her underwear. "It's just, uh, how I sit when I'm comfortable."

"That's so cute," Ray said and hopped over the back of the sofa to sit next to her. "It's the same way you hold a beer."

"What are you talking about?" Charlie closed her book.

"Actually, it's not necessarily a beer. It's any drink. And only when we're at home. You sort of turn your hand so the drink is cradled against your inner wrist and then you rest it against your sternum." Ray demonstrated. "Like so."

Charlie looked down at her chest. "Do I really?" She practiced it a few times. "It feels funny."

"That's only because you're aware now. I'll point it out next time you do it," said Ray.

Charlie stopped miming. She looked at Ray very seriously for a moment. "You're unlike anyone I've ever known."

"Oh, I'm sure that's not true. I've got everything that almost everyone else has. Two eyes, two ears, an okay set of teeth."

"You know what I mean. No one's ever really cared to know things about me. Certainly not silly little things like how I hold my chosen beverage when at home."

"Here's where I get all diabolical and say in my crazy, evil voice, 'There's nothing I don't know about you, Charlie Lester.'"

Charlie blinked thrice. "Don't ever talk in that voice again," she said.

Ray chortled.

Charlie stared at her.

"Dude. I'm serious. That was Goddamned creepy."

The phone rang and Charlie debated not getting it. Ray was at work but she rarely got a chance to call from there. Charlie's curiosity got the best of her and she grabbed it just before the machine would've picked up.

"This better not be a solicitation," said Charlie.

"Lucky for me, I have nothing to sell," Gwen replied.

"Gwen, hey!" Charlie cried. "It's been forever! What's up?"

"Not much…not to give you a lecture or anything, but I was really upset to hear that you moved without saying goodbye. It took me forever to track you down," Gwen replied. "What happened?"

"I'm a bad friend and I apologize. But Ray smiled at me in that way that won't let me deny her anything. So, we moved to Hartford."

"You moved too? I will never understand the allure of a big city."

"Hartford's not a big city," Charlie told her. "Wait, I take that back. It's big, but it's not exciting. Most things are closed on Sundays and the city part is mostly offices. It's as enthralling as Linnmoore ever was."

"Which is certainly the lesser for your leaving. With both you and Spot in Hartford now, I feel like an abandoned ship," said Gwen.

"Hartford?" Charlie said. "I thought Spot moved to Stamford."

"No, last I heard, he left Stamford for cheaper digs."

"Know what would be awesome? You come visit, help me find Spot and then Spot and I stop you from leaving."

"I just might," said Gwen. "So, what else are you up to? How's the acting?"

"I don't know," said Charlie. She let her head loll back as far as it would go. "I still want to do the whole acting thing, I guess. But I haven't been in anything for years. And now I'm writing more again. I haven't written on a regular basis since I was in, like, seventh grade. Ugh, I can't believe I just said *like*. I swear, the longer I'm out of school, the dumber I become. Is it possible for someone to go through de-evolution?"

"You're not devolving," Gwen assured her.

"I don't know. I feel like ridiculously young sometimes. I have to take time to think when someone asks how old I am. I have to remember that I'm not seventeen. Has my mentality just stopped? Have I not grown since then? I guess I expected to know more by now. Or at least to be doing more with myself."

"I know what you mean. I'm certainly not using my degree selling coffee."

"But you have ceramics," Charlie offered.

"Yeah, but where does that get me? I make stuff that someone might eventually buy."

"But you're good at something. You are undoubtedly talented," Charlie said.

"So are you," Gwen insisted.

"You sound like Ray."

"Is that a bad thing?" Gwen asked.

"No. She's just so ready to let me do whatever I think would be interesting. But she has no perspective on it. Like when you ask a kid what he or she wants to do with his or her life, and the kid says, 'I want to be a princess' or, 'I want to be a cowboy.' And you laugh because you think that's cute. I have a feeling I could say that to Ray and she would tell me, 'No, you should pursue that. You could really make that work.' It's sort of irritating."

"She has faith in you," said Gwen.

"But it's so much more than that. She thinks I can do anything. I'm not even good at that many things, but she really believes that if I apply myself, I could do whatever I wanted to. She's like a guidance counselor. It kind of drives me crazy."

"It drives you crazy that she thinks you can accomplish things?" Gwen asked.

"Okay, not crazy, but it can be suffocating. She'll say that I'm talented but she's never seen me act. She wants me to succeed so badly and I don't know how to tell her that it doesn't really matter to me anymore. But I feel like I owe it to her. She believes in me so blindly; how can I let her down? Also, the fact that I don't agree with her on the question of my talent kind of throws a wrench into things."

"I think you're just going through a transitional period," Gwen told her. "Or at least, that's what it sounds like. You're trying to figure out who you want to be and you've met someone who loves you for who you are now. You have to be comfortable with yourself before dragging someone else into the mess."

"I guess so. So, can you seriously come visit? I would love to see a familiar face," said Charlie.

"As much as I'd love to, I can't. Emily and I are on kiln duty today."

"Aw, crap."

"Why don't you call Spot?" Gwen asked. "You're out in his neck of the woods again."

"I don't have his number. I don't even know where he lives."

"It's called a phone book, genius," Gwen teased.

"Eh, maybe I'll call him later. I don't feel like doing anything. I feel like having things done for me right now."

"That's the ambitious attitude we all should have," said Gwen. "I am so proud of you, lassie."

"I'm hanging up."

"Okay, bye."

"Bye."

Charlie was making a sandwich for herself when she called out to Ray. "Honey, I'm making lunch. Would you like anything?"

"Whatever you're having is fine," Ray answered from the other room. Shortly thereafter, she appeared in the doorway of the kitchen. She gripped a copy of *The Hartford Courant*. "Did you know the *Courant* lists auditions in their Calendar segment?"

"I did not know that, no," Charlie replied while spreading mayonnaise over wheat bread.

"They do. There's an ad in this very issue that lists an open casting call for a musical to be put on next spring."

"Hmm. That'd be great if I could sing," replied Charlie icily.

"Ooh! You could go to a workshop!" Ray said excitedly, waving the paper about.

"Ray. I am not attending a theatre workshop."

"Why not?"

"Because they're a waste of money and I don't have a job. Because anyone who truly wants to be an actor doesn't need to go to a fucking workshop to do it. Besides, the word choice is all wrong. *Workshop.* It sounds like elves make shoes there. Do you want your sandwich cut diagonally or perpendicularly?"

Ray didn't respond. Her eyes were downcast and her expression sullen.

"I'm sorry. I don't mean to be bitchy. I appreciate the suggestion."

"Maybe you could get an agent," Ray said.

"With what? I haven't acted since high school."

"I'm just trying to help," Ray mumbled.

"Oh, honey, I know." Charlie sighed. "I'm sorry for being snippy. C'mere." Charlie hugged her. "I'll try harder."

"I just want you to be happy," Ray said from Charlie's embrace.

"You make me happy. I just suck. That's not your fault."

Ray shook her head. "You're wonderful."

"Shh..."

Chapter 8.5 - A Not So Pleasant Interlude

"You ever see *Biloxi Blues?*" Spot asked Charlie as they were opening the day's shipment. It was a humid August Monday and the air conditioner was emitting hot air.

"Umm...sounds vaguely familiar...refresh my memory," she said.

"Matthew Broderick, Christopher Walken...sequel to *Brighton Beach Memoirs* by Neil Simon..."

"I do know what you're talking about, but, no, I've never seen it. Hand me the box cutter," said Charlie.

"Great movie," said Spot, passing her the X-acto knife. "Anyway, there was a part in the beginning when Eugene, that's the protagonist, arrives in Mississippi for the first time. And it's hot, I mean, really fucking hot..."

"Spot, if you think that this is helping my frame of mind," said Charlie.

"No, there's a point. I swear. Anyway, Eugene is from New York and he's just astounded by this heat and he keeps going on and on about it. 'Geez I didn't think it was going to be this hot. It never got this hot back in Brooklyn.' And then there's like ten minutes of completely unrelated dialogue and then next thing he says is, 'It's like Africa hot!' It's so funny." Spot looked up from the box of books.

Charlie stood, glaring, sweat running down her face and said, "After that story, you are so going to buy a fucking fan."

The heat made Charlie irascible. Normal things which one can usually shrug off pushed her closer to the edge. She handed Spot a twenty-dollar bill and said, "Go." He took it and promised to return in about fifteen minutes. Charlie looked at the piles of books and the invoice and her soaking wet hands and decided to take a little break. She sat on a folding chair and let her mind wander. Eventually, a little against her will, it ended up in a stifling apartment in July of 2001.

Charlie and Ray were next to each other in bed. Ray lay on her stomach. Charlie sat up, knees tucked beneath her chin, hugging her shins. They were both very sticky and very nude. From a remote corner, a fan whirred, sifting the warm recycled air about the room. Over it, Charlie moaned a loud and wearisome groan.

Ray lifted her head, sopping wet, from her pillow and said, "Hmm?"

"Nothing," replied Charlie grumpily. "I just hate this fucking heat." She swung her legs over the side of the bed and plodded over to the mirror. The skin around her nose wrinkled at the sight of her reflection. Her hair hung around her face and neck in straggly clumps. It was at the intermediate stage when one has two options: cut it off or wait.

Her skin was dotted sporadically with heat rash. She poked at the skin around her waist and it bloated back in response. Charlie growled. "I was not meant to live in these conditions. My hair looks like shit, I'm breaking out from the humidity, and I'm so upset over losing my job that I don't have the energy to hold in my gut!" she whined.

"Oh, for Christ's sake," said Ray. "You are *not* fat."

"I am!" Charlie protested, falling into a heap. "I'm a fat, ugly, acne ridden, unemployed dyke!"

Ray moved from the bed to the crumpled mess which was Charlie. "C'mon, is sex with me really that bad?" she asked. After some consideration, Charlie shook her head. "Well, then, I don't think you should put 'dyke' on your list of complaints," said Ray. "Besides, you're not a dyke. Not really. Discounting the thing with Danielle, I'm the only girl you've ever slept with and you basically said it yourself that you don't usually go for girls. You're bisexual at best. You are, in actuality, a straight girl, whom I, in my wicked homosexual deviant fashion, have lured over to the dark side."

Charlie had said nothing through this. She remained immobile, curled up on the floor.

"And, you're not ugly," Ray added as an afterthought.

Charlie lifted up her head at this. She sniffled a bit. "Really?"

"Really," said Ray and poked her side.

"I am unemployed though," said Charlie.

"Yes, but you're better off. No one should be forced to pour their heart into a job that gives nothing in return save a few measly dollars and a kick in the teeth. You were wasting your talents there," said Ray.

"Yeah. What, with all those directors banging down my door, I was squandering all my ability working retail," Charlie moaned. She rolled her eyes and looked in the mirror again. "I don't have what it takes anyway. I'm not pretty enough for Hollywood. Hell, I'm not even pretty enough for stage where they can't see you very well. I haven't set foot on a stage in three years and you can't put high school plays on a resume."

Ray walked between Charlie and her reflection. "I think that's your aunt talking. It's nothing to do with how pretty you are, even though you're incredibly attractive and never give yourself enough credit. It has to do with your talent. And you need to show it. You need to get out there and say, 'This is what I have and you're an idiot if you don't want it,'" said Ray.

"I can't," Charlie rolled away from her reflection. "I don't believe enough. I used to and I just can't anymore. I used to want it so badly. I miss it. I miss working on one scene for eight hours until it's pristine. Until it's so crystal, you can see your reflection in it. But I can't do it anymore. No matter how badly I want it, it's just not enough," said Charlie matter-of-factly. "I'm not enough."

Ray wanted to mend the part of Charlie which held her self-image. But she didn't know how. She walked around to face Charlie again. She pressed on, "Well, what about your writing? I've read your stuff and it's really quite good."

Charlie shrugged it off. "I can't..."

"Can't. You've said that about twenty times in the past three minutes," said Ray. "What's stopping you from doing what you want to? I know you're not afraid of failing, you've nothing to lose. What is it?"

"I—I don't know," replied Charlie. She got up and stood in front of the fan. "Fuck, it's hot."

"You do know. Why won't you tell me?" said Ray.

"You...you just wouldn't get it. You know what you want. You always have. It's not as easy for me," said Charlie.

"It is. Just say it."

"I'm just afraid, all right? I'm not afraid of failing...it's something else. I can't tell you about it. You know what you want. You want to write your music and you want women and you want what you want. I thought I knew what I wanted and then it wasn't what I wanted anymore. I thought I knew what I wanted out of life and then the passion for it just went out of me and I don't know how to get it back.

"I thought I had everything planned and I met you and you just fucked it all up and I can't explain that without hurting you and I don't want to hurt you but I don't know how else to say it. Motherfucker, I cannot believe this fucking heat!" Charlie's head hung down toward her chest. She looked up and Ray's eyes were teary. "Oh no...please, don't." She went toward her. Ray backed away.

"Don't..." said Ray. "Just...don't."

Charlie pushed the sweat from her brow with the heel of her hand. "I just feel like I don't know anything anymore. Who I thought I was is just being wiped away and I'm left with nothing. I have...nothing."

Ray cleared her throat, but her voice cracked and gurgled anyway. "You had me. But, apparently that's not important..." She pulled her clothes on at a frantic pace.

"Where are you going?" Charlie asked. Her face was a soggy mess of sweat and tears.

"Away," Ray answered. "I've never been the clingy type and I can see you need time alone right now. Give me a call when you're not so confused, okay?"

"Please don't leave," Charlie pleaded. "I'm sorry..."

"We're all sorry, Charlie," said Ray as she closed the door.

Charlie picked up the phone and returned it to its base almost immediately. There was a heavy weight in her stomach and its name was Guilt. She checked the clock. Ten forty-five PM.

She's probably at work. I'll just call and leave a message...

The phone rang loudly on the wall of Ray's kitchen. Charlie had figured after five days of silence and absence, Ray wasn't talking to her nor was she coming back. She took it upon herself to throw most of her stuff into storage and haul the rest back home, the rest being a bag full of clothes, a bottle of shampoo, her toothbrush, a journal and a pen. Until she sorted everything out, Charlie had been staying with Gwen. It seemed her haven in time of need.

Ray sat, with her legs out, pigeon toed on the floor. She gazed at the phone balefully...

One ring...two rings...three...

Her hand reached for the receiver. Ray nodded in acquiescence.

"Hello?"

"Hello?" said Charlie, her voice timid and hesitant. "Ray? Are you there?" Charlie asked the void.

Ray took in quick uneven breaths. Her eyebrows pleaded. She shook her head.

"Ray? Please...I just wanted to say—"

"You're going to have to try *very* hard for me not to hang up." Ray didn't attempt to disguise that she was already crying.

Charlie was taken aback by the abrupt order. "I—I just..." Tears flowed from her eyes and audibly clogged her voice. "I wanted to apologize."

"That's not..." Ray started to say.

"Please...let me say this and then you won't have to deal with me ever again. The things I said...the other night. Part of it was out of frustration about the stage my life has reached right now...just career-wise, I feel like I've reached a stalemate." She spoke through her sobs. "You're been incredibly supportive and that's great." She paused here, not knowing how to continue.

"But I don't believe in what I'm doing right now because I don't know what I want. My relationship with you also falls under that category. I love you. I do. You have shown me so much...about myself and what's important when all the useless bullshit is taken away...what really matters. But at the same time, I will never be comfortable with us because I'm not comfortable with myself." She wiped her tears away with the back of her sleeve. "I love you...in a way I didn't know existed and I know that I don't deserve you—"

Ray shook her head, but said nothing. Her face was sopping wet.

"But I can't right now." Charlie's voice was so quiet. "I'm sorry for what I've done. I'm really very sorry." Slowly, noiselessly, Charlie hung up the phone.

Ray let the receiver slip to the floor. She buried her head in her hands and had a long, loud cry.

Positive Reinforcement

Late September, 2001, Charles Lester was out for a morning constitutional.
There wasn't a skip in her step and she didn't rejoice in "God's wondrous creation."
She shuffled along, mopey and despondent. After a while, she found herself
downtown. The ghost of an old bookshop was to her right. She walked over,
under the awning, to get a closer look.

Charlie's reflection seemed to gawk at her from inside the store. A spectral
version of her from years ago. She cupped her hands at her temples, ridding herself
of the image. Looking at the empty shelves and barren slatwall, Charlie imagined
what Ray would think. Charlie could hear Ray's voice in her head.

"Barnes & Noble's mission statement is to close every independent
bookshop. Every damn one."

*Which is sadder? No more indepedent bookshops or the fact that I have to
conjure Ray's presence in memory only?*

She pressed on.

At the corner of Main and Asylum, Charlie stopped to get her cigarette.
When she did, a straggly male appeared beside her. They waited for the light to
turn green. Charlie took a sideways glance at him. He looked about twenty-five,
sported blue jeans faded at the knee, a dirty T-shirt, what looked like seventy-year-
old Chucks and seven days of scruff. The light was green. They walked.

He was leading at first, but soon, Charlie pulled ahead. Whenever she
encountered anyone on the street, if they were walking in the same direction, she
had to either pass them or keep pace. It was her only competitive streak, but it was

strong and powerful and stubborn. She toyed with her cigarette as she walked. She bobbed it up and down between her index and middle finger. She looked down to make sure she didn't drop it. It was only a second.

He passed her.

Son of a bitch.

The cigarette was in her mouth. She quickened her pace. She nudged into the lead. His footsteps came quicker. They were neck and neck. She elongated her stride. Charlie turned her head in attempts to stare him down. They walked like this for twenty more paces or so. Then he slowed, her eyebrows pushed downward and her cigarette went slack. She'd been swinging her arms furiously and at the last possible instant, he caught her by the wrist. A car whizzed by her face blaring its horn.

Charlie looked back at the unkempt fellow. He released her wrist and with his now free hand—the other was in his pocket—he lit her cigarette and moved it from her mouth to his.

"Truce?" he said.

"You stole my cigarette," said Charlie.

"That I did. I owe you one. So, truce?" he said again.

"Yeah. Truce, I guess."

"Great. I'm Eli."

"Charlie."

And so was an interesting relationship formed.

Eli and Charlie walked on for two hours: seven miles, all told. She spoke of her lack of drive and writing and Ray.

"I don't know what I'm supposed to do with my life, in any respect. I grew up with someone telling me about all the things I couldn't do and I pushed away the one person who was convinced I could do anything. I think I'm fundamentally messed up."

"That is what we call the human condition," he told her.

Eli talked of his nomadic lifestyle. He lived on the road.

"Like Kerouac!" she said.

"Kinda, but not nearly so romantic. It's mostly being asked to leave because you're disturbing the customers because you're soaked from the waist down. And all you want to do is buy a pack of smokes with the change you stole from the fountain in the mall."

"How can you live like that?" He gave her a you-should-know-better look. "No, really. What do you eat? Where do you sleep?"

"Well, I sleep in my car. It's a jalopy with a huge back seat. I'm sure at least one human was borne back there. I usually look for restaurants with signs that say, 'Open Late.' I'll roll in there for a quick power nap and then keep going until I hit a motel and that's pay dirt. Motel parking lots mean eight or nine hours of sleep at least. It's awesome.

"As for how I eat, I usually go, once a week, to donate blood and after getting paid, I go to a grocery store and buy one bar of soap, one bag of ice, one head lettuce, one onion, one cucumber, one tomato and one packet olive oil. I have one bowl and one fork and I eat salad every day."

"Yum," said Charlie, grimacing.

"Don't knock it," said Eli. "It's better than starving. I bathe and shave once a week at the rest stops and other than that, it's just me, the highway and the sky."

"And you don't miss stuff?" Charlie asked.

"Such as? TV? Working retail for slave wages? Dealing with the same bullshit day in and day out?"

"Civilization?" Charlie asked.

"If that's civilized, then take my thumbs and call me an ape," said Eli.

"How about seeing a familiar face every now and then? There's no one that you'd like to come home to each night?"

Eli shook his head. "Not really. I can usually rely on meeting a new pretty face in each town." Charlie scoffed at that. "I met you, didn't I?"

She smiled wanly, looked at the odd stranger and sighed. They were near West Service Road. "Well, Eli, it's been a little slice of something, but I ought to be getting home."

"Where's home?" he asked.

"About ten miles that way," Charlie replied and pointed the way whence they came.

"Mind if I walk with you?" asked Eli.

Charlie shrugged. "Why not?"

They walked a while in silence. Then, "So, Ms. Charlie Lester, what do you do for fun in Hartford?" Eli asked.

"Um…I walk. And I write," she replied after some thought.

"Your work must be very fulfilling," Eli mused.

"Not really," Charlie responded. "Right now, I'm working as a barrista in a little coffee shop called Xando."

"I meant your writing."

"Oh. Well, there's not much to do in Hartford. Nothing for young people anyway. You want to go to the opera? Sure. You want to visit a museum? Yeah, we have that. And for the tourists, of course, there's the Mark Twain House. But beyond that, it's the loneliest metropolis I've ever encountered."

"You don't seem affected by it," Eli told her.

"I don't follow," she replied.

"You don't seem lonely."

"I'm not, I suppose. Then again, I haven't been here long." She grew pensive for a moment before saying, "It's funny, ya know? The way things turn out."

"What do you mean?" Eli asked.

"When Ray suggested we move here, it was so we could finally live in a big city."

"Not what you thought it would be?" Eli asked.

Charlie shook her head. "I had…misconceptions. I thought I'd meet all these cool kids and we'd relate through art but I get here and there's nothing. Just…not a thing. Downtown is like a cement building block. There's no getting around it. It's just so depressing. But on the other hand, there's home."

"Home?" Eli was hoping she'd extrapolate.

"Linnmoore. Where I'm from. About two hours from here. Completely McDonald's-ized cultural graveyard. It's like there's no middle ground. No in-between. No give and take. Either run you over with a billboard," she gestured in one hand, "or don a suit and grimace through your day," she balanced with her other hand. "It's like…there's art here but it's without feeling. There's no community. No real audience. What an empty gesture."

"Maybe this just isn't the right town," Eli offered.

Charlie shrugged, "I hear West Hartford is nice though."

"Never been there?" Eli asked.

"Nope. Don't have a car and I hate the bus," Charlie replied simply.

"Would you like to go now?" Eli offered.

Charlie smiled in amazement. "I'd love to, but…"

"But you don't want to get in a car with a guy you've just met who could potentially be psycho," Eli finished her sentence.

"Actually, no, it's not that. I'm broke, so we wouldn't be able to do anything anyway, plus I don't know where anything is."

"We could find out," said Eli. "Besides, the best things in life are free."

"The best things in life aren't things," Charlie corrected.

Eli nodded sagely.

Charlie looked at the trees against the streetlamp light. Everything seemed black. The foliage, her favorite part of autumn, was unable to be seen at night.

She thought about everything Eli had experienced and everything she hadn't. Then something occurred to her.

"What's the ice for?" she asked.

"Hmm?" Eli replied.

"The ice. You said you bought a bag of ice. What for?"

"I have a cooler in my car. It's for the vegetables," he answered.

"Oh."

"Don't worry. I don't harvest organs out of my trunk or anything."

"Just checking," she said as they approached her building. "I suppose I should ask you in. At least to rest after that walk."

"You don't even look winded," Eli told her.

"I'm used to it," she said.

"So, is that an invitation inside?" Eli asked.

"Yes, I suppose it is. I warn you, there's a TV in there," Charlie joked.

"As long as we don't watch MTV. Like I need to see prostitots throwing themselves at Carson Daly."

She unlocked her front door and motioned Eli inside.

"Brace yourself," said Charlie. She flicked the overhead light on.

"It looks like the inside of my car," Eli commented.

"Is that a compliment?" Charlie asked.

"No."

It must be taken into consideration that while the normal onlooker would see Charlie's apartment as a pigsty, she knew where everything was. She never misplaced a thing.

"It all has a system," she said. "This is my makeshift desk," she pointed to the edge of her futon, in the couch position. Between that and the wall was a small end table. Stacks of papers were piled haphazardly. Among them was a pocket dictionary and a cup full of pens. An open notebook sat on the end of the futon. Next to it was a bald patch of the mattress which had been worn raw by Charlie sitting with her foot underneath her without removing her boots. The rest of the futon had pants draped over the back.

"Why is that your desk?" Eli asked. "There's a desk right over there." He meant Charlie's mother's desk. Modest and old, it was made of solid oak. It would've served as a fine desk.

"Can't use that," said Charlie. "That was Mom's."

"The cigars too?" Eli inquired.

"No. Those were my father's. He only smoked that brand. I don't know why. They weren't even Cuban," she answered.

"Why do you have them? Your Dad quit smoking?"

"He's dead," Charlie replied.

"Oh. I'm sorry," Eli responded.

"Don't worry about it. My parents weren't the greatest people. I keep these as reminders," she said, waving her arm toward the desk and the cigar box.

"I'd sooner forget my parents," said Eli.

"It's not an homage or anything like that," Charlie explained. "I just don't want to become like them. They each had their vices, their way of tuning out the world. Mom would sit at her desk, doing cross-stitch or writing out thank you cards for something or another. And Dad would sit and read his paper and smoke those God-awful cigars. They were both introverted, so it was easy to sit and ignore everything. Including the person they had married. I just don't want to get to that point. They were completely disaffected." She paused and looked at him.

"How did they die?" he asked softly.

"Car accident. They were driving home from a party. Dad had had too much to drink. He swerved to avoid what was presumed to be a small animal. When he did, he drove into the lane of oncoming traffic. When I heard about it later, I imagined he'd done it to get away from everything. From my Mom, from life…" She laughed nervously and trailed off. "I really know how to warm up a room, huh? Sorry."

He shook his head. "Not at all."

Looking down at herself, she said, "I'm all gross from the walk, so I'm gonna run a bath. You can stick around if you want, watch a movie or something."

"May I join you?" Eli ventured.

"Um," a million thoughts went through Charlie's mind in a matter of seconds—*I don't even know this guy. Why did I ask him in? What about STDs? AIDS? Do I even have a condom in here? Would he even fucking use it?* "Sure," she replied without faltering.

Charlie went to the bathroom and lit some candles. She started the water and said, "Set your temperature, cap'n." Eli knelt by the tub and messed with the faucet. When he turned around, Charlie was wrapped in a towel.

"Did you want the heat on?" she asked.

"Heat in the bathroom? What'll they think of next?" She smiled. "I think the water will be sufficient," he said.

He stared at her, waiting for the towel to be removed.

"You wearing that in the tub?" he asked.

"You're one to talk," she replied.

"Good point," he said. He quickly removed his shirt, shoes and socks. He stopped.

"You're still wearing your pants," she said.

"You're still wearing your towel," he responded.

"That's barely a comparison," she argued.

"Okay, give me a towel."

"All right." She removed her towel and tossed it at his face lightning quick. By the time he moved the towel, she was in the tub, too dark to be seen. She thought he would laugh or be mad or complain of unfairness. Instead, he sat on the edge of the tub and leaned down and kissed her, once, gently. When she opened her eyes, he was in the tub next to her. She breathed a laugh.

"So," said Charlie. She looked at the sink and then at Eli. "Do you come here often?"

He laughed. "If this is awkward or I'm making you uncomfortable, I can get out," he said.

"No, it's okay. I don't mind," Charlie replied.

"Good. It's been an age since I've had a bath."

"Yeah, me too. I was going to put bubbles in it," Charlie said.

"But you wanted to see my dick?" Eli finished.

"Actually, yes. But the lack of bubbles is because most guys dislike them," Charlie replied.

"Ahh," he said. Water dripped against his back. He was sitting at the end with the faucet. "Ya know, I figured you wouldn't want to see my dick," he added as an afterthought.

"Why not?" she asked.

"Just got out of a long-term lesbian relationship, I just figured," he trailed off.

"Oh no, I think that would be the best reason to want to see it." She giggled. "Cunt overload."

"No such thing," said Eli. Charlie shook her head.

"My relationship with Ray had very little to do with an attraction to women. I mean, yes, I found her attractive, I don't deny that. But it was about who she was. Yes, the sex was incredible, but I loved *her*, ya know?"

"Nothing's better than sex with love," said Eli. "Except for sex with your pets."

Charlie nodded. "So, what did you do before becoming a vagabond?"

"Not much. Had a string of pointless jobs, didn't go to college..."

"Was there something you wanted to do? Any aspirations?" Charlie asked.

"No, not really. You'd think I'd want to be an artist or something. But all I really wanted was to live without strings," Eli responded.

"I'd miss books," said Charlie wistfully.

"That's why there are libraries," Eli reasoned.

"Not for me. I've always had a problem giving the books back." She swirled her fingers through the water. They danced atop the surface, rushing and splishing.

"Hey," said Eli. "No splashing, young lady."

"Why not? You're already wet," Charlie protested. Eli splashed her back.

"Do you like it?" he said.

"Maybe." She splashed more. He grabbed her arm.

"Stop, silly girl," he said.

"Make me," she replied.

He pulled her close. She touched the side of his face, casting a looming shadow over his features. With her eyes closed, Charlie heard all the bathroom noises. The water against Eli's back, the water in the tub moving and settling. They stopped kissing.

"Eli," she whispered.

"Charlie," he replied.

There was more kissing and handling. She guided him inside. It hurt. It hurt so much she gasped and yelled a bit.

"You okay?" he asked.

"Yeah, sorry. It's been quite a while," she replied.

He reached down and rubbed her clit. He kept pumping but he didn't let go. At one point, she accidentally flipped the switch that drained the water, but he didn't stop. Spasmodically, she came. He pulled out.

"Aren't you going to…?" she asked. "I mean, don't you want to?"

"Nope," he said simply.

"Why not?" she asked.

"I—you'll laugh," he said.

"No, I won't. I promise."

"Okay," he said. "I can't come during sex."

"Are you mocking me?" she asked skeptically.

"No! Really… I just can't," he said.

"Would you be crushed if I said I didn't believe you?"

"C'mon." His eyes locked on hers and he didn't look away.

"Wow," she said. "What about oral sex?"

His face broke into a grin.

Charlie woke feeling fine. She stretched and grinned and looked around the room. Eli wasn't there. Part of her was let down, but part of her wasn't surprised. She padded into the kitchen. A note was on the counter.

Charlie,

Thanks for last night. It was grand. Forgive the snooping, but you left your notebook open and I read a page. Grade A. If I'm ever in CT again, I'll look you up. Be well.

Eli

At the bottom of the note was a cigarette.

"You would not believe what a customer said to me the other day," Charlie told Gwen. They were at The Cutting Board, the sandwich shop which had opened when Cool Beans went under. Charlie was referring to her new position as bookseller at an independent bookshop in Hartford called The Book Asylum. Gwen waited patiently while Charlie chewed and swallowed a large bite of her pastrami on rye. "I was just ringing this guy out when he squints at me and says, 'How old are you?' And I say, 'Excuse me?' I guess I looked insulted because he immediately changed his question to, 'Are you in college?'

"'No, I'm not,' I reply, wondering where this is going.

"So he tells me, 'You look no more than 23 years old and you're wasting your life in a bookshop.'

"Well, at this point, I'm pissed, but I'm so shocked by his audacity that I say nothing in response. He goes on to tell me that if I were in school, I could look at my life in five years and feel that I've accomplished something rather than just drifting aimlessly with nothing to show for it."

"So, what did you say?" Gwen asked.

"What the fuck could I say? I gritted my teeth, gave him a bookmark and flipped him off under the counter."

"That should've made you feel a little better," said Gwen.

"It didn't, actually. The whole thing was depressing. I've spent the past four days examining my life and its complete lack of direction and all I keep seeing is this jackass's face telling me I'll never amount to anything. God, it reminded so much me of Jean." Charlie made a face like her sandwich had turned sour.

"We have no idea the effect our actions have on other people," said Gwen.

"I know," Charlie groused.

"What's worse is he probably thought he was helping you, obviously not taking into consideration that there are people who can't afford college."

"Not just that, but what fucking business is it of his what I do with my time? For all he knows, I could be independently wealthy and just working retail to blend in with the little people."

"The little people? Like Lilliputians? Have we entered the world of Jonathan Swift?" Gwen teased.

Charlie shuddered. "Anything but that. I loathed Gulliver's Travels."

"Yeah, me too," said Gwen. "It's one of the few books that I was unable to finish."

"I finished it and then vowed to never again discuss it. Thanks for dredging up the memories."

"No problem. So, other than the idiot, how's the new job?" Gwen asked and dabbed her mouth with a flimsy napkin.

"It's all right," Charlie replied. "I hate that I can't wear a T-shirt to work anymore. And, since it's still a bookstore, it's chock full of crazy."

"What are you talking about?" asked Gwen.

"A woman came in the other day and said, 'Oh, that's a beautiful cross!' in reference to my ankh. So I told her it wasn't a cross. And she said, 'Well, it means the same thing, doesn't it? Christianity?'" Charlie laughed.

"Oh no," said Gwen.

"Just wait; it gets worse. So I tell her it's an ankh, the Egyptian symbol of immortality and she says that it's clearly a rip-off of a cross design. I tell her it came first, seeing as how the first civilization known to man was that of the Babylonians, right near Egypt. She looks me up and down and says that I'm wrong. I just smile and say you learn something new everyday. Now this woman is at least sixty-five years old. She looks me right in the eye and says, 'Some of us have lived long enough that there's nothing left to learn!' And she walks out." Charlie slurped the last of her lemonade through her straw. "Can you imagine that? Having learned everything and lived to tell the tale. Idiot."

"Okay, so, other than the stupid customers, is the job okay?" asked Gwen.

"It's not bad. Since it's an independent shop, there are only a few floor staff employees. Two full-timers, a woman named Tory and myself, and a handful of part-timers. But, mainly, it's a skeleton crew."

"Is that a bad thing?" Gwen asked.

"No. Since we're an independent, we don't get nearly as much business and so don't need so much stock. And once the books are shelved and things are straightened and stuff is clean, I'm just stuck."

"Stuck?" Gwen asked.

"In my head," Charlie replied. "I have all this time to think about my lack of direction. And when I'm not thinking about it, some kind soul comes in specifically to remind me of it," Charlie chuckled. "It's like a mantra. 'Just remember, you're a failure.'"

"You're not a failure," Gwen said.

"I'm not exactly succeeding at anything either. I've no long-term goals, I'm working in retail, a specific branch of retail in fact, in which I'm at the top of my game. Higher up is unattractive and you can't get much lower than floor staff, so I'm at an impasse. Plus my one lifelong dream is basically dead," Charlie moped.

"Well, I suppose the question is," said Gwen, rolling up her straw wrapper to throw it at Charlie, "what do you want to do instead?" Charlie giggled and lifted her palms skyward.

The Book Asylum was set up like an ongoing series of tunnels. It had expanded three times in its fifty years. The newest addition occurred five years prior to Charlie's hiring. They'd knocked out the wall between the children's book department and the next storefront and made it all one department. Customers were always commenting on how big it was. "You turn a corner and you think it's the end, but it just keeps going," they'd say. The entire shop sprawled over five storefronts and had three separate entrances. The actual book department only took up seventy-five percent of the store. All things related to books that weren't the actual article occupied the other quarter. Bookmarks, bookshelves, Mylar covers, bookends, bookplates, stationery, book lights, everything one could think of. Charlie loved it from the moment she walked in. She went immediately to the nearest employee and asked for an application. She was hired within the week.

Once she'd gotten situated, grown accustomed to her coworkers and fostered a friendship with her boss, she felt better. She didn't think of Ray quite so often and she was good at her job. Greta, her general manager, felt Charlie was an asset to the store.

Tory, the full-timer that trained Charlie, was manning the register while Charlie shelved and dusted. Tory called for assistance and Charlie joined her at the counter. After the customers had left, Charlie talked to Tory for a bit.

"How've things been?" she asked.

"Not bad," Tory replied. "Matt and I are visiting his family next week…"

An elderly couple approached the desk. "May I help you?" Tory asked.

The man exuded a faint odor of mothballs. His head was a deep pink and closely resembled a misshapen peach. He had the lips of the dead. A common feature in men his age, his lips were purple, his mouth a bruise. He wore what Charlie thought of as a golfing hat, oval shaped, snug at the back and jutting out in the front. Add his polo shirt and plaid pants, he could've been on the back nine.

His companion, a woman in her early 70's, was a sight to be seen. She wore a multi-colored lamé windbreaker. She complemented this with gold ballet flats and black stretch pants. She carried a green suede purse the size of Tulsa. She had two inches of white growing out under her otherwise artificially yellowed hair. She styled it like a delicate halo. Her make-up was applied heavily and evenly. If it had been paler, she could've participated in an Atlantic City Kabuki show.

"May I help you?" Tory asked them.

The woman spoke first, slowly. "I'm looking…" she said, reaching into her body bag, "for this book." She pulled out a gold change purse and sifted through it to find a miniscule slip of paper with one word scribbled across it. "I think it's called…*Bell*."

"Okay," said Charlie, standing closer to the computer. She stamped *bell* into the database. "There's no title that's just called *Bell*."

"I think…it's…" The woman stopped. Her next word was drawn out and painful. Charlie wanted to drag it out of her mouth. "Poetry," she said finally.

"All right…" Charlie awaited more information. When it was clear she wasn't going to receive any, she offered, "I can check to see if we can order it for you."

"Is that the title?" the man yelled. He was hard of hearing.

"Shush, Edward," the woman waved her hand, dismissing him. "You don't… have…it here?"

"Well, I don't pull that title up," said Charlie.

"Are you sure it's not just part of the title?" Tory asked. "Maybe it's *Bel Canto*? Or was it possibly written by Bell Hooks?"

"All I know…is…it had something…to do with…bell." Charlie strained to concentrate.

"Maybe it was Alexander Graham Bell!" Edward yelled. The three women ignored him.

"I'll go look up bell and poetry," said Tory going to check Books-In-Print. *Bell and poetry…*

"Ma'am, is it *The Bell Jar* by Sylvia Plath? She was a poet," said Charlie.

"Yes, I think…that might be it," she said.

"Okay, we have that in fiction." Charlie ran to get it. She didn't want to bear witness to the pace at which this woman walked. She returned out of breath. "I can ring you up right here," she said.

"Okay…" the woman replied.

"Are you a store club member?" Charlie asked.

"What?" Edward yelled. His wife took his hand.

"No, we're…not," the woman answered.

"Okay, then your total is $13.72," Charlie said.

Five years later, when the woman was finished counting her exact change, Charlie wished her a good day and thought good riddance.

Tory returned and said, "I didn't find anything."

"It was *The Bell Jar*," Charlie said.

"Eek."

"I know. Did you see her hair?" said Charlie. "All I kept thinking was, don't eat the yellow snow."

"You're awful," Tory looked past Charlie to a customer behind her. "May I help you?" she asked.

Charlie turned to see a painfully obese woman approach the counter of The Book Asylum. She held a study guide in her corpulent, sweaty hand.

"This book was printed last year. Do you have a more current edition?" she asked.

It was January fifth of 2002. The book was copyrighted for 2001. Nonetheless, Charlie dutifully checked the database.

"No, ma'am, this is the most current edition. The next publication is due out in May," Charlie replied.

"Oh," the customer exhaled loudly. "Well, I don't want to wait that long. Can I just have a discount on this one?"

Charlie looked to Tory.

"Greta," Tory said.

"I'm not sure, but I believe that our policy is not to discount a title until a more recent edition is released," said Charlie, a bit taken aback by the woman's attempt to parley with her.

"Would it be too much trouble to make sure?" the woman asked. She smiled widely as she said it.

Charlie again looked to Tory.

"Greta," she repeated.

"Ah…no, not at all," Charlie told the woman. "I'll be right back."

"Thanks, hon," the customer cooed.

Hon?

Charlie poked her head into her manager's, Greta's, office. "Got a minute?"

"Sure. Come in, please," replied the older woman.

"A customer wants a discount on this book," Charlie explained, extending the study guide to Greta. The latter lowered her glasses to give it a once-over.

"Is it damaged?" Greta asked.

"Not that I know of. She wants a more recent edition, but the new one's not due out until May."

"Then it's still the list price," said Greta flatly.

"That's what I told her. She wanted me to make sure," Charlie grimaced at the absurdity of such a request.

"Don't you just hate people?" asked Greta, winking and returning the study guide to Charlie.

"Yes. Yes, I do."

Upon telling the customer the book would not be discounted, she decided against the study guide and instead chose a small bookmark for a dollar twenty-five.

"Are you a store club member?" Charlie asked her when she reached the register.

"No, does it benefit frequent shoppers?" asked the woman, dabbing sweat from her ribbed forehead.

"Yes, ma'am."

"Do you have any stores in New York?" the customer asked.

"No, ma'am," Charlie replied. "This is an independent book shop."

"Oh…so there are more throughout Connecticut?" the woman asked.

"No, ma'am," said Charlie, unwaveringly. "This is an *independent* book shop."

"Oh…"

Jesus Christ.

"There's only one of its kind. It's not a chain," Charlie explained slowly.

"Oh! Well…" she said, looking around as though absorbing it for the first time, "isn't that…nice?"

"Isn't it?" said Charlie, crinkling up her nose. "That'll be $1.31." She hated the word *nice*. It was simply a way to candy coat one's apathy or disdain for something in an attempt to not sound insulting. Charlie preferred not to have sunshine blown up her ass.

The woman paid the dollar and thirty-one cents and huffed and puffed her way out of the door.

"Wow, all the winners are coming in today," Charlie muttered.

"Are they gone?" Charlie heard Tory ask from around the corner.

"Who?" said Charlie.

"The stupid people."

"I'm afraid they're everywhere," Charlie replied.

"I swear, the madhouses let them out every full moon. We get the dumbest people in here. While you were asking Greta about that book, a guy came in and asked where our large print audio books were," Tory spoke quietly just in case any of the customers were still lurking.

"That's okay. A woman came in last week and wanted to know if we had any of Anne Geddes's books in audio," said Charlie. At that, Tory doubled over in laughter. She laughed until her face was purple. "Tory, it wasn't that funny," Charlie said, finally.

"No," she said through her tears. "Can't you just hear it? Page one…" She took a deep breathe and tried to focus. "A dead baby in a pea pod." Charlie snickered. "Page two…a dead baby dressed like a sunflower." Charlie muffled a laugh.

"Page three," Charlie joined in, "a dead baby on a man's naked chest…"

"You look like you're contemplating the meaning of life," Tory told Charlie. Charlie had been staring at the Olsen Twins' books for fifteen minutes.

"Hardly," Charlie scoffed. "Have you ever noticed that the Olsen Twins look like monkeys?"

"Very well groomed for simians," Tory returned.

"Yeah, I guess," said Charlie. "I'm just waiting for them to pose for Playboy or Penthouse."

"That'll be the day."

"I'm serious," Charlie insisted. "You know there would be a picture of them making out. Well, not making out per se, but one of those pictures that makes lesbians look like they only have sex because men think it's hot. So they wouldn't so much be kissing as they would be licking each other's tongues."

"Interesting theory," Tory said, with a handful of the latest from John Irving.

"Oh my God, I *know*!" Charlie and Tory heard from the front of the store. Charlie exchanged a fearful look with Tory.

"Do you know them?" Tory asked.

"No…but they sound like every girl I've ever avoided," Charlie said fearfully. Upon seeing them, a crack formed in Charlie's carefully stacked self-esteem.

"Hi!" Two candidates for homecoming queen, tanned and preening, greeted Charlie upon her arrival.

"May I help you?" Charlie asked, trying to swallow any venomous judgments until after they left.

"Um," said the blonder of the two, "where's your…non…fiction section?"

"Well," said Charlie, "there are several non-fiction sections. History, art, business, sociology…"

"No, we want *non*-fiction," the second, less blonde, specified.

"Those are non-fiction," said Charlie.

"We want the books that aren't true," said the first.

"Non-fiction is true, fiction is not," Charlie explained. "If you want a novel, that's fiction."

They both started giggling.

"Sorry," the second apologized, "we've been out of school for almost two months."

"I see," said Charlie and walked to the fiction wall. "Paperbacks are here. Hardcovers are on that table." Charlie pointed to the New Hardcover display. "If you need anything else, please feel free to ask."

"Oh, one more thing," the first asked excitedly. "Do you have Ethan Hawke's new book?"

"He's totally hot," the other whispered.

"Uh, yeah, we should," said Charlie and disappeared for a second. She returned with it in hand. "Here you go."

"Wow," the girls said in unison. They ogled his author picture.

"Yeah, so, if you need anything else…" Charlie's voice trailed off as she backpedaled away.

She heard the sound of determined footsteps quickly approaching. Greta.

"Good afternoon, Charlie," her manager greeted her.

"Hi, Greta. How are you?"

"Fine, thank you. How are you?" Greta asked, coolly polite.

"I'm...all right."

"Note the hesitation," said Greta.

When Greta made a point, she tended to sound like a nature show host.

"I just..." Charlie looked over the shelves to make sure the girls were still engrossed by Ethan Hawke. They were. Charlie lowered her voice. "There are a couple girls back there who can't even tell the difference between fiction and non-fiction. Right now, they're raping Ethan Hawke vicariously through his new book," Greta suppressed a laugh. "In roughly seven years, they'll be out of college and each with a degree which could get them a desk job and a pension."

"...and?" Greta prompted her.

"And they can't tell the fucking difference between fiction and non-fiction," Charlie said despairingly.

Greta leaned in closely so she only had to speak in a gruff whisper. "Fuck 'em. Do you really want a desk job and a pension?" she asked Charlie.

"Not really, but I'd like to get to a point in my life when I actually have some money and I'm not just scraping by," said Charlie.

Greta smiled. "I know," she said. "But remember, you're smarter than they are. Try to think about what it's like to walk around with their intuition. Not only do they not have the capability to grasp concepts beyond which sweaters are on sale this week at The Gap, but they lack the insight to know when two people who make their living in retail are ripping them to shreds not twenty feet away."

Charlie grinned. "Thanks, Greta. You always know just what to say."

"Eh, it's a gift," said Greta.

In her next paycheck, Charlie got a raise.

She was going over her pay stub like she normally did and when she realized the difference, she went off in search of the Book Asylum's accountant. His name was Kenneth. He was a very fussy and yet incompetent man. He had his job because he was Greta's nephew.

Charlie knocked on Kenneth's door.

Kenneth looked at her over his glasses which perched at the end of his nose. "Yes?" he said.

"Hi Kenneth," she half-waved and started meandering toward his desk. "Um, my check."

"You got a pay increase," he told her.

Charlie stopped meandering. "Oh. Um, thanks."

"Thank Greta," he told her and went back to punching numbers.

Greta's office was across the hall. The light was off and the door was locked. Charlie thought about leaving a note. She didn't want someone else to find it. She went to the nearest phone and left Greta a voicemail.

"Hi Greta, it's Charlie. I'm actually calling from work, oddly enough. Just wanted to say thanks...for the, um, paycheck. Yeah. Okay, anyway, I'll see you at work. Um, thanks again. Bye," Charlie said, hanging up.

The rest of her day was a blur. She flitted around the book department, reorganizing and straightening things, whistling as she went along and generally enjoying her everyday normality. She was feeling so up, she even flirted with the handsome twenty-something who agreed to ordering a copy of *Fargo Rock City*. He was from out-of-state and she figured, why not?

Charlie treated herself to some Chinese takeout for dinner and walked home with a spring in her step.

Chapter Nine – Big Brother is Calling

"Book End, this is Spot," Spot said into the receiver. "Yeah, just a second."
He put the mouthpiece to his shoulder and yelled, "Charlie! Phone."

Charlie looked up from the travel section. Guides to Washington D.C.
and Bolivia, San Francisco and Monaco, Iran and Cuba sat around her feet. She
sighed at having to leave the shelf in such a condition. "Uh, give me a sec, Spot,"
she replied. Charlie picked up all the books in her arms and quickly alphabetized
them. She left them in a pile and ran to the order desk to get a scrap of paper. Oh
it, she scrawled WORK IN PROGRESS, snapped a piece of tape and attached it to
the stack. She went to the front counter.

"Say what now?" Charlie asked Spot in a voice which sounded strained from
helium inhalation.

"Phone's for you, geek," he replied.

"Thanks." She went behind the counter and picked up the phone. "This is
Charlie, may I help you?"

"Hi," replied a voice on the other line. It sounded frail and almost skittish.

"Uh, hi" Charlie said, not knowing how to proceed. "Can I help you?"

"This, uh…can you give me directions to your store?" replied the voice. It
was male.

Charlie's eyes squinted, giving her a perturbed and confused expression.
"Sure," she said slowly, "where are you now?"

"Across the street," he answered. Charlie's face relaxed. She leaned over the
counter to look out the window.

"May I put you on hold, sir?" She didn't wait for him to reply. Charlie pressed the button for line one and put the receiver down. Spot looked at her.

"You okay?" he asked.

"Not really, no. I think there's some weird prank caller guy across the street," she said.

"What are you talking about?" Spot asked.

"The guy on the phone...did he ask for me by first name or by first and last name?" asked Charlie.

"Um...I think he just asked for the owner," replied Spot.

"Okay...listen, I'll be right back. Watch from the window. If I get attacked, call 911," she said.

"Wait a minute—" Charlie walked out before Spot could finish. A man, smallish, stood talking on the payphone with his back to Charlie. His hair lay, stringy, about his shoulders. It was dyed black, but his brown roots were growing out. She stood behind him and waited for him to say something. She wanted to make sure it was him.

"Uh," she started, "excuse me, sir?"

He hung up the phone, turned around, grinning widely, and said, "Yes?"

Charlie's mouth fell open. He had a few days' growth of beard and he was wearing glasses, unusual for him. His cheeks which were once prone to baby fat were emaciated, but as she stared, she knew. "You fucking asshole!" she threw her arms around his neck. "What are you doing here?"

It was Lee, her brother.

"Nice greeting...what has it been? Three? Four years? And you call me an asshole. I'm going to develop a complex," he said and mocked wiping a tear from his eye.

"Fuck you, man," she said. "Four years...try more like eight." She pulled back to look at him. "What happened? Did you shrink or something?" She was two inches taller than him.

"No...when I left, you were only sixteen, if I recall. You had some growing yet to do," he said. "Besides...tall women love shorter men."

"Spare me. You've yet to answer my question. What are you doing here?" Charlie pressed. She didn't trust anything from her past, especially not Lee.

"I came to see you. I actually had to take two planes to do it. First I thought you were still in Linnmoore, so I flew back there, but you were nowhere to be found," he said.

"I needed new surroundings," said Charlie.

"So, then I went to the library and did one of those people find things on the internet. Miraculous thing, the internet," Lee reflected.

"Yeah, something like that," replied Charlie.

"And, here I am," he said, inhaling deeply to puff out his chest. "And look at you!" He put a hand out to touch the tips of her hair. "Jesus, you almost look respectable. Have your own business, let the hair grow out. No makeup either... but I see you still wear the ankh. And you have that one blonde streak." He spoke of the highlighted section she'd bleached earlier that month.

"Can't forget where we came from," she said, leaning in emphatically, "now can we?"

"Give it a rest. Aren't you going to give me a tour of your establishment?" he asked cheekily.

"Oh...*sure*," Charlie replied. They made their way back across the street.

Spot looked up as they entered the store. Gwen was at the counter now as well. "So, I guess it's good I didn't dial 911," Spot said to Charlie.

"Yeah...though it would've been mildly entertaining for a little while," she said. "Lee, this is Spot and Gwen. Gwen, Spot, this is my brother, Lee."

"I didn't know you had any siblings, Charlie," said Gwen.

"What kind of name is Spot?" Lee asked.

"You're one to talk. You have a girl's name and your sister has a boy's. At least I chose my name," Spot quipped.

"Fair enough," replied Lee. He looked around. "Not a bad place you've got here. Very nice indeed."

"Thanks...do me a favor to help prolong its life and buy something," said Charlie.

Lee wandered toward the back of the store. Spot looked at Charlie. "Wow. Did you guys swim in different gene pools?" he said.

"Actually, when Lee left, we were very similar. It just seems that he's still exactly the same. We are kind of the same personality wise though," Charlie replied.

"Hey, we should invite him out with us tonight! That would be so cool!" said Gwen.

"I don't know. Drinking with Lee." She pondered it a bit. "Neither of us were old enough to drink when last I saw him. It'd be weird," she said, scrunching up her face.

"Oh, come on, boss lady, you afraid he'll tell embarrassing stories about you?" said Spot.

Charlie looked from Gwen to Spot to Gwen again. "Fine."

Every Man For Himself

Charlie awoke to the muffled sound of a blaring radio. Tainted Love was playing from Lee's room. It was his alarm. No one turned it off.

"Lee! Turn off your Goddamned alarm!" shouted Charlie from under a pillow. The song ended and began again. Charlie got up and thumped into Lee's room.

She stopped in the doorway. The walls had been stripped of posters. His mattress was bare. Most of the drawers had been pulled open, the contents pulled out hastily. The only thing left besides the empty, lonely furniture was the stereo with a note taped on the front of it. The paper shook from the bass. It read: *The stereo and CD are yours. Love you. Lee*

Charlie crossed to see the note. She read it and reread it. Jean banged on the door. "Would you turn that fucking garbage off?" Charlie ran and opened the door.

"He's gone."

"What do you mean, gone?" Jean pushed Charlie aside to look into the room. Charlie leapt at her, pounding her aunt's back with the side of her forearms as hard as she could. "This is all your fault, you witch!" Jean backhanded her and Charlie fell to the floor. Jean seized a fistful of Charlie's hair and pulled back her head so they were face to face.

"Watch your mouth, young lady," said Jean. "And don't you ever hit me." She released Charlie's hair, stepped over her into the room and yanked the stereo plug out of the wall. "Have this shit out of here before dinner," Jean said and went downstairs.

Chapter Ten - After Hours

"So, what are you reading now?" Spot asked Charlie. The foursome had just arrived and grabbed a booth. Lee was in the men's room.

"*101 Reykjavik*. It was originally released in Icelandic in 1995. It was translated a while back to English and I just picked it up last week."

"How is it?" he asked.

"It's really quite funny. As I'm reading it though, I'm thinking, is it this funny because of the translation or because of the author himself?"

"Maybe it was even funnier in Icelandic," said Spot.

"Mayhap," said Charlie. After a few sips of her drink, she changed gears, "I can't read and write at the same time. Invariably, whatever I'm reading seems to influence my writing and then I feel like a hack. So, despite enjoying the books I'm reading now, I'm getting nothing done. And it sucks because I really want to work on my writing. It makes me feel like I'm not pissing my life away."

"You could be a lot worse off," said Gwen. "I mean, you have the store. It's not as thought you've accomplished nothing."

"This is true," said Charlie.

"What's true?" asked Lee, returning to the table and sipping the head off his beer.

"Nothing. What've you been up to, my errant brother?" asked Charlie.

"Well, believe it or not, I spent four years serving our country," said Lee with chagrin.

"Get the fuck out of here. You? A soldier?" She shook her head. "I don't believe it. Sorry, but there's no way."

"I'm serious," Lee protested. He rolled up his sleeve. An eagle was tattooed on his shoulder, with the letters USMC below it.

"Oh my God, and a Marine no less. So, what did you do with the other four years?" asked Charlie, still in disbelief.

"Well, I realized that the government we have is complete bullshit, so I took their money and spent it on women, beer and pot," said Lee, grinning.

"How very responsible of you," said his sister.

Lee went on telling funny boot camp stories and tales of all the places he'd been. Every city held a different story of some girl he'd bedded down. When Spot and Gwen went out to the dance floor, Lee decided it was time to drop the bomb.

"So, there was this one time I was in Savannah," he began. "I met this girl, Megan." He stopped there.

"And?" prompted Charlie.

"We're getting married," replied Lee.

Charlie put her drink down. She pushed it away from her. "That's it. I'm done for the night. I thought you just said you were getting married," she said.

"I did. She's beautiful. She's got hair the color of wheat and eyes bluer than the sky," said Lee.

"Please, stop. I may well vomit," said Charlie.

"Oh, come on, tell me you've been in love since I've been gone," said Lee.

"Twice, actually, very deeply, but I still wouldn't describe either of them like a fucking Hallmark card," quipped Charlie.

"Really? Twice? With whom?" asked Lee.

"Irrelevant. We're talking about you here. So, tell me more about this Megan chick," pressed Charlie.

"She's a real Southern belle. She's sweet and generous and loving," said Lee. Then he said something Charlie didn't hear.

"What?"

"And kind of...pregnant," said Lee.

"I knew it," said Charlie. "Jesus Christ...you're back from an eight-year hiatus, you're getting married and you're going to be a father. I think I'm going to have a massive coronary in my sleep tonight."

Lee squinted at her and then raised his eyebrows as though giving up on something. "Wow," he said.

"What?" said Charlie.

"I can't believe how much you've changed while staying the same," said Lee. "You're so grown up and responsible and you know stuff. Not that you were stupid before, but you know real stuff now. Like, if I were in trouble and needed advice, I'd ask you. But you're still just as jaded and cynical as when I left."

"Is that an insult?" Charlie asked.

"Not at all," Lee answered. "I was hoping you would be."

Charlie nodded. "Always happy to be of service," she said.

"Well?" said Lee as though he'd just asked something monumentally important.

"Well what?" repeated Charlie.

"Are you coming to my wedding or not?"

"Is that a multiple choice question?" said Charlie.

"Sure, but if you say no, I'll hate you forever," said Lee.

"*You'll* hate *me*...you jackass. You're lucky I'm even fucking talking to you right now. I was so hurt when you left," said Charlie.

"I would apologize, but you turned out fine. You're self-reliant and you made it through. I'm proud of you, kid," he said, mussing her hair.

"Don't call me that," she replied, fixing her hair. "I seriously thought you were never coming back. Not that you care. I didn't even get a letter. Thanks a lot."

Lee shrugged innocently and went to play pool with Spot. Gwen returned to the booth and Charlie.

"Can I ask you a question?" Gwen asked her upon her arrival.

"Sure," Charlie replied.

"I know there was a...thing...that happened between you and Spot..." Charlie waited for her to continue, hoping there was a question and not just that statement hanging in the air.

"Yeah," said Charlie hoping to goad Gwen into proceeding with her line of questioning.

"I was just wondering what happened."

"Oh." Charlie took a sip of her amber cider. "I found out that Spot was very drunk that night and didn't remember most of what happened." Charlie wondered how much Gwen knew. She decided to leave out the sexual reprise and summed it up with, "It was just easier for us to be friends." Gwen nodded and watched the guys pace around the pool table. "Why do you ask?" Charlie said.

"I was just thinking..." She didn't move her gaze from Spot and Lee.

"You and Spot, huh?" Charlie asked.

"I don't know. Do you think it's stupid?" Gwen asked, slightly embarrassed.

"Not at all. I just thought you were still...ya know, upset over—" Charlie hedged the subject of Gregory.

"I am. I just miss having someone there." Gwen stared down to her lap. "I miss him so much sometimes. The stupid little things, ya know? He used to do this thing anytime we were listening to a song; it didn't matter which one. He'd put my name in the lyrics and sing them in this silly voice. It was so cute. When I'd blow him kisses, he'd catch them in his teeth. And he made the best faces when he orgasmed."

"Didn't see that one coming," Charlie teased.

"He really did though," Gwen insisted. "Most guys look like they're in pain when they're coming. He would shut his eyes so tight and his mouth would fall open slightly. He didn't clench his jaw or anything. He almost looked graceful." Charlie nodded. She missed Ray. When she looked over to Gwen, she saw she was crying.

"Oh, Jesus, don't do that," said Charlie. She moved over to put an arm around her. "It's okay." Gwen shook her head.

"No," she sniffled. "How am I going to find someone like him again? We agreed on almost everything. I never had as much fun with anyone else." She looked at Charlie. "No offense."

"None taken," said Charlie.

"The worst part is," Gwen continued, "I'm worried that I gave my best years to him."

"Don't do that to yourself," Charlie warned. "If you do, the next person you're with will only be a disappointment."

"But what if I'm right? I looked in the mirror this morning and found, not one, but three gray hairs. I'm getting old, Charlie."

"Gwen. You're 27. You're a sweet, funny, talented girl. You're not old. You're not getting old. Just two months ago, you were chasing after Mark. What happened to that?" Charlie gently pried.

"Don't ask," said Gwen. She nursed her beer.

"Why? What happened?"

Gwen shot her a look. "He's gay."

Charlie shut her eyes and inhaled sharply through her nose. She held her breath. She opened her eyes and spoke. "Gwen, you can't let that discourage you. I know it's hard to be alone and I know that you're still very hurt by what happened, but not all guys are like Gregory and once you relax, you'll allow yourself to be happy again."

"I just don't know what I want anymore," Gwen said sadly. "For the past year and a half, I've been trying to forget about what happened. I've been telling myself that it wasn't my fault. That there's nothing wrong with me. But that doesn't make it easier. I've had more one night stands in those fifteen months than I'd care to admit, and that just leaves me feeling like a whore. But I'm scared to start over with someone.

"I don't remember how to be single. I'm couple-minded. I don't want to go through all the bullshit that comes with meeting someone new. I don't want to have to worry about what'll happen the first time he sees me naked. I don't want to have to worry that he'll have an STD. I don't want to have to worry about whether or not he'll know what he's doing in bed. I don't want to have to think about meeting his parents and him meeting mine and does he want kids and all that other stupid crap. I just want a simple, 'Do you like me? Great, I like you. Let's like each other and just be happy.' Why can't I find that? Why doesn't that exist?"

"Because the world sucks and we all have to go through that stuff. But…if you act now," said Charlie pointing toward Spot with the neck of her bottle, "you may be able to find a comely soul with whom you can commiserate."

Mogul

Charlie paid her rent on time every month without fail. She'd hand deliver it to her rental office and it was often early. She praised herself on being a responsible and quiet tenant.

Imagine her surprise when her landlady called to tell her the rent check had bounced.

"That can't be," said Charlie. "My paychecks are directly deposited into my account."

"Honey, I'm not accusing you of anything," said Mel, her landlady. "I just don't want you to have a hassle with the bank and overdraft fees and the rest of that. You've consistently paid me on time since you've been here. You may want to go and make sure everything is squared away."

It was already past six and the banks were closed. Charlie decided to wake early the next morning and go before she had to be at work.

She made it to the bank thirty minutes before she was due at the Book Asylum. Not knowing if a teller could help her, she went instead to the section where one normally opens an account.

"May I help you?" asked a fresh-faced woman behind a bland desk.

"I'm not sure, actually," Charlie began. "I was told one of my checks bounced and I wanted to make sure all my normal deposits had gone through."

Charlie fired off her account number and the clerks fingers were dashing over the keys.

"There should have been a deposit last Friday. From the Book Asylum."

"Let me just pull that up," said the clerk. After another instant, "Mmm. Looks like that didn't go through."

"Okay… What does that mean?"

"The code I have states insufficient funds," the girl told her.

"My paycheck wasn't deposited because I didn't have enough money?" Charlie asked. "I'm confused."

"No, the check wasn't deposited because the Book Asylum didn't have the money to cover it."

"That can't be. It must've been a mistake. That's a paycheck," Charlie insisted.

The clerk shook her head, "I'm sorry. I would take it up with your employer."

Charlie was flummoxed. She went to work and paged Greta immediately. There was no answer.

She paged her again.

"She's on the phone, I think," Tory called from the biography section.

She tiptoed over to where Tory stood. Charlie spoke deliberately under her breath. "Tor, have you had any problem with your paycheck?"

"No, should I have?"

Charlie explained the previous evening's and that morning's events.

"How is that even possible?" Tory asked. "It's not a personal checking account. Maybe you should take it up with Kenneth."

"Maybe…" Charlie mused. She walked back to the counter and picked up the phone. She was about to page Kenneth when she heard the click-clacking of Greta's heels approaching.

Greta spoke before Charlie could say anything. "I need you to page everyone over to the book department please." Greta's face gave nothing away. Charlie did as she was told.

In a matter of minutes, Charlie, Tory and Greta were joined by Allison from HR, Sam from shipping and receiving and Elaine from the accessories department.

Greta folded her hands in front of her, partially to keep herself from wringing them. "I'm sure that some of you have already ascertained knowledge of the financial problems we've been having…"

Charlie was in Linnmoore visiting Gwen. They were at their usual table in The Greasy Spoon when a dream of a man walked through the door. Charlie put down her coffee and stared, unblinking and unwavering.

"What?" Gwen turned to look.

"That. Is a dream of a man."

See? I told you.

Charlie stood and smoothed her shirt. She rearranged her jeans until they looked sufficiently relaxed. "Where are you going?" Gwen asked.

"To the bathroom. I want to have a better look," said Charlie.

"If you want a better look, put your glasses on," said Gwen.

"All right…I want a *closer* look," said Charlie and made her way over to get a closer look.

Charlie was unsure which feature struck her first. His hair was coifed into a black jungle. Each strand and clump carefully arranged into unintentional-looking bedhead.

Beautiful.

Maybe it was the choice of clothing. Black boots, blue jeans, black snug T-shirt, three silver rings. Always a good look.

Charming.

It could've been his square jaw and strong chin. Maybe it was his toned arms.

Stunning.

No. It was, she saw when he looked up and smiled, his eyes. Clear and green as an open field in May.

Perfect.

When he looked up, she stopped. She forgot where she was going. She returned his smile with an awkward uplift of the corner of her mouth. Just as she remembered she was on her way to the bathroom, he said, "I'd like a cup of black coffee and the short stack please," and handed her his menu.

"Right," she said after a few seconds. "I'll be sure to tell your server." She took his menu and turned to give it to the hostess.

"That guy over there wants black coffee and a short stack of pancakes." At the quizzical look she gave, Charlie followed that up with, "Don't ask, really," and returned to Gwen who gave a short snicker at her return.

"You are *smooth.*"

Charlie laughed. "Don't act like you don't think I'm cool."

Gwen looked at her very seriously and said, "Charlie. You're very cool."

Charlie ignored this and added sugar to her decaf. "So..."

There was a pause.

"Is this the part where you say, 'I'm sure you're wondering why I've called you all here,'" Gwen asked.

"Nothing so formal," Charlie told her. "I actually have to ask you a favor. If you can't swing it, I completely understand. But I need to borrow a few hundred dollars."

"Sure," Gwen said. "What's up?"

Charlie sighed. "The Book Asylum closed."

Gwen's eyebrows shot up. "What happened?"

"You want the long version or the short version?" Charlie asked.

"The long version, of course," Gwen smiled.

"Well, a few months ago, I got a raise. Remember when I told you that?"

"Yeah, that was, what? Six, seven months ago?"

"Thereabouts, yeah. That was my first real interaction with the accountant at work. Kenneth. Typical OCD, hates his life kind of guy, right? Anyway, two weeks ago, my landlady calls. She tells me my rent check bounced. I'm shocked, obviously. So I go to the bank. They tell me my paycheck didn't go through. As in, my employer didn't have enough money to pay me for one week's wages."

Gwen's jaw dropped a bit.

"Oh, it gets better," Charlie continued. "So, I go from the bank to work and Greta, my boss, calls us all in one spot. She tells us that she's really sorry, but the

Book Asylum is closing. She knows none of us have been paid, but she'll pay us the last week out of petty cash from the safe. We're all silent. None of us can say anything. Finally, someone locates their voice and asks what happened. It seems Kenneth was taking the money that's set aside for sales tax and squirreling it away into a private account. Then, when the letters from the Department of Revenue started accruing, he hid them from Greta.

"This went on for well over a year. Greta had no idea, and why would she even suspect? Kenneth is her nephew. Finally, when he had enough money put away to leave and never come back, he writes out a check covering half the money owed in back taxes, cleaning out the account and leaving Greta holding the bag."

"Isn't there anything that can be done? They still have stock, don't they?" Gwen asked.

"They do, yeah, but they're selling that off wholesale to pay for the rest of the back taxes."

"Wow," was all Gwen could say.

"Yeah. I know." Charlie looked out the window and gave Gwen some time to let it all sink in. "There are actually two parts to the favor I need."

"What's the second part?" Gwen asked.

"Would you ever consider leaving Linnmoore?"

"Why?"

"Well, I'm not qualified to do much. But if I could get the money together, I'm thinking I could open my very own independent bookshop. I checked into it and since I've never been to college, the government figures instead of having me turn around and sell drugs to make money, they'll give me all these grants and loans to start my own business," Charlie said.

"That's awesome," said Gwen.

"I'm glad you think so. I want you to work there," said Charlie.

"In Hartford?" Gwen asked. "I don't know. I'm not sure Gregory would want to move. And I can't afford to commute."

"It would actually be in West Hartford. The rent is just as expensive but there are more people there and a better chance of the store surviving."

Charlie told Gwen to think it over and to call when she had decided.

Gwen hummed along with the radio as she drove home. She was wondering how to broach the subject of moving to Gregory. "Hey, sweetie," she said aloud to herself in the car. "Charlie's opening a bookshop in Hartford and I think it would fun to move there. We've been here for so long, I think it's time for a change. New scenery would do us good." She pulled into the parking garage and trotted the block and a half to her street. Gregory had a sweet tooth, so Gwen had stopped at a bakery to buy a chocolate cake to soften him up. She arrived at her apartment building and headed upstairs. She was excited to tell him. They'd lived together for nearly four years. A new place would add some thrill to their relationship, which, truth be told, had been lacking of late. She unlocked the front door and hid the cake behind her back.

Gregory wasn't in the living room. She sneaked past the bathroom, in case he was in there, she didn't want to alert him of her presence just yet. She peered into the bedroom. No sign of him. "Maybe he went out," she thought. She debated leaving the cake for him in the bed, but thought better of it and set off for the kitchen.

Gwen and Gregory's apartment building had once been a house. It was then quartered off into separate sections and rented out accordingly. The room that Gwen and Gregory usually prepared food in was probably formerly a bedroom. When the building was remodeled, they simply added a stove, refrigerator and tile floor to make the transition. In the process, the door was never removed from the frame. It's for this reason that there was a door leading to the kitchen. It was old and the knob had been painted over and no longer had the ability to lock.

Upon entering the kitchen that afternoon, Gwen wished the lock still worked. Gregory was being pressed against the refrigerator and sodomized by his racquetball partner and next door neighbor, Thomas. The cake fell to the floor. A tear hastily made its way down Gwen's cheek.

"Shit," Thomas said and exited Gregory. He grabbed his clothes and left.

Gregory had been facing the refrigerator and did not turn to look at Gwen. She didn't bother to wait for an explanation. She returned to the bedroom, packed a duffel bag of clothes, grabbed her toothbrush and a towel and made way for the door. Gregory, now clad from the waist down, stopped her.

"Where are you going?" he asked.

"Does it matter?" she said. She did not want to deal with him. She needed to leave.

"Yes. It matters," he replied. "We should talk about this."

"No. We shouldn't. You need to figure things out for yourself and I am not a part of that. I'm no longer your concern. I want you out by the end of the week."

Gregory didn't bother to argue the point. She was justified in her anger.

"I'm sorry."

"You should be."

She sat in her car and sobbed. She cried loudly every possible expletive that came to her mind. By the time she called Charlie, Gwen was beyond hoarse.

"Hello?" Charlie said. She'd been reading *The Cheese Monkeys*.

"Charlie?" Gwen murmured.

"Gwen? Are you okay?" Charlie asked worriedly.

"Can I stay with you for a week?" Gwen requested dejectedly.

"Of course you can. Are you okay?" Charlie repeated.

"I'll tell you when I get there."

Gwen arrived at Charlie's door two hours later. Over dinner and ice cream, she told Charlie what had happened.

"Gwen, I am so sorry," Charlie said when she'd finished. Charlie didn't know what else to do. She wanted to offer any consolation she could to this woman who'd gotten her through so many crises. She felt helpless.

"It's okay. I mean, it's *not* okay. But, there's nothing to be done. I know you're only saying that you empathize, and I appreciate that. I just feel like shit," said Gwen. After a brief pause, she asked, "Can I ask you a question?"

"Sure," said Charlie.

"Can I still come work for you?"

"Are you sure? You'd have to move out here."

"I know."

"You could stay with me for a little while," Charlie offered.

"Thank you." Gwen paused to collect her thoughts. Tears crept in while she wasn't looking. "No matter how much I cry, I never seem finished."

"Oh, honey," Charlie hugged her dearest friend. "It's just karma, ya know? It's because I've done this to you so many times.

"If it meant this had never happened," Gwen mumbled, "I'd say we could call it even," Gwen sighed. She needed to think about something else. "Any luck finding Spot?"

"I found his phone number, but I haven't called him yet. I should make him work with us too."

"My God, the old team together again."

"It's like a Muppet movie," said Charlie.

"Shush."

Charlie called Gwen to check on any last minute changes. Everything seemed to be in place. "How are you holding up?" Charlie asked.

"Mmm," Gwen replied indifferently. "I've been better obviously." A scratchy batch of static clawed its way into Charlie's ear.

"Is that your phone or mine?" she asked.

"Neither," Gwen answered. "It's me."

"What are you doing?"

"Sniffing porcelain," said Gwen.

"I'm sorry?" Charlie said.

"I'm sniffing porcelain. It has this wonderful earthy scent. There's no other clay like it. It smells better than a book," Gwen said.

"Liar," said Charlie.

"No, really," Gwen insisted. "When I get there, you can smell it before I use it."

"What're you going to make?" Charlie asked.

"I'm not sure yet. A handbuild seeing that I lost my space at the gallery," Gwen replied nonchalantly.

"You did? Because you're moving?"

"No, I lost it a few weeks ago. Gregory moved out. That was always our agreement. Cheater leaves. And that means I'm paying for this whole place myself. Plus I was saving up money to move out there—"

"Gwen, I'm sorry," Charlie said.

"No, don't worry about it," Gwen insisted. "I was just trying to cut corners. My space at the gallery was a pretty expensive corner. Lucky for me, I still have some clay lying around and Emily will fire the pieces for me."

"Nice."

"Yeah. Listen, I have to get going. I still have to pack the last of my stuff. I'll see you in a few hours?"

"Definitely." Charlie checked her hipwatch. "I'll be there at…four."

"See you then."

"Bye."

Charlie hung up and got ready to go. As she was leaving, she started thinking about something Gwen had said. She grabbed her notebook and started to write.

Three hours later, she showed up at Gwen's place.

"Hey, I got caught up in stuff. I have something for you," she said, digging in her bag. She retrieved her notebook and flipped to the correct page. "Here," said Charlie. "I wrote this for you…or because of you, or whatever. Anyway, I hope it cheers you up." Gwen scanned the pages.

"But you're not a writer…" Gwen teased. She flipped through the stack of paper. "Christ, Charlie, it's almost fifty pages."

"It's okay. Sit and read it. Have you eaten yet?" she asked.

"No."

"I'll run down to The Cutting Board and grab some sandwiches."

"Can't. They closed," said Gwen.

Charlie's first reaction was to ask why, but she stopped herself. "Fuck, I hate people. What's still open that doesn't suck?" she asked.

"Go to Edgeboro and Main," said Gwen. "Across the street from the movie theater, there's a Chinese place. Grab some chicken mei fun and whatever you want for you."

"Okay, what's it called?" Charlie asked.

"Hard Wok Buffet."

"Gotcha. Be back in a few."

When Charlie returned, Gwen saw she had picked up some plastic utensils and foam cups. She had a bottle of seltzer under her arm.

"Good," said Gwen. "I was worried about the beverage thing."

Charlie sat down on the floor in front of Gwen. Gwen was still reading. "The place looks weird with everything in boxes," Charlie commented.

"I know," Gwen replied without looking up.

"Want your food now or when you finish?" Charlie asked.

"Hang on, I'm almost done," Gwen replied.

Charlie removed the take out containers from their bags. She ripped the plastic off the plates and piled food out for each of them. "Do you have any ice?" Charlie asked.

"Yeah, in the freezer," said Gwen, whose pinky fingernail was in her mouth as she read the last two pages. Charlie smiled, retrieved the ice and poured the seltzer. She returned and sat cross-legged next to Gwen. She watched the steam rising off the food. Ten minutes later, Gwen looked up.

"That was…" she searched for the right phrase, "painful. But also very good."

The story was about a couple that had met through a mutual friend and had started dating because of a hypothetical question. He'd asked her, if she hadn't just ended a relationship, would she consider dating him? She said, "If I hadn't just ended a relationship, yes, I'd consider it." He took that to mean that she was interested in him and, shortly thereafter, they started living together.

Besides having incredible powers of self-delusion, he was also a control freak. They would talk about everything to the most insane, minute detail. The topics varied from what would happen should she get in a car accident—if she were in a coma and died, he would consider that as her leaving him and a lack of faith in their relationship—to what would happen were either of them unfaithful. Since they shared a living space, the decision was that the cheater would move out. And he said that was "all her" because he believed wholeheartedly in monogamy.

Despite his belittling her character and his psychotic need to dominate every situation, including the hypothetical, she foolishly loved him.

Until one day, she came home early from work to find him fornicating with her own mother over their stove.

He moved out and she went to therapy. Just under a month, she stopped seeing her psychiatrist when he prescribed Prozac. She slipped into depression. She debated suicide. But then she had a better idea…she would kill him instead.

A week later, she was on the eleven o'clock news. Her mother was quoted at calling her "a raving lunatic." There was footage of the girl being dragged from her apartment, the one they'd shared, mumbling incoherently and covered in blood.

"Were there any parts you didn't like?" Charlie asked Gwen.

"Yeah, the won ton soup was cold," she teased.

"You know what I mean."

"Well…it was sick. But I like sick. I mean, her own mother?"

"I know!" said Charlie, laughing.

"And it was funny…"

"Funny's good," said Charlie.

"Why don't you send it to a magazine or something?" Gwen asked.

"Eh, I don't know. It's the first thing I've written in a while that I didn't immediately hate. I'm not sure I can so blindly offer it up for rejection," Charlie said hesitantly.

"You've got to try," Gwen reasoned. "You'll never know if you don't try."

"Yeah…" Charlie said. "I'll think about it. So, how do you want to do this? Boxes and then furniture or vice versa?"

"Well, we can put the furniture in the truck first, then the boxes and whatever doesn't fit, I'll grab when I come back for my car."

They filled the truck in two hours.

"Good thing I'm poor, huh?" Gwen said. She and Charlie exchanged knowing looks.

"Once you work at the shop, we'll be all set. Speaking of," said Charlie as they jumped in the cab of the truck. "I need help thinking of a name for the store."

"Uh, how about The Cracked Spine?" said Gwen, starting the engine.

"I don't know. That smacks of used bookstore to me," Charlie reasoned.

"That's true," Gwen nodded. "Hey, look in the glove compartment."

She did. There was the insurance pamphlet for the truck and a map of Connecticut. She pulled out the map.

"I take it this is the object up for discussion in that little open-ended synapse misfire?" Charlie asked.

"Dude, where do you come up with these sentences?" Gwen asked. "Most people would say, is this what you wanted? Not you, you're like Damon Wayans on

'In Living Color,' that guy in prison. What was his name?"

"I don't know. But I know who you're talking about. And fuck you, that's not what I sound like," Charlie protested.

"Yeah, keep telling yourself that. Anyway, the point of the map is…you're the navigator."

"Are you serious? I don't know where the fuck I'm going," Charlie whined.

"That's why you have the map, genius."

"Shut up. I'm serious. I'm directionally impaired," said Charlie.

"Listen, it's not hard, all you need to do is trace the route from here to Hartford and tell me what routes to take."

"All right," Charlie said uneasily. "So, about the store's name?"

"Oh, right…I don't know. What are you aiming for? Clever? Serious? Fun?"

"I'm not sure," Charlie replied. "I just want something memorable."

"Well, you don't have to name it today. Just think about what you want to say with this shop and go from there."

"We have to find Spot," Charlie mentioned distantly.

"You haven't called him yet?" Gwen asked.

"No. Take this next exit."

Gwen took the next exit.

"Not a great plan, huh?" Charlie laughed. "'Sure, Gwen, come on out. Spot, you and I will work at the shop, but I don't know where the shop will be or what to call it and I'm not really sure that Spot would even want to work there,'" Charlie laughed. "Aren't you glad you decided to join us?"

"I just hope we don't drive it into a lake and drown," Gwen quipped. "And don't worry about Spot. He'll be in. I guarantee it."

"Have you spoken to him?" Charlie asked.

"No," Gwen answered curtly.

"You sound pretty sure of yourself."

"No, sure of *yourself*."

"What does that mean?" Charlie asked.

"I just have faith in your ability to successfully run this store. You'll be great."

Charlie half smiled. "Thanks, Gwen."

Spot said yes. Charlie watched him and Gwen do lemon drops. They were at Spot's apartment and it was four in the morning. Charlie had briefed him on the bookshop idea and he was all for it. She was waiting to hear back from the landlord about the building she wanted to rent and, as long as they were willing, she'd have a store. She'd already gotten a loan from the bank and Gwen and Spot had other part time jobs, so staffing wouldn't be a problem. They'd decided to do some preemptive celebratory drinking. They'd been at it for seven hours. Charlie had sensed impending vomit and switched to drinking water around one AM.

It was now a contest between Gwen and Spot. After downing the last shot, Gwen slammed the glass down and yelled, "It is I who will rule the world!" before shoving the lemon slice in her mouth.

"Great, another drunk president," said Charlie.

"Not president," Spot corrected as he licked the sugar off his teeth, "but ruler."

"Yeah," Gwen whispered, staring moodily into her empty shot glass. "I am…utterly fucking drunk."

"Ranting about ruling the world? Yeah, I'd say those are the ramblings of a mad drunk," Charlie mused.

"I'm not mad," Gwen grinned sloppily. "I'm happy."

"You certainly are," Charlie chuckled.

"Before you've drunk yourself into a giggly stupor, I'd like to lay down some ground rules. One, I don't want work to ever stop being fun. If I ever become that boss that you have to go out and drink to get away from, I want one of you to hold me down and the other to beat me unmercifully with a brick. Okay?"

"Yes," said Gwen.

"I do the brick," said Spot.

"Okay, good for you," Charlie continued. "Now, I want to continue doing celebratory things like this, so anytime you want to hang out and drink after work, we'll just go."

"Fun."

"Yay."

"Also, last thing and then you can continue working toward DT's. We will not, I repeat, not be carrying children's literature. We can order it, but I don't want to have it normally in the store."

"Why not?" asked Gwen.

"Because I hate kids. And they only want to read Harry Potter anyway."

There was a period of silence and Charlie's speech had a slightly sobering effect on Spot. "But…at least kids are reading," he reasoned.

"No!" Charlie slammed her hand, palm down, on the table. "It's people like you that fuck things up for the children. All children really need to do is watch TV and drink. So fuck reading and fuck you."

Lots more silence.

"No, I'm kidding, I kid you. We'll have kids' books. Now get the hell out of here," Charlie teased. Gwen and Spot slowly shook off their shock and laughed a bit. They both stood and turned to leave.

"Gwen, are you going to be okay to drive?" Spot asked blearily.

"I live right across the street."

"Oh yeah."

They reached the door and Gwen stopped.

"Spot," she said.

"Yeah?"

"You live here."

"Right."

"I would've let you back in," Charlie said behind him. "See you tomorrow."

"Bye chickie," said Gwen.

"Chickie…"

"So," Spot slurred at Charlie as he closed the door. "Wanna do another shot?"

"I can't, remember?" said Charlie, sitting down. He joined her.

"Stupid gag reflex."

"Lucky for you, it's only when I do shots," she replied.

Spot thought on that. "How does that make me lucky?" he asked.

"It was a joke, Spot."

She could see in his face that it didn't register.

"About fellatio…"

He stared at her, nonplussed.

"Head. Me sucking your dick."

Charlie shifted her fist from her lips to an inch away and back while pushing her tongue into her cheek.

Spot blinked thrice and then raised his eyebrows and inhaled deeply. "Oh!"

Charlie nodded. "Um, speaking of, uh…sucking dickage…"

"God, you're a drunk Pauly Shore," Charlie said.

"Dick-age!" Spot laughed. "No, really," he said, "I was just wondering, since you, uh, like chicks and all now…" Charlie thought better of interrupting him at this point. "I was just wondering, is there no chance for us to ever, ya know…"

"Fuck?" Charlie finished.

"Yeah."

"I didn't know you wanted to, Spot."

"Since I first saw you," he replied. "But you had just split with Pyre and I was with Jenn. I didn't know how to ask. Then when I quit and moved out here, I realized I'd never get a chance to ask."

"And that would've been a travesty," said Charlie.

"No, I mean it. I don't meet girls like you every day."

She never knew how to take a compliment, especially not of that caliber. She turned away and quickly wiped her tears.

"Spot, I think you should go lie down and I should be getting home." She stood up. He followed.

"Is that a no?" he asked.

"You're drunk," she said.

"You're not exactly sober either."

"All the more reason why we should have this conversation another time."

He looked at her with an expression Charlie didn't recognize. And in that instance, she thought of Eli.

Has it been that long?

"Just so I don't feel like a complete asshole tomorrow…how many fingers am I holding up?" Charlie asked Spot. He squinted.

"Including the thumb?"

"Dude."

"What?"

"I'm not holding up my thumb."

"I knew that," Spot countered.

"We can't do this." She dropped her hand.

"What was the answer?" Spot asked.

"Two."

"I was gonna say that. I swear."

He crossed to her, closing the space between them. "Aw, Spot…" She hugged him.

With his head still over her shoulder, Spot asked, "Can I just—I mean, just one?"

He stood up straight to look at her.

No going back…

She opened her eyes to see Spot looking at her in a way which made her feel loved and so, so lonely.

"Do you want to?" he asked.

A floodgate of memories opened on her. Stephen, first meeting Spot, his relationship with Jenn, their friendship, Ray, Eli again, and then the past year of no one. She didn't want to make this decision now. Not like this.

"Yes," she heard herself say.

Charlie opened her eyes as the first sign of daylight spilled into the room. She squeezed them shut again and stretched stiffly. She was not in her room. She was not in her apartment.

Spot.

She recalled the previous evening's events with surprising clarity. Spot had smelled like a blend of sandalwood, deodorant and pheromones. When she had told him so, he just smiled and softly thanked her. The sex had been everything she thought it wouldn't be. There was foreplay—something she'd never experienced with a male, save the failed attempt with Stephen. She was expecting it to be drunken and sloppily done, but he was considerate and patient during penetration and cradled her and carried her to different positions.

Charlie rolled over to look at him.

What have I done?

She looked at the ceiling. *It's not like you've never had a one night stand*, she told herself. *But I never saw him again. I certainly didn't have to deal with him on a daily basis, much less at a potential work situation.* Her mind then immediately jumped to, *Maybe it was only sex for him too. That would be all right.* She looked again at Spot. *I should go.*

Noiselessly, she located her clothing and got dressed. As she bent to tie her boots, the floorboards released a loud creak. Spot squinted his eyes open and lifted his head. He sat up steadily and continued squinting until his gaze fell on Charlie.

"Hey," she said. Charlie felt like a parent caught having sex by her four-year-old. No, there's no one else in bed with Mommy. Do you want some juice? But more along the lines of: no, I'm not leaving. I just wanted to slip into something more comfortable. I always lounge around in my boots at dawn.

"Hi," he replied. She smiled at him.

"You're cute early in the morning," she said.

"Aww, you're only saying that because I have a hangover and the always sexy post-sex morning wood."

"No, really," she insisted. "It's a little kid, my hair's messed up but I'm still cute and sleepy sort of thing you have going."

"No, really," he responded, "I know I'm not cute. I'm *Spot*."

Charlie's words echoed back to her. "I didn't mean that the way it sounded…"

"Didn't know I knew you said that, huh?"

"When did Gwen tell you?" she asked.

"About an hour after you said it," he replied.

"Shit."

"Don't worry about it," Spot sighed. "It's kind of my own fault. It just came up, ya know, what did you do today? Oh? How's Charlie? Yeah, what did you talk about? Ahh, I didn't know she felt that way. That kind of thing. You were with Ray at the time and I had just moved to Hartford. I was wondering how you were doing but I didn't want to be all weird and call and say hey, I miss, I was wondering if you were interested in the penis sampling program I'm involved in right now. It's kind of a one-man gig, you just test it out, fill out the review card, mail it back and get your five dollar check in seven days."

"Same old Spot," Charlie grinned. He noticed her half-tied boot.

"You leaving?" he asked.

She debated lying. She mentally scolded herself. For thinking about lying or getting caught, she couldn't be sure. "Yeah, I need to get the taste of cock out of my mouth, so I figured I'd go get some breakfast." He masked his hurt with an eyebrow raise. "You wanna come with me?" she asked.

"Sure," he replied. "I fucking hate that cock taste."

"One coffee and one hot chocolate with whipped cream," said the waitress, handing out the beverages, to Spot and Charlie, respectively. Charlie ordered a bagel, toasted.

"Thanks for not ordering eggs," said Spot, grimacing. "The smell would've made me puke."

"What a way to start the day. Projectile vomiting," said Charlie.

"Best vomit ever, Linda Blair, *The Exorcist*," Spot mused.

"Agreed," Charlie said, without hesitation. "But the book was better." She scooped and ate a spoonful of whipped cream.

"The remake was scarier than the first movie," said Spot, "and better than the book."

"I cannot possibly communicate how wrong you are."

"Did you even watch the movie? Hmm? Little girl?" Spot, mock anxious to hear Charlie's response, raised a hand to his ear.

"A? Shut the fuck up. B? Scary books always win because I can imagine more frightening shit than can ever be caught on film. You can't argue that point because you can't see what I can."

"That's true," Spot nodded.

"And you're hungover." Charlie sipped sagely at her hot chocolate.

"Also true. …the stuff, um, last night," Spot began. He was concentrating on his coffee, so he didn't see the layer of whipped cream left along Charlie's upper lip. "I didn't mean to make things odd between us," he looked at her then and started laughing. "I wish I could grow a moustache that quickly."

Charlie's expression read confused. Slowly, comically, her gaze dropped to right below her nose. She saw white in the periphery. Her eyes crossed. "Oh Christ..." Charlie mumbled, hiding her face with her hands. Spot couldn't suppress his smile and passed her a napkin. "Thanks," she said and held the napkin to her mouth, wishing her whole face could be wiped away with a cursory swipe. "Sorry," she said. "I unintentionally interrupted you..."

"No, it's okay," he smirked.

"Actually, before you go on, I want you to know that I had a good time. I don't know if you feel the same way, but..."

"No," he nodded. "I mean, yeah! I mean...I had a good time too," he replied.

The waitress returned with Charlie's bagel. "Sure I can't get anything for you, hon?" she asked Spot.

"Thanks, I'm set."

"Okay, enjoy."

"Anyway, what I wanted to say—" Spot continued.

BEEPBEEPBEEPBEEPBEEP...

"What is that?" Spot asked. It was coming from Charlie's hip.

"Oh Jesus, I'm sorry. It's my pager," she said.

"You have a pager?"

"I know," Charlie sighed. "It makes me feel like a drug dealer or something. I got it so I could find out about the store front for the bookshop as soon as possible. I was going to get a cell phone, but I know I'd never use it and they're really expensive." Charlie nodded to herself. "I guess this is the moment of truth. I'll be right back." She left to find a payphone.

Spot watched her walk away. He tried not to think about his headache. He tried to remember the previous evening's events. "She said she wanted to get the cock taste out of her mouth, so did she suck my dick? Maybe I don't remember because it wasn't all that memorable... On the other hand, some girls don't even give head. Certainly not the ones that have sex with other girls..." He was so angry with himself. So much build up for something that he could barely remember. He waded through it again. He remembered talking... "Did I tell her how I feel? How do I feel? Do I love her? The whole thing is so Goddamned blurry. Does she remember it? Maybe it was just sex for her. That would be okay...wouldn't it?"

She was at the table.

"How'd it go?" he asked.

She modestly beamed. "I'm a shop owner."

"Congratulations," said Spot and he got up to hug her. It was their first physical contact since last night.

"Thanks," she almost whispered. He still smelled the same, only fainter. Her mind was wandering.

"You okay?" he asked, bringing her back mentally. They had returned to the table.

"Yeah, I guess I'm just absorbing everything," she said.

"I just figured you would be more excited."

"I am," she said unconvincingly. "I guess I'm just waiting for the other shoe to drop," she reasoned. "It's scary. Having things this close to where I want them."

He wondered if she was still talking about the shop.

Change the subject…

"Ideal mate, what would she look like?" said Charlie. She loved lines of questioning like this. It let her know more about the person she was spending time with and needed no segue at all.

Spot knew what she was doing and so replied, "I'm going to have to be vague with these answers. Hair color and eye color don't matter. Depending on the rest of you, those things are incidental. Having said that, I'm pretty sure she'd have to be at least three hundred pounds with…stretch marks, lots of stretch marks. On her face. And she'd have to be *covered* in varicose veins."

Charlie started to giggle. Spot continued, "Her neck would have to resemble a package of hot dog rolls, and if she has one chin, she has to have several. Her hair should never be done up, in fact, she's going bald and has a comb over."

Charlie made the mistake of drinking her hot chocolate as she heard this and so had to cease her laughter as hot chocolate lapped against the back of her front teeth. Her lips were pursed in a tight smile. She panted through her nose and her eyes were screwed shut. She couldn't stop laughing. Spot went on, "She has to have two tattoos. One on her arm that says, *I heart Twinkies.* The other on her forever growing abdomen which says simply BEER."

Charlie clapped her hand over her mouth. Her face was practically purple. "As far as fashion sense goes, I'm thinking muumuus. All muumuus, all the time." That was too much. Hot chocolate, lukewarm at that point, forced its way out of Charlie's nose. She didn't even care. She let her mouth fall open and she roared with laughter.

"Oh my God," she said through a napkin. "You asshole." She couldn't control her giggle fit. About five minutes later, it finally subsided. "Hoo…" she whispered, mopping the tears from her eyes and chocolate from her face. "My cheeks hurt. I can't believe you did that."

"Me? I wasn't the one who made a scene. I bet they charge us double now," he teased.

"Well, after that little stunt, you're footing the bill."

On the way to her apartment, Charlie absentmindedly drummed her index fingers against Spot's dashboard. She heard him stifle a laugh. "What?" she smiled.

"Abusing my car now too?" he joked.

Mocking offense, she asked, "When have I ever abused you?"

He stifled a grin. "Forget it," he said.

"What? Why?" She thought he was playing with her.

"Nothing. Nevermind."

"Spot," she whined, trying to coax him into being fair.

"Nothing. I just…I meant last night."

"Oh," Charlie mumbled. "Is that an off-limits topic?"

"No...I mean, I'll talk about it...ya know, if you want to," he trailed off.

"I just didn't know if you regretted it or something."

"No! Well...not the parts I remember anyway," Spot smiled.

"You were so drunk," Charlie laughed.

Spot grinned nervously and half-laughed. "Yeah. Um...I remember talking for what felt like a long time. Did I say anything completely embarrassing?"

"Well, you didn't confess your undying love to me or anything. But, yeah, the stuff you said was nice."

They made eye contact for the first time since they got in the car. "I'm a suave drunk," said Spot. He parked the car, but neither of them got out. "Why does it feel like we're still not talking about it?" Spot asked Charlie. "I mean, we've acknowledged it. Kinda like, 'Hey, remember that time when we...?' But we haven't really *talked* about it, ya know?"

"Well," said Charlie, "go ahead. Talk."

"Okay..." Spot replied. He looked as though he was about to announce something monumental and then stopped. "Before I do, I just want to say that I'm going to just blurt things out and I don't want you to get mad or anything. Okay?"

"Sure," said Charlie.

"Well, it's like I said. I don't really remember that much of it. I remember talking, but I don't remember what about. I remember kissing you...a lot. I remember finishing. That's about it."

"Do you want me to fill in the blanks for you?" Charlie asked.

"Well, no. I was actually sort of wondering...if we could do it again. Ya know...when I'm...not...drunk." Charlie laughed. "Thank God," Spot smiled.

"What?"

"That's the part I figured you'd get mad over."

"Oh," Charlie said softly. "Spot, before I say yes or no, I have to ask you something. Last night, you basically made it clear that you've been interested in me ever since we first met. And, not to say that you've held a torch for me or anything, but I don't want to screw things up if this holds more emotional value for you than you're letting on. I mean, I was with Stephen for a long time and he knew I was in love with him, but he fucked me anyway because it was convenient at the time. Not only do I not want to hurt you, but I don't want you to think that I would knowingly play with your feelings like that."

Spot shifted his gaze from her to the dashboard. A silence lingered.

Oh fuck. Please say something.

"Should I take that as, you don't want to wear my class ring?" Spot asked quietly.

"You should take that as my looking out for you just in case this turns out to be nothing beyond sex," Charlie explained. "We'll still be friends and we'll still hang out and I will still love you more than I can articulate with my piddling knowledge of our language."

Spot grinned with only one corner of his mouth. "I think I can steel myself to your womanly wiles," he said.

"Okay," Charlie smiled.

"Is that an okay, okay?" he asked.

"If you're asking if I'm saying yes, yes, I'm saying yes."

"Score."

With the exception of a few minor differences—Spot being a little more lucid, his hang time lasting longer—the sex for Charlie was very similar. No better, no worse. Before they'd started, Charlie prefaced it with, "If any of this makes you feel uncomfortable, for whatever reason, we can stop."

That's why it surprised Spot when toward the end, Charlie looked at him and started to well up. At first, he thought she was sweating. When they were done, he heard her breathing laboriously and he asked her, "You okay?"

She covered her eyes with her hands and nodded silently.

"Shouldn't I be the one crying?" he asked, sitting next to her.

"I know," she laughed. "Talk about role reversal. I'm sorry."

"Nothing to be sorry for," he said.

"I just miss Ray. I miss being this close to someone all the time. I miss making her happy."

Spot put his arm around her. "Maybe you just miss girls," he suggested. "I could understand that."

Charlie shrugged. "I don't know. It just happened when I stopped to look at you. I was just reminded that I was alone."

"You're not alone. You have Gwen," he said. After a while, he added, "You have me." Charlie nodded. "I know, it's not the same." Charlie shook her head. "Why don't you call her? I'm sure she'd love to know you still care about her."

Charlie opened her mouth to speak several times before giving up. Finally, she said, "I can't. I'm still the same person I was when things ended. Until I sort myself out, I can't be with anyone."

"Well, if you ever need a quick fix, I'm there for you," Spot offered.

"Thanks. I take it that means we're still friends," said Charlie.

"Why would we not still be friends?" Spot asked.

"Because you're sober this time."

"Oh yeah… The sex was terrible, get out."

She punched his arm. "Jerk. But seriously, we're okay?"

"Yes," he said.

"Good."

"Okay."

"Definitely."

"Yeah."

"Okay."

"Said that one already."

"Right."

"Shower?" he asked.

"I'm there."

"Great."

Gwen, Spot and Charlie were at one of those non-descript chain restaurants whose décor consists of various license plates, pictures of celebrities, vintage movie posters and old Coca-Cola advertisements hung randomly on each wall. Spot had convinced Charlie to go because he insisted she try their onion rings. She was less than impressed. It was her 24th birthday. The store had been open for a month and she was wound tighter than a broken music box.

"Are we having fun yet?" Charlie asked.

Gwen and Spot looked at each other. "Aw, c'mon, boss lady. We just want to cheer you up," said Spot. "You've been all busy with opening the store and it's your fucking birthday. Now, be a man, suck it up, and enjoy yourself."

"You, of all people, should know that I'm not a man," Charlie said to Spot. "That being said, I'm going to the bathroom." With that, she stood and exited stage left.

"What was that about?" Gwen asked.

"Oh Christ," thought Spot. "Well," he said. "Remember the night we found out the store was practically definite and we got drunk and you left early?"

"Yeah…" Gwen sensed impending doom.

"Charlie and I…uh…" With his eyes shut, Spot inserted his right index finger into his left fist and pulled it just far enough to show motion before shoving it back in. He repeated this several times.

"Oh my God," Gwen smiled. "Why didn't you tell me?"

He decided to leave out the part about round two. "I was drunk. I only remember bits and pieces of it. Besides, all the stuff with the store was happening at the time and I didn't get a chance to mention it."

"Are things all weird now?" Gwen asked.

"No. We talked it over and things are fine. I don't know what's wrong."

"It's probably a bit of everything and the usual," Gwen mused.

"The usual?" Spot repeated.

"She misses Ray."

"Right. Well, the cake ought to cheer her up, right?" Spot asked.

"Let's hope so."

By the end of their meal, moods were lighter. Their server returned to their table and asked, "Can I bring you anything else tonight?"

"Not for me," said Charlie.

"Just the check, please," said Gwen.

A few moments later, the waitress returned with three plates and an ice cream cake holding twenty-five candles.

"Happy birthday," she told Charlie.

Shocked, Charlie replied, "Uh, thanks."

The icing on the cake read: *Hither, Pry a Bad Play Chi!*

"Chi?" Charlie asked.

"What," Spot said defensively. "Chi is a word. Like tai chi. Like balance in all parts of life. Chi is a fucking word."

Charlie snickered. "How did you get them to write that on the cake, anyway?"

"Eh, I slipped the waitress a large bill," Gwen replied.

"Can you guess what it says?" Spot asked.

"I'm thinking…happy birthday, we quit?" Charlie teased.

"Wow," said Gwen, "she got it on the first try."

"Funny," said the birthday girl.

"You have to make a wish," said Spot.

Charlie smiled and thought her normal bittersweet birthday thoughts.

"Hurry," said Gwen. "Or we'll be eating ice cream wax."

Charlie wished to see Ray again and blew out all her candles.

Chapter Eleven – Sibling Rivalry

Lee awoke groggily to the muffled whirr of a hairdryer. It reminded him of his fiancée. She dried her hair slowly, letting the hot air blow against it strand by strand. Charlie moved the dryer as though she wanted her hair dry instantaneously. She whipped it back and forth manically, running her fingers through her hair. But it was so thick, she usually gave up before it was completely dry. She emerged from the bathroom looking nothing like the little sister Lee had left behind.

"Morning," she said.

"Hey," he replied hoarsely. He was a mouth-breather when he slept, so chronically had drymouth when he woke. "So," Lee cleared his throat, "what are we doing today?"

"*We* aren't doing anything," said Charlie on her way to the kitchen. "*I* am going to work. You can do…I don't know," she yelled from the kitchen, "whatever it is you do."

"Dude, I came to visit you," Lee argued, following her to the adjoining room. Once there, she handed him a bowl of cereal. "Thanks." He shoveled a heap of cereal into his mouth, pushed it to his cheek with his tongue and repeated, "I came to visit you."

"Rather unexpectedly," she finished. "You can't expect me to drop everything because my estranged brother returns from the fray."

"Estranged? That's a bit much," said Lee.

"We haven't spoken in over eight years, man. What do you call it?" Charlie asked calmly.

"It's not like we had a disagreement. I was just going my own way. And you weren't exactly the easiest person to find," he responded.

"Lee, regardless, I have things to do." She tipped back the bowl and drank the leftover sugary milk.

"I can't believe you. Don't you want to spend time with me?" Lee asked.

"Sure…*later*." She reached over to the windowsill, grabbed her glasses and slid them on.

"Oh my God. What are those?" Lee teased.

"They're called glasses, dear brother. They're what I use because I have impaired vision." She spoke slowly.

"Ha ha," he said in staccato. "Since when do you need glasses?"

"Since the year after I graduated high school. You're not the only one who's changed," Charlie said and rinsed her dish. She turned and saw his arm outstretched with a dirty bowl. She rolled her eyes and cleaned it. She turned again and Lee had half a hot dog sticking out of his mouth. "What the fuck is that?" she asked.

"It's called a hot dog, dear sister. It's made of dead pig amongst other things and it's what one eats to maintain his or her good health." He spoke slowly. She looked at him and blinked, once.

"But it's raw. And I hate hot dogs. Where'd it come from?"

"I bought a pack last night," he answered. "How could you hate hot dogs? We ate them all the time when we were younger."

"Lee, contrary to what you may think, my memories of our childhood aren't glimmering rays of sunshine."

"Well, yeah. But it wasn't all bad," he said.

"Name one thing that didn't suck," she challenged him.

"When Mom used to let us eat raw hot dogs."

Charlie shuddered, "That's disgusting."

"But you ate them," he said.

"What alternative did I have? I was four years old. I ate whatever was in front of me."

"True," said Lee.

"I can't believe you still eat those," she said, grimacing.

"I can't believe you don't. They're good," he munched happily. "Dad hated that she let us eat them."

"Dad hated everything," said Charlie.

"That's not true," Lee protested.

"He certainly hated Mom," said Charlie, staring at the floor, then her brother. "The last few years they were alive, all I remember is the lengths to which they'd go not to talk to each other."

Quietly, Lee asked, "Don't you miss them?" It hurt Charlie to hear so much pain in his voice. She tried to remember something about her parents that was worthwhile. Her father's smoking and brooding and avoiding his wife…her mother's complacency and negligence. The way they'd pretend to be a real family in front of other people. "I was younger than you," she told him. "I don't really remember them that well."

"You remember the bad stuff," Lee reasoned.

"There was a lot of it," Charlie touched her still damp hair and then... "I miss the way Mom brushed my hair," she said after a while. "Never too hard. She didn't push me to wear bows or barrettes or anything. As much as she wanted me to... She didn't yell at me for not playing with dolls or wearing dresses. Not like Jean."

"Can we please not talk about Jean?" Lee asked.

"I had to deal with her longer than you did," said Charlie.

"Okay, fine. I get the Worst Sibling Award. I deserted you. I didn't call. I suck, okay?" Charlie sat down next to her brother and hugged him with one arm.

"Nah, you're all right. I think I'll keep you," she smiled.

"How generous of you," he scoffed.

Charlie shook him. "Don't be a grump. I know you loved Mom and Dad..."

"Didn't you?" Lee asked.

"Of course. But it was harder for me. They liked you better," Charlie said in all seriousness.

"Don't even...they loved us both equally," Lee insisted.

"I'm not disputing that. But they *liked* you better. You and Dad would go to baseball games and be outside for hours. You were best friends. And Mom loved that; you were 'her boys.' And when I was born, I guess I was supposed to be her equivalent. What a disappointment I must've been. Yes, Mom loved me because I was her child and she felt she had to, but we had nothing in common. I didn't want to watch soap operas and she resented that I liked Dad better. He was more fun. And I wanted him to like me as much as he liked you. If I'd been a boy, like I should've been—*Charles*—it would've been no problem. Just more of the same. I tried everything to make him proud of me, like the theatre and the rest, but he didn't care. And despite her silence, I felt Mom's disapproval. She hated that I wanted that additional attention. I was everything she never wanted me to be." Lee looked at her face so full of sorrow. He wished he knew what to say.

"By the time I had started to become my own person," Charlie continued, "she'd become indifferent toward me and the rest of the world anyway. She hated Dad because I preferred him to her and Dad hated her for growing despondent. They shouldn't have gotten married in the first place, but by the time he realized that, there were mortgages and kids involved. Rocks and hard places."

"I'm sorry," was all Lee could say.

"Don't be," she told him. "Really, don't. It doesn't mean anything to me anymore. They're dead. Nothing can be done about that. And maybe it was good they died when they did. I only would've been more screwed up had they stuck around. Guilt over why I'm not in college. Why I'm not in a 'meaningful relationship,' and all that other bullshit. I like not having to explain myself to anyone. It allows me to figure things out for myself."

"But maybe if you'd had a little more mothering, you wouldn't feel that way," said Lee.

Charlie shrugged and stood. "I guess we'll never know."

"I wish you weren't so apathetic about this," said Lee.

"Sweetheart. They're dead. I'm not hurting their feelings. I'm not hurting anyone. Neither of us turned out so badly, so why be upset over it?"

"That's exactly my point though. Neither of us is terribly fucked up because of our parents," Lee reasoned.

"We have self-reliance to thank for that. You can learn one of two ways from your parents: good example or bad example. Either way, there's no excuse for growing up to be an asshole." She leaned down and grabbed her canvas bag. "I get out of work at six. It usually takes me about an hour to get home, so I'll see you later, okay?"

"All right. I may stop by," said Lee.

"Okay." She walked halfway to the door before turning to say, "I hope I haven't depressed you too much or ruined your memories of Mom and Dad. Like I said, I know you loved them a lot."

Lee shook his head. "I still remember them somewhat fondly."

"Good to hear," she smiled sincerely and walked out the door.

"Chicks have it easy. They control the ebb and flow of sex in the relationship. No means no, and that closes the book."

"Yeah, right on his dick."

The setting is Connecticut. Hartford. Jason's, also known as Spot's, house. The basement. Five figures are at the pool table. Four guys and one girl…female…woman. She lays on the table. The others sit, counterclockwise, at each corner. Spot, one of his roommates, Lee, and Spot's neighbor, respectively.

"Chicks have it easy," said the roommate, Andy. "They control the ebb and flow of sex in the relationship. No means no, and that closes the book."

"Yeah, right on his dick," replied Spot's neighbor, Chad. They all had a hearty laugh.

"I don't think that's always true," Charlie, the one on the table, interjected. "I can think of several times in which I wanted to have sex and Stephen said no. So…we didn't have sex."

"I don't think Pyre should be serving as a representative of all males," Spot told Charlie.

"I don't have much other experience otherwise."

"You've only dated one person since I left?" Lee asked.

"No." Charlie let the answer sit, not wanting to continue on. Chad made the decision for her.

"For argument's sake," he said, "since you've been in a relationship in which there was no male, what's it like for two girls?"

Charlie took a deep breath. "Give me an example," she said.

"You're horny. She says she has a headache. Is that a valid excuse?" asked Chad.

Charlie pondered it. "It wasn't quite like that. There were no bullshit excuses. We were both secure enough that if one of us said she was tired, the other accepted that and either went to sleep or violated herself."

"Why don't you tell us more about that part?" asked Spot, smiling and leaning over her.

Charlie laughed. "Shut up. I think when it comes down to both sex and foreplay, girls are crowd pleasers. Unless she thinks she might fall asleep in the act, a girl will go out of her way to make the other person happy. Be it male or female."

"That's only if love is involved," said Spot. "What if the relationship is only based on sex?"

"Well," Charlie began, "if you only see this person for fucking purposes, why would you say no?"

"You're not in the mood," said Spot.

"Tell them," Charlie responded.

"You'll hurt their feelings."

"If it's all for sex, it shouldn't matter," said Charlie.

"That's cruel," said Andy.

Charlie shrugged. "I do feel sorry for guys sexually though."

"How so?" asked Chad.

"Girls may be the ones who have to go that extra mile all the time, but guys have to struggle just to make it the first mile. Guys, in general, are slapped with this predetermined reputation for fucking and fleeing. I know so many girls, gay and straight, that automatically pigeonhole all men as dogs or assume that all a guy wants is sex. I know for a fact, present company excluded, that there are plenty of guys who want more than sex."

Lots of laughing. One "Hey!" comes from the engaged member of the crowd.

"Most guys I know bend over backwards just to have a woman agree to a date. Then, at the end of the evening, because every woman on earth is so worried about having to make the walk of shame, they pass up what could've been a pretty good fuck.

"Also, solely because of most women's inability to forget anything, you have to suffer through months of blue balls because her last two boyfriends screwed her over…like that's your fault."

"You can't just expect her to forget and go into a new relationship blindly," said Chad. "There's bound to be some trepidation."

"I'm not saying she should have her guard down, I'm just saying she shouldn't have three guys with rifles guarding an impenetrable wall. Besides, even if these past experiences didn't mean anything to her, she will never give you the upper hand. That's another thing…women are so fucking fickle. Let's say there's Mr. Mysterious who she spends as many as thirty whole minutes to cajole into a dinner date. It turns out that Mr. Mysterious is actually Mr. Nice Guy who treats her well, loves her and would never think of putting their relationship in jeopardy. She dumps him for the next Mr. Mysterious because most girls don't want Mr. Nice Guy. Mr. Nice Guy has a reputation for being Mr. Boring As Hell, and so women go out in search of Mr. Doesn't Treat Me Very Well, But Has Long Hair and a Dark Side and Three Other Girls as Competition. Women are so stupid."

"You know, you're the first woman-hating dyke I've ever met," said Andy.

Charlie sighed. "I'm actually not a dyke. I still like men. So, I'm one of those annoying bisexual girls that truly seasoned lesbians loathe. And I don't hate all women. It's just that a lot of them have these stupid guidelines they live by that supposedly help them catch the right man or whatever. As though any trickery needs to be involved.

"I know a lot of guys on the verge of giving up on women because women just don't try anymore. They won't call. They won't do anything spontaneous. They need to be wooed. God forbid it would go two ways. And if the guy doesn't want to put up with it, she says he doesn't care and that he's just like every other man out there.

"Some men are just as shy as women and they're completely afraid of approaching a woman, not for fear of being shot down. There's no shame in that. They just don't want to put the effort forth if there's already a preconceived opinion." She looked toward Lee. "You've been awfully quiet, big brother. What's on your mind?"

"You fucked a girl?" he asked.

"Dude, shut up."

The make-shift game broke up and the room became divided into friends and family.

"So, you're working retail for life now?" Lee asked through a yawn.

"Well-placed," said his sister of his yawn. "It leaves you sounding disgusted and disinterested."

"Give me a fucking break. If you guys hadn't kept me out so late last night…" Lee's words trailed off.

"The cries of a weary old man. 'Boo hoo, my life is so hard.' You're not even here doing anything. I'm the one who has to go to work tomorrow."

"Leading us back to my original question," said Lee.

"Which was?"

"Your occupation. Why aren't you doing theatre anymore?" He hefted the cue ball and waved it about as if weighing it against his words. "You're a writer now?" She nodded. "Since when?"

"Since I decided to grow up," she replied. Her words were pointed, more so than was her intent. "It stopped me from figuring things out. It gave me something to hide behind. It allowed me to be the same person I'd been for ten years. And I didn't want that anymore."

"But you were so good at it," Lee told her.

"But that's all I was. There was nothing else to me. I needed room to grow," she said.

"To change," he corrected.

"Change is growth," she pointed out.

"Not always."

"Maybe not. But in my case, it was," she said. Lee wore a defeated expression. "Dude, it wasn't an easy loss. It was necessary." Confusion set in. "Why does it matter anyway? It's not like you stayed exactly the same."

"Well, no," he admitted. "But at least I'm recognizable. Not to sound old-fashioned, but it's like I don't even know you anymore."

"Whose fault is that?" Charlie asked.

"I said I was sorry."

"I know," she nodded. "Listen, did you really even like the old me all that much?"

Lee cocked his head to one side and squinted. After a while, he shrugged, "I don't know, I didn't really know you. We were kids, ya know?"

"Exactly. I didn't have any memorable qualities because I wasn't me yet."

"Yeah, but we connected on stuff."

"Did we? Did we really? As you said, we were kids. We connected on things like, 'Hey, it's cool when we run through sprinklers,' and 'Wow, this is a good burrito.' It wasn't as if we had something to really bind us together other than our mutual hatred for Jean and even that didn't last long since we both got out."

"Wait, you don't hate Jean?" Lee's face fell. "That's it, we can't be friends anymore."

"It's not that I'm running back into Jean's arms. Hardly. I'm just indifferent to her. I like that I don't have to see her. I want no harm to come to her. I just want her to leave me the hell alone."

"Fair enough," said Lee.

"Can I ask you something?" Charlie said.

"You just did."

"Okay, smartass, I won't ask next time. What did you expect in coming here? I mean, did you really expect to find me completely unchanged, still wearing all black and moping through my life?"

"I don't know," he replied after a moment's thought. "I guess I just figured I could relive my youth a little bit before having to become respectable."

"Marriage doesn't equate respectability, my friend," said Charlie. "You can still do whatever you want."

"Is it wrong that I'm envying that twelve-year-old's hairless, cellulite-free legs?" Gwen asked Charlie. They were at a used furniture store looking for a cheap bookcase for Charlie. Charlie refused to believe that a storage unit should cost ten times more than one of whatever it was storing. She hadn't been listening to a word Gwen was saying.

"Hrm?" she responded.

"I said, is it wrong that I'm envying that twelve-year-old's hairless, cellulite free legs?" Gwen repeated.

Charlie looked in the direction of said twelve-year-old. "Yes," she said without hesitation.

Barely hearing her response, Gwen continued, "You know what I found last week?"

"Another gray hair?" Charlie quipped.

"Worse. A varicose vein. I'm not even 30 yet. Why do I have to deal with this shit now?" lamented Gwen.

"Gwen, you are beautiful," Charlie said while searching for a price on a large oak shelf. "Your legs are fine and you have nothing to—ooh! This one's only thirty dollars!" Charlie's face lit up. She looked at Gwen. Gwen wore the same expression that Jeannie Bueller did when she found out Ferris was staying home from school. "Okay, okay, sorry. C'mon," Charlie beckoned her over to a used sofa covered in love bugs and flower power daisies. "Here, sit down for a sec." Gwen sat.

"Have you spoken to Spot yet?"

"No," Gwen mumbled.

"Why not?" Charlie asked.

"Because I'm an idiot."

"No, try again," said Charlie.

"Because I don't know if he likes me," said Gwen.

"Nonsense," said Charlie, touching the tip of Gwen's nose. "Pretty girl like you..."

"You sound like my mother," said Gwen. "I guess I'm just afraid that he'll be all like, eww, you have cooties. Or whatever the grownup equivalent of that is."

"I think he has more tact than that," Charlie told her.

"But I don't want to screw things up," Gwen sighed.

"Gwen. Think about what you're saying. This is Spot. You and he are best friends. You tell each other everything. Even things I wish you wouldn't..."

"Like what?" said Gwen.

"Like when you told him that I didn't think he was cute," Charlie replied.

"But you didn't!"

"I know that," said Charlie, "but you didn't have to tell him that I said that."

"Well, I'm sorry," said Gwen. "I still don't understand how you could not find him cute."

"He's not my type. But see? This is what I mean. It almost doesn't make sense that you aren't together. Besides that, I had sex with Spot. We work together and things aren't screwed up. And weighing your fear of rejection against the alternative, the scales don't exactly balance out. If he says no, you'll still be friends and everything will remain the same. But if he says yes, things will be even better."

Gwen gave her a "You really think so?" look and said, "I don't know. I can't make a decision right now. I'm all fucked up. It would make me feel better if I knew that Gregory was unable to move on. Then I wouldn't feel like a mental case."

"He has his own set of problems. At least you know who you are."

"That's difficult enough," Gwen sighed.

"You know what I meant," said Charlie.

"No, I know. Sorry. I guess I'm just feeling mopey."

Charlie wrapped Gwen in a hug. "I know what you mean."

The Book End was open six days a week. Thursdays through Tuesdays from ten to seven. Closed Wednesdays for Mental Health as the sign on the door said. Gwen, Spot and Mark made their own schedules for Thursdays through Tuesdays. Charlie worked everyday, her favorite, of course, being Wednesday. She could listen to whatever music she wanted, she didn't have to worry about the counter or answering the phones and, best of all, no customers. Since she was salaried and technically didn't have to be there, she could spend all day reading if she wanted to. Mostly, she shelved. Acquainted herself with titles, authors and covers. She enjoyed the time alone. No one bothered her and she had plenty of time to think. She often found herself staring at an open catalogue in her lap that she was pretending to read.

A few days after her twenty-sixth birthday, Charlie realized she'd been staring at page twenty-three of the Andrews McMeel winter catalogue for almost forty-five minutes. As she was trying to focus her mind on work, she heard the unmistakable sound of a key sliding in a lock.

Click.

But the only other person who has the key is…
"Gwen," Spot scolded. His tone was one of comfort and ease. A tone usually reserved for a…
Girlfriend?
"Jason," Gwen returned.
Jason?
"Stop it!" He pinched her sides. "You sound like my mother." She shrieked with laughter and turned to lock the door.

The Book End had been open a little over two years. Charlie had never told Gwen and Spot that she worked Wednesdays. When they came in, she was sitting on the floor behind her desk. Her head just barely peeked over the counter. She felt guilty about pseudo-eavesdropping, but she didn't know what to say, so didn't alert them of her presence.

"So…" she heard Gwen say, "what do you want to do?"
Loaded question.
"Oh, I don't know," Spot replied. "We have this whole big store all to ourselves…"
Not really.
"I'm sure we could think of something," said Spot.

Charlie took that as her cue to noiselessly set the catalogue on the ground and start crawling for the door. She guessed from their voices that Spot and Gwen were far enough from the front windows so no one could see them from outside.
Just a few more feet…
She grabbed her keys with her kung fu grip so they'd be completely silent. She sifted through them looking for the right one.
Apartment, laundry, deadbolt…
All she had to do was unlock the door and slip out unnoticed.

"Me like to go down to the church…"

"What the hell?" said Spot.
Fuck. Fuck. Fuck. Fuck. Fuck. Fuck. Fuck.
"What is that?" Gwen asked.

Spot started to walk past the counter. He got as far as the Dover Thrift rack about twenty feet from the door when he saw Charlie crouched on the floor.
"It's Mindless Self Indulgence, actually," she said. She couldn't help but to laugh. Spot started laughing too.
"What are you doing here?" he asked.
"Well, I was working," said Charlie. "But then two of my employees came in and wanted to have sex in the store. And, since I'm such a cool boss and didn't

want to interrupt their act of teenage hormonal overload which could have clearly been executed elsewhere, I tried to leave the premises as quietly as I could. And I would have if it hadn't been for that fucking hidden track." Spot turned red. "Speaking of, where's your partner in crime?"

Spot looked around. "Gwen? It's okay. It's just Charlie."

"Yeah," she yelled. "I know."

Charlie looked down a few aisles until she saw Gwen cringing in fiction, her hands over her face.

"Gwen? You okay?" Charlie asked.

"No."

"What's wrong?" said Charlie.

Peeking between her fingers with only one eye open, Gwen mumbled, "This is fucking embarrassing."

"Aww, it's okay," Charlie smiled. "You only came in here because you thought there was a slim chance of getting caught. You just underestimated the getting caught factor. Don't worry about it. That's what exhibitionism is all about."

"Thanks. That makes me feel so much better," Gwen grumbled.

Charlie knelt down next to her. She whispered, "But the sex is good, yeah?"

Gwen grinned impishly. "Yeah."

"See? I told you." Charlie stood. "All right, you two crazy, horny kids. I'm gonna go. Gwen, I'll see you tomorrow. Spot," she slapped him on the shoulder as she walked past him, "don't stain my carpet." She unlocked the door, walked outside and turned to relock it. As she was starting to leave, she noticed a man getting out of a minivan. He walked to the door and tried it.

"Sorry, sir, we're closed today," Charlie told him with a smile. "We reopen tomorrow at ten am."

"You work here?" he asked.

"You could say that."

"All right. If you'd be kind enough to pass this along to your boss." He handed her an envelope with the Book End's address on it. "Have a good day." And he curtly walked back to his minivan and drove away. Charlie opened the envelope and read the generic letter enclosed.

She knocked on the front door to warn Gwen and Spot before just barging in. She unlocked it. "Guys. I don't mean to interrupt and if either of you is indecent right now, you don't have to come out. I just thought I might tell you. They're raising the rent. I have to close the store."

"What?" she heard Spot say.

"I'll leave the notice on the counter," Charlie told them. She put the paper next to the register and sluggishly made her way home.

Later that evening, Spot called Charlie's apartment. "Let's hope I'm writing. Leave a message."

After the beep, Spot's voice began, "Charlie, hey, it's Spot. Listen, give me a call and—"

"Hey," said Charlie. "I'm screening just in case my mother calls."

"Charlie," said Spot. "Your mother's dead."

"Oh yeah…" Charlie's voice faded. "What's up?"

"Gwen and I are worried about you. You left without saying anything," Spot said.

"I think the paper said more than I could manage at that point," said Charlie. "Don't worry about me. I'm fine. I just need time to think."

"Are you sure you're okay? I can come over or something," Spot offered.

"Nah. Don't worry about it. Really," Charlie said.

"It's no problem. I can come over if you want," Spot repeated.

"I'm all right. I'll see you tomorrow."

"Um, okay."

"Have a good night."

Spot let his phone snap shut.

"What did she say?" Gwen asked.

"She seems remarkably calm."

"Numb," Gwen corrected, reaching for the phone book.

"What are you doing?"

"Trying to fix things," Gwen replied.

Charlie hung up and looked out her window. The light spilling from the clouds was orange. She headed outside.

It was late November, almost Thanksgiving and the setting was thoroughly autumnal. The sun had already fallen past the hills and there was a gradual fade on the horizon from indigo to lavender to mild orange. Charlie thought of Ray. She wanted to call to ask her if she could see the sky from where she was.

A bird flew quickly past Charlie's view. Then two more, then five. As she watched, more birds appeared. They were all blackbirds from that distance. They weren't blackbirds, but against her sky, at that time of night, they were harbingers of the evening and rightly dark. Charlie found that she couldn't look away. She thought how perfect they looked, almost computer generated. Their outlines were crisp and precise and hypnotic. They would diminish and then, when she thought they were gone, more would appear. Like they were dancing just for her. They almost filled the sky.

She looked down for an instant. She sought through her mind for options other than closing the store. She found none.

When she looked back, her birds had vanished. Every one of them, gone. She turned to go inside. She looked back only once, seeing one bird flutter alone into the darkness.

Gwen waited patiently for Charlie to open the door. She heard a muffled call of, "Just a second!" before the deadbolt unlocked.

"Holy shit," Gwen whispered upon seeing what remained of Charlie's apartment.

"Yeah, I know," Charlie looked around. "Um, you can sit on whatever. Want anything to drink?"

"That's all right," Gwen replied. "I'm not staying."

Charlie looked up to ask why not and that's when she saw that Gwen wasn't alone.

"Hey Charlie," Ray said quietly.

Tears fell immediately from Charlie's eyes, but she didn't shut them. She was afraid to look away.

"I'll talk to you later," said Gwen before guiding Ray through the doorway and shutting them in together.

Ray stood, unmoving. She watched Charlie, who looked as if she were gravitating away from frazzled and nearing ever closer to decimation. Ray waited for an explanation of all the boxes and the harried state of affairs. When she was left without, she prompted, "How are things?"

"Um, ya know. Much the same. Falling apart," Charlie laughed humorlessly.

"You look good," Ray offered.

"I look awful," said Charlie.

"I didn't say you looked well. But the hair's nice. And the glasses."

"Oh," Charlie absent-mindedly touched her hair. "Thanks. How are you?"

"Worried," Ray responded, her gaze darting from Charlie to the boxes and back.

"Yeah. I have this bookstore. And we just barely scrape by now. The landlord is raising the rent. Actually, let me correct that. The landlord is making the rent impossible to pay."

"How much?" Ray asked.

"Another fifteen hundred dollars per month."

"So, you're going to, what? Close it?"

"I was thinking of trying to sell all my books, thus the boxes. But then I realized that was hopeless. Only temporary. Then I thought I could sublet my apartment. But I'd have no place to shower or put my stuff."

"Or sleep."

"That too."

"Your friend's nice," Ray said, motioning toward the door. "Are you two—?" Charlie raised her eyebrows. "I'm sorry. That's none of my business."

"Wait, me and Gwen? Jesus, no," she smiled. "Gwen is definitely not my type. Not to mention she only likes boys."

"I didn't realize that was Gwen. We'd never actually met."

"No, you hadn't," Charlie repeated. "What did she tell you?"

"She said she was a friend of yours and that you needed help."

"That's it?"

"There was a lot left unsaid."

Charlie nodded and crossed the room to sit on a box. "I'm glad she called," she told Ray.

Ray bit her bottom lip and pursed a little smile. "Yeah."

"Ray, I—"

"Don't," Ray cut her off. "I know that you're sorry."

"I'm not sure what else to say."

"Think about why your friend would call me and something might come to you."

"I miss you," Charlie said simply.

"That's a start."

"Are you with? I mean, is there anybody?" Charlie faltered.

"Not currently, no. A few since, but nothing now." Charlie's expression remained blank. "It's okay."

"What?"

"You can smile," Ray told her. So she did.

"First time all day," Charlie said. "Ray, I don't know what to do."

"How so?"

"About this," she waved her hand to the room's state of dishevelment, "the store, my job."

"I just wanted to make sure we were still discussing business matters." Ray let that stand. "How much would you get subletting?"

"This place? Eight hundred a month."

"Is this all your stuff?" Ray waved her hand toward the boxes.

"Well, these are the books. There's also the futon. The desk and the bean bag chair. The guitar case..."

"I was hoping you still had that," said Ray.

"I couldn't part with it."

"The guitar's a little worse for the wear."

"You can have it back if you want," Charlie offered.

"Funny you should mention that." Ray didn't turn to face her. "I have a suggestion, if you're interested."

"Go ahead."

"I have a small space in my apartment," Ray said. "I use it as a studio right now. You could store your stuff there if you needed to."

"I, um."

"You don't have to sleep there—"

"No, I want to! Sleep there. I mean, not in the room with all my stuff, though that would definitely be fine, I mean, I don't want to impose. I could just stay with Gwen," Charlie spat out all at once.

"Wait, I get your books and you sleep at your straight girlfriend's apartment? That's hardly fair."

"I feel like this is what it's like when people have a conversation with me."

"Meaning?" Ray asked.

"I can't tell if you're kidding." Charlie let her lids shield her eyes. "Would it bother you to have me around?" She opened her eyes and looked up to where Ray still stood.

"I forgave you years ago if that's what you're asking."

"Will you sit next to me?" Charlie asked.

"Why can't you stand?" Ray countered.

"Meet me half way?"

They both got on their knees and faced each other.

"Ray," Charlie began. "Amidst these boxes, with all my literature as our witnesses, will you give me another chance?

Ray looked ponderous for a moment. "Yeah, sure."

Charlie closed the distance between them and, with her head over Ray's shoulder, whispered, "Thank you."

Acknowledgments

I heap a large amount of gratitude atop the following individuals: Stephanie Anderson, Susan Fisher, and Emily Rizzo for reading the first draft; Emily Rizzo (doubly) for answering all my questions regarding ceramics and for giving me a crash course where she did most of the work while I spectated; Randolph Pfaff for reading every draft that followed the first; Scot and Laurie Larabee for giving me a place to edit; Paul Marques for Alister's poem; the staff at the Brattle Theater in Cambridge, Massachusetts for allowing us to take photos for the cover; the entire crew at the Moravian Bookshop in Bethlehem, Pennsylvania, up to and including Dana DeVito and Jane Clugston, for making every day a good day to be a bookseller.

I am utterly obligated to thank Randolph again and again and again for being the best editor I know, for laying out the interior of this book in its entirety, for helping me design the exterior, and for being stubborn when he needed to be, but also a generally likeable fellow.

ABOUT THE AUTHOR

Carissa Halston lives in New York with her groom. She is one half of
Aforementioned Productions as well as the contributing editor of *apt*,
an online literary magazine. Her work has been published online and in
print, in the United States and the UK. She is glad you bought this book.